D0961165

Praise for Shannon Lee Alexander's
Love and Other Unknown Variables

"A quirky and heartbreaking coming-of-age novel. Fans of The Fault In Our Stars *will fall in love with Charlie and Charlotte's story!"*
—International bestselling author Julie Cross

"A heartwarming YA story of love and entering the unknown territories of adulthood."
—Kirkus Reviews

"It took me 1.00749 seconds to fall in love with this book. Love And Other Unknown Variables *shines with the light of a thousand stars, and Shannon Lee Alexander's smart and emotive storytelling creates a chemical reaction called: Love At First Sentence."*
—Regina at Mel, Erin, & Regina Read-A-Lot

"Heartbreaking and real, Love And Other Unknown Variables *will have readers experiencing the soaring heights of fi rst-time love with whip-smart characters reminiscent of a John Green novel."*
—Swoony Boys Podcast

"Brilliantly poetic and touching, this book ripped the heart out of my chest, stomped on it, and then fluffed it back up and stuffed it back inside me. An utterly fantastic read!"
—A TiffyFit's Reading Corner

"(Humor + Snark) x (Love + Strength) / Tears = a book that I couldn't put down. Shannon Lee Alexander has written a story that will stay with me for a very long time."
—Flutters and Flails

life after juliet

life after juliet

SHANNON LEE ALEXANDER

Entangled Publishing, LLC
2614 South Timberline Road
Suite 109
Fort Collins, CO 80525

Entangled Teen is an imprint of Entangled Publishing, LLC.

Visit our website at www.entangledpublishing.com.

Edited by Heather Howland and Jenn Mishler
Cover design by Lousia Maggio
Interior design by Toni Kerr

ISBN 9781633753235
Ebook ISBN 9781633753242

Manufactured in the United States of America

First Edition July 2016

10 9 8 7 6 5 4 3 2 1

For those who can see the Thestrals—carry on, always

You may think you know me,
but you don't. I am yet to be made

Prologue

[A funeral]

It's a small church. Everything in this town is small—everything but the mountains that frame it. Those are giants bowing before the sky. But the church is small, and everything feels too close. I can see every brush stroke on the painting of The Last Supper hanging above the altar. I'm choking on the scent of the lemony polish that's been used on the great oak doors at the back of the church. And I feel as though I could reach out and touch Charlotte where she's lying in her coffin. I could take her hand in mine. I could hold it. But I don't. Don't really want to because while the body in the coffin may look just like my best friend, I know it isn't.

The fingertips of that body are free of charcoal residue and ink stains. The lips on that body are smiling—too pretty, too perfect. Charlotte's smile was always a little crooked and almost always accompanied by laughter. The raven-hued curls on the girl before us are all in place. My Charlotte's curls were a beautiful mess.

But the biggest hint that we're all being deceived is

that the body lying in this coffin is much too still to be Charlotte. Much too still. In the short year that I knew her, I never saw her be so still. Charlotte moved like the wind, pushing and pulling whatever was in her path, bending life to her whims.

Charlotte's body was alive. This one is not.

The woman at the altar asks if anyone else would like to say a few words. I look at my older brother out of the corner of my eye. Charlie's tall frame is squashed beside me, his knees pressing into the back of the pew ahead of us. His head is bent so low that his chin rests on his chest, a golden blond lock of hair across his forehead. He's concentrating on a difficult task—holding himself together. I think he has counted every thread in the weave of his dress slacks. His jaw tightens, and I know that he will not be saying a few words.

He's barely said anything since day one, the day we had to start over, the day Charlotte died. That day he had words to say, but I think he was on autopilot, an adrenaline rush, shock, whatever you want to call it. It's not every day a boy gets a phone call in the earliest hours of morning telling him that his girlfriend is dead.

He's said four words today. "We'll be okay, Becca." Then he hugged me before opening my car door.

Thank goodness Charlie's friends James and Greta rode along with us for the funeral. Charlotte will be buried here in the mountains, in her old hometown, four hours away from where we live. Four hours is a long time to survive on only four words.

No, Charlie won't be saying anything at this funeral.

"Anyone?" the woman asks again.

Around us, the small crowd shifts in their seats. I have something to say. I'm just not sure I have the courage to speak. I lean forward in my seat. I take a deep breath. My heart flies, and my fingers feel electric. I have something to say.

When I stand, Charlie glances up. His eyes, underlined with dark circles, search my face. I touch his shoulder as I step over him. He watches me down the aisle. I'm doing it. I have something to say, and I'm going to say it.

But when I get to the coffin, I falter. This body is not Charlotte. This body is—I look at the woman standing to the left of the coffin. Her hands are loosely gripping the podium. She's so calm. She smiles at me, and I know it's meant to be encouraging, but a flicker of rage dances inside my chest.

How can she be so calm? This body is all wrong. This body is a joke. This body is not Charlotte. It is nothing.

I'm choking on the syrupy sadness in my throat. Behind me, someone is crying. I move away from the coffin with the too-still body and take the three steps up to the podium. The woman welcomes me, opening her arms to me, embracing me before stepping away so I can say my few words.

From here I can watch the sea of sadness as it rolls in waves across everyone's faces. My brother is no longer counting threads. He is sitting tall, watching me, his golden hair catching fire in the red light from one of the stained glass windows. He has things to say, too, but no way to say them. I will say the things. I will be brave.

For Charlotte.

But when I open my mouth, nothing comes out.

Act First
Scene One

[A classroom]

I'm not sure how long I've been back in school. I don't really do days anymore. Time is measured in pages. I've read 3,718 pages since Dad dropped me off on the first day. It's been 108,023 pages since Charlotte died. I've read 150 pages since I stepped on the bus this morning. It's been ten pages since I thought of Charlotte.

She's not coming back, and I don't know what else to do, so I keep turning the pages.

However long I've been back at Sandstone High, the advanced literature and composition teacher, Mrs. Jonah, informed me yesterday that I am no longer allowed to "sit like a bump on a log, reading books" in her class. I find this strange, but then, I don't understand the real world. I've given up trying to make any kind of sense of it. Today in class, I am sitting like a bump on a log, staring out the window.

Sandstone is a typical high school, unlike the fancy

math and science school on the other side of town that Charlie graduated from last spring. It's the kind of building that's been pieced together—add a wing here, convert a gym there, dump mobile units here—throughout the decades as the town's population grew and it had to be quickly expanded. There's no one defining style. It's a mishmash. The kids who go here are also diverse, so it's not hard for me to fade into the background.

Lit and Comp is a junior course. The guidance counselor signed me up for it at the end of last year. She described it as a lively class full of opportunities for personal and artistic growth. In other words, it's my worst nightmare. I've decided growth is overrated.

Mrs. Jonah's classroom is long and narrow, with a wall of windows down the side. She's decorated the wide windowsill with spindly spider plants, stacks of books, empty vintage Coke bottles that catch the sunlight, and a bust of Sir Isaac Newton, which is strange since she's not a science teacher.

Mrs. Jonah raps on her desk now to get our attention. She stands and brushes invisible lint off her black pencil skirt. Tall and unafraid of wearing high heels, she towers over everyone in the school, even the basketball coach. Her pixie haircut and makeup are always perfect. She's the most *with it* human I've ever seen.

"Time's up," she says. "Please, pass your quizzes forward."

I've been done with my quiz for what would have been about twenty pages, if reading were still allowed in Lit class. I pass my paper to the boy in front of me. He runs his hand through his choppy black hair and smiles. His lips are chapped, and the smiling pulls the raw skin too tight. It makes me wince. I instantly feel bad, because

I remember this guy.

Max. He was in Mr. Bunting's World History class with Charlotte and me last year. He was the only student at Sandstone who spoke directly to me after Charlotte died. He came right up to me in history, cleared his throat so I'd look up from my book and said, "Sorry for your loss."

I remember I got up and left the room. It was either that or start crying.

He's still looking at me now. I should say something, something nice, like "Thank you for your condolences." Instead, I look out the window again.

Max sighs, soft like the riffle of book pages, as he turns around and passes our quizzes forward. I'm used to that sound. It's the sound of my father when I refuse to put my book down and come join my mother and him. The sound of my mother when she realizes I've been listening to the book characters in my head instead of her. Lately, I'm really only safe lost in the pages of a book. Outside, in the real world, it's like I'm walking around with no skin. Everything hurts.

"Okay, people," Mrs. Jonah says, clapping her hands. The sound snaps my attention back into her classroom. "I'm going to assign your critique partners for this quarter. You'll be partnering with this person on various writing assignments, sharing constructive criticism, ideas, and support throughout the writing process. Your job as partners is to help each other improve. My hope is that many of you will connect over your writing and that these partnerships will become valuable to you outside of the classroom, too. So for the remainder of class, I want you to get acquainted with your new writing buddies."

The class murmurs and scuffles in their seats, excited that they'll get to work with other people. If Charlotte were here, I would whisper to her, "Partners?"

Charlotte would roll her blue eyes at me. "Of course," she'd mouth back.

But that's not going to happen, so I turn back to the window to watch a gray-tinged cloud morph from a blob into a Volkswagen Beetle. No, that's a silver Honda with a dented fender just like Charlotte's. And despite not wanting to remember, I'm caught in a memory that won't let me go.

"You remember how we met, don't you?" Charlotte asks. My room is dark. I'd thought she'd fallen asleep. Her sleeping was so erratic then. "Remember?" she says, "Mr. Bunting assigned us that history project? I thought for sure it was going to be a disaster, until you looked up at me with those big old doe eyes of yours and this funny smile on your face, and I knew right then that we'd be friends."

But I remember it differently. "I was so nervous I started babbling."

Charlotte laughs, her wind chime laugh that makes the air around her shimmer. "That's right. You said you didn't want a partner—actually you kind of yelled, 'NO'—but he insisted, and I stuck out my hand and said, 'You can call me Charley.' And then you said"—she waits for me to fill in the blank.

I laugh and bury my face in my pillow.

"Go ahead, Bec. What'd you say?"

I toss my pillow at her. "'My brother's name is Charlie and that would be weird.' That's what I said. Little did I know how weird it would get."

She fakes insult and hugs my pillow to her chest. "You mean how awesome it would get?"

I didn't ask for my first real friend to start dating my older brother, but life is full of surprises.

Some of them more deadly than others.

"Quiet down, folks," Mrs. Jonah says to the class now. The excitement about partner work has continued to build around me. "*I'll* be assigning the partners."

Everyone groans, and my insides bunch up thinking of Charlotte again. My fingers are getting tingly, my eyes sting, and my head feels too big. I realize I'm holding my breath. This is why the memories are so dangerous.

Mrs. Jonah pulls out a slip of paper and reads off the partner assignments. As names are called small bubbles of excitement burst around the classroom. There are four of us left, and we eye one another like we're the final four tributes in the Hunger Games—the dark-haired Max, a blond guy with an unfortunate case of acne, and a girl whose purple fingernails match her purple cowboy boots. Her hands are fisted on her knees, and the tips of her ears are rosy. It reminds me of my brother Charlie. His ears go red whenever he's embarrassed. But I don't think this girl is embarrassed.

And then there's me, fighting to keep the anxiety in my stomach curled into a nice, tight, controllable ball.

"Max," Mrs. Jonah says, reading from a clipboard. He nods. "You and Brian will work together, and—"

"Mrs. Jonah," Purple Boots interrupts.

"Yes, Darby?"

"Meggie and I work really well together and I thought maybe—"

"You'll work with Becca."

Darby of the purple boots looks once at the girl to her left—Meggie?—before sighing and unclenching her fists. "Yes, ma'am," she says with a tight-lipped smile. When she glances at me, I notice a flutter of dread in her gray eyes.

I'm amazed at the strange power I now wield as *the dead girl's friend*. My classmates may have never noticed me before Charlotte. But now that she's dead, their eyes slide right off me like I'm wearing an invisibility cloak. They don't want to see me. I make them feel things they don't like. I get it. I feel lots of things now that I don't like.

Mrs. Jonah addresses the class. "Now, with these last ten minutes, get together with your partners, get acquainted, and discuss your expectations and any ground rules for critique you'd like to establish."

Whatever discomfort Darby felt a moment ago passes quickly. She has long dreadlocks, and she tosses them, whip-like, over her shoulder, and I'm struck by how different we are—like if we were books she'd be shelved with the thrillers and I'd be something like, I don't know, candlemaking.

Instead of moving to meet with me, she glares at Mrs. Jonah, her purple boot tapping out an angry rhythm on the metal leg of her desk.

There is no way I'm getting up and approaching her. It'd be akin to poking a pissed-off badger with sharp purple claws. The room hums as everyone shifts desks and chairs around. Max glances between Darby and me once before he moves to sit across from his partner.

Mrs. Jonah keeps looking at me. She's noticed that we're the only pair that hasn't moved. She had to have known this was a bad idea. There should be a bulletin board in the teacher's lounge with posters of troublemaker kids—like the wanted posters in the post office—so that teachers know what they're getting before you walk in their doors.

Mine would say:

WANTED

FOR THE OBSTINATE REFUSAL TO WORK WITH OTHERS

And it'd have my yearbook photo, the one where I look like the camera is a zombie about to eat my face off, smack-dab in the middle. I don't know. Maybe they do have stuff like that. Maybe teachers just like to think they can change us. The way Mrs. Jonah keeps looking at me makes me think she believes she can get me to move with sheer will.

It's creeping me out. Normally, I'd stuff my face in a book so I wouldn't even notice her looking, but this is English class, and I'm not allowed to read in English so…

I don't know what else to do. I force myself to stand and walk toward Darby, giving Mrs. Jonah my best when-she-maims-me-I'm-blaming-you look. My heart alternates between wedging itself in my throat and fisting itself into my stomach. Mrs. Jonah smiles.

I tell myself that Charlotte would be proud of me. I'm taking initiative. I'm putting myself out there. I'm walking through fate's open door. I'm not paying attention to where I'm going, and now I'm tripping over the blond, acne-prone boy's bag.

I gasp, and my hands do a flailing thing, like a fast-pitch softball pitcher throwing two balls at once. I stumble forward, my ankle trapped in one of the backpack straps, arms still flapping, and I face-plant into Max's lap.

Hello, Max's lap.

Max jumps because it's obviously not every day that a girl's face ends up in his lap.

That's not fair. Maybe it is normal for him. I don't know him. Either way, it probably doesn't happen in class. So Max jumps up, swearing under his breath, but he manages to grab my head before my temple smacks into the desk beside him.

I'm not sure I'm painting this picture too well. I'm now on my knees. Max is standing and holding my head. Everyone is laughing. Except the acne kid, who is swearing because I've ripped the strap of his backpack.

And Darby. Darby's not laughing. She's just watching.

The bell rings, and everyone leaves as Max helps me to a seat. "Are you okay?"

"Yes, Becca," Mrs. Jonah says, walking up the aisle, "that was quite a fall."

"I'm fine."

Mrs. Jonah looks from me to Max. "Well, then, Mr. Herrera, I'll let you handle this." She nods, a quick bob of the head.

Darby is lingering in the doorway. "Please, Mrs. Jonah," Darby says, "couldn't I work with Meggie?" Mrs. Jonah shoos her into the hallway.

Max shifts his weight as he stands in front of me. I can't look at his face, but if I look straight ahead, I'm staring at his crotch, which only reminds me that my face was just smashed into said crotch.

I look up and focus on his T-shirt instead. It's faded gray with a picture of the first edition cover of *A Wrinkle in Time*. The cover is blue with three green circles and many black circles all interconnected. Each green circle has a silhouette inside. It's one of my favorite books—has a great first line.

It was a dark and stormy night.

"She's amazing," I say.

Max crosses his arms, covering the middle of the three green circles and the man standing inside it. "Darby's a drama qu—"

"Madeline L'Engle is amazing." I point at his chest.

Max's skin is the color of a well-worn penny, but his cheeks brighten to a coppery glow as he drops his arms to pull on the hem of his shirt and studies it. "Oh. Yes. She is."

"It's a cool shirt," I say.

He licks his lips and smiles, sliding into the seat across the narrow aisle from me. "Thanks."

I finally take a moment to study his face. It's a nice face, deep brown eyes, longish nose, wide, sharp cheekbones and, although his lips are chapped, they are full and a delicious shade of—what the heck is wrong with me?

I jump up, knocking our knees together. "Sorry," I say, only it comes out wobbly sounding. "I'm sorry for"—*using your manly bits as a landing pad? Um, no*—"for, you know, the thing." I grimace at him instead of smiling, probably looking a bit like a skittish dog baring its teeth. Then I rush for the door.

"Becca, wait," Max calls as I'm two steps shy of the hallway. I drop my chin to my chest and turn around. There's no way I'm looking at his face ever again.

"Your books," he says, scooping up my bag. When I reach for the strap, he doesn't let go. "Are you sure you're okay?"

Without my brain allowing it, I look up at him. Yep. He's still adorable. "No, I'm not okay. But thanks for asking." He calls my name again as I'm running away, but I don't turn around.

Without Charlotte, I've been forced to ride the bus home from school each day. It's not as bad as it seems. No one on the bus cares if I read. If you sit near the front and keep your head down, even the bus driver ignores you. It's kind of the best part of my school day.

I've just left my locker for the bus lot. I've already got my copy of *Jane Eyre* open to my page and can't help but read as I walk, because the faster I can leave school and get back to Thornfield the better. Of course, I'm not looking where I'm going (book nerd problem number seventy-two) so it doesn't take long for me to run into someone in the crowded hallway.

The someone turns around and I'm facing *A Wrinkle in Time* again.

"Hey, Becca."

I look up at his face. "Max." My glance skitters away, bouncing from the red lockers across the hall, to the shiny tile floor, to the way Max's hand—his fingernails short and square—grasps the strap of his backpack.

Max shifts his weight, leaning back to get a glimpse of the book cover in my hand. "Walking and reading, eh?" He nods at my open book. "Always knew you liked to live on the edge."

I frown at the joke, because it's been months since I've been expected to interact with real live humans, and I'm a little rusty.

Max licks his bottom lip and presses on. "So, are you—?"

"Thank you for your condolences." I instantly want to punch my brain. *What is wrong with you? Why can't you just say normal things?*

Max's whole face is flickering with a thousand expressions as he stutters, "Wha—oh, um, you're welcome." Then he smiles.

"Okay, well, I have to go." I refocus on my book and head toward the bus lot.

"Do you want a ride home?"

"No."

"It's no problem. My friend Victor lives around the corner from you, and I take him home every day. We pass your house."

"You know where I live?" My hands are clammy from all the adrenaline, and I try to wipe them on my jeans without him noticing.

"Um, yeah."

"How?"

"I'm not a stalker or a creeper or whatever." He presses his lips together. "Saying that kind of makes me sound like one, huh?"

I nod.

"It's just—Victor and I, we've seen you get off the bus. It sucks to ride the bus—I know—and it's no trouble."

I take a deep breath, trying to slow everything down, and in that breath I pause. Max smells like honey and boy soap, sharper and spicier than girlie soaps. It reminds me of the cedar wood behind Gram's house. The smell of him makes me want to close my eyes and rest my head on his chest and just breathe.

"Uh, no, thank you. I like the bus." I take a step away.

"You do?" One of Max's dark brows arches upward.

I take another step, this time in the direction of the buses. "Yes."

"No one likes the bus, Becca." Max falls in step with me.

I grab a piece of hair and begin tangling it around my index finger. "I do."

"You didn't ride it last year."

I yank at the tangle of hair. "What?"

"Victor and I were on that bus last year. I'd have noticed you."

"That was different."

"How?"

"I had a friend—"

"Who offered you a ride? How's this different?"

She smelled like vanilla, and you smell like clean, spicy bees. "No. Thank you, but no."

"Okay, well, remember not to read and walk," he says, tucking a red flyer in the crease of my book as a bookmark. I close the book around the flyer and hug it to my chest, trying to think of a funny remark, but I end up with—

"So yeah, thanks for the bookmark."

Before I can take in another breath of him, I scoot past. I make it all the way to the end of the empty corridor before I peek back over my shoulder.

He holds up one hand in a wave, and I wish I could fold time over itself like a blanket, trapping us in that moment when he first said, *"Sorry for your loss."*

"Thank you for your condolences, Max."

"You're welcome, Becca."

And then I'd smile, not a splintered half smile, but a real one. Maybe we could have been friends.

Scene Two

[Becca's home]

The bus pulls away from my house in a whir of strained gears and hot wind. I stare at the housefront, dappled in shade from the pecan tree. I blink to adjust to the light, my gaze settling on the curb. There are faint black scuff marks in the spot Charlotte always parked her car. When are they going to fade away entirely? And why couldn't that girl park her stupid car without hitting the curb?

But now the curb is empty. The driveway is empty. The house, waiting for me, is empty.

Dad teaches science at the middle school. Mom's an elementary school principal. Their schools dismiss later than mine, plus they're both super dedicated, which means I'm always home before them.

I wish I were back on the bus.

I take a deep breath and look around my room, dropping my bag at my feet. Everything I see reminds me of Charlotte and the life I lived when she was around. My bulletin board is covered in sketches she drew, movie ticket stubs she saved, and even a flag she secured from a valiant knight at the cheesy Renaissance restaurant we went to once.

I've got clothes she left in my closet—a pair of jeans with *Starry, Starry Night* drawn on the left pant leg in Sharpie marker, a stretched-out hoodie sweatshirt she slept in, and a pair of shoes covered in doodles of black, feathery wings. Her earrings are in my jewelry box. A few of her books are on my overflowing bookshelf.

She's everywhere.

And nowhere.

I curl up in a nest of blankets on my floor and pull *Jane Eyre* from my backpack. I want the world around me to slip away, the shapes of my room to melt into the dark textures of Thornfield Hall. But as Mr. Rochester rides up on his horse, his dog Pilot—good Pilot—trailing behind him, something is different.

He's ruined me. Stupid boy.

Mr. Rochester has never had lips quite as full as the ones I keep picturing in my mind's eye, and his cheeks have never shone like pennies in a fountain. It's distracting.

I close the book and toss it aside. The house is too quiet without the company of Jane and Mr. Rochester. Quiet never bothered me before.

My life is divided into two halves now—the before and the after. And I wonder, not for the first time, if this is normal, one of those stages of grief you read about. Will I ever stitch the two halves back together?

Before Charlotte, I don't know that I even noticed quiet. There were so many voices in my head—characters rehashing dialogue from whatever book I was reading. I never felt alone.

I hear a car drive by outside. I think I can even hear

the refrigerator humming below me in the kitchen. Too quiet.

I stand and run my fingers along the spines of the books on my shelf, listening to the ruh-tut-tut sound they make as they bounce along the bindings and remembering the day I first brought Charlotte home with me.

"I think you've got almost as many books as my sister," Charlotte had said then. I'm still not sure how she ended up coming home with me. I know I didn't invite her. I must have blacked out.

She'd pulled the slender copy of *Romeo and Juliet* off my shelf, and then ran her fingers over the gold inlaid letters on the red cover. "Have you read them all?"

I wanted to pull one of my blankets over my head and pretend there wasn't a strange girl in my room.

When she asked which book was my favorite, I blurted, "They're like friends. I can't choose." And then I wanted to strangle myself with the blanket, because who says that stuff out loud? And why couldn't I just pretend to be human for one afternoon?

But when she laughed—because how could you not laugh at something so ridiculous—it sounded like she was laughing not because I was embarrassing, but because I was right. Her laugh filled my normally quiet room to overflowing. And, I don't know, I guess I got used to the loudness of life when Charlotte was around.

Because it was loud—so very loud. Charlotte couldn't abide silence. She said it made her feel empty. She played music and sang and told stories to fill the emptiness. I glance at the spot on the rug where she was usually sprawled with her pencils and paints. There's a black stain on the carpet from her charcoal pencils.

I get what she meant about the silence now. The

emptiness is seeping through my skin—its cold and clammy fingers probing my insides—so I scramble out of my blankets and dig through my bag for my phone. Pulling up Charlotte's favorite playlist, I let the music battle the silence.

The speakers on my phone just aren't loud enough. The emptiness is winning. Downstairs, Dad has a set of Bose speakers that ought to do. I plug the phone in and crank up the volume. I can feel the bass in my chest.

Still not loud enough.

She's gone. I can't get her back. This hole cannot be filled.

I turn the volume up as high as it will go. Now the sound is everywhere. It rattles the windows and presses on my shoulders, pushing me to the ground. I curl up and will the music to crush me. With my head pounding to the beat of the music, it's easy to forget the sound of Charlotte's voice, the laughter in her eyes, the unforgiving pain in my chest.

"Becca?" Mom's lips move, but I can't hear her. She's leaning over me, one hand on my shoulder, the other reaching for my phone. The music stops.

Mom sits me up, pushing my thick brown hair out of my face. There are worried wrinkles at the corners of her eyes. "What's going on? Sweetie, are you okay?"

I hate that question. Since Charlotte died, it's everyone's favorite thing to ask me. I'm not sure what I'm supposed to be okay with. The silence? The loss? The abject loneliness? Who would be okay with any of that?

I'm no dummy, though. I know they just want me to nod. To say I'm okay so they can feel some sense of ease. And I've been playing by the rules for months now. But for the second time today, I just can't find the will to lie.

"No."

"What's wrong?"

"Everything." Which is an unfair exaggeration, but at the moment, it feels right.

Mom pulls me into a hug. I want to melt into it, but it's like my skin is raw, and the pressure of her arms around me makes me want to scream. She feels it, too, and releases me from the embrace, trying to hide the worry blooming on her face. "I'm calling Dr. McCaulley. I'll set up an appointment."

Dr. McCaulley is the psychiatrist mom of Charlie's best friend, Greta. In the spring, right after Charlotte's death, the whole family went for a few sessions. Charlie went to a GriefShare group all summer. He's found one up at school in Cambridge, too.

I hated GriefShare. I didn't want to share anything, and watching other people cry just made me feel worse. Dr. McCaulley had reassured Mom that perhaps it just wasn't my time. She said I'd know when I was ready.

"I don't want an appointment," I say, untangling myself. "I want—"

I cut myself off. It doesn't matter what I want. I can't have it.

"I'm fine, Mom, really. I just had a rough day at school, and I'm overreacting. But, seriously, I'm okay. I don't need to talk to Dr. McCaulley—not again—not yet."

The wrinkles around Mom's eyes deepen. "What happened?"

I force a half smile. "Oh, typical high school stuff. Some girl in English thinks I'm a freak, and then I fell and face-planted in a guy's lap. You know, just to prove her right."

Mom's eyebrows shoot up as her jaw falls open. "You did what?"

"Face-planted in a guy's lap."

"Oh, dear." The wrinkles on her forehead recede. "Oh, my poor girl." She's trying to swallow a laugh.

"He was cute, too."

"Of course he was. Isn't that always the way?"

I squeeze Mom's hand. "I'm okay. Tomorrow is a new day."

Mom smiles. "I know this is hard, Becca." She squeezes my shoulder as she stands. "If you won't let me call Greta's mom, then please, promise me you'll stop by and see your school counselor. Charlotte always liked Dr. Wallace."

"Mom, I— "

"Please," she says, her voice vibrating with worry.

"Okay."

"Promise?"

I nod. "I promise."

She kisses the top of my head before crossing the room to the kitchen. She pauses, looking over her shoulder at me. "And maybe tomorrow you could keep the volume a little lower?"

I fake a smile. "Sure."

Tomorrow?

My gut burns. I have to do this all over again tomorrow.

Scene Three

[Becca's room]

Back in my room I pick up *Jane Eyre* and pull out the red flyer Max gave me. I close the book without reading a line. Instead I read over the flyer for the first time. I don't get farther than the first line.

Romeo and Juliet.

He gave me *Romeo and Juliet*. What does it mean?

Nothing. It means nothing. But my fingers tingle as they trace the letters in the play title. I try to stay grounded here in the present and not slip back into memories of pillows and blankets and popcorn, of the dim light from the screen as Charlotte and I watched version after version of *Romeo and Juliet*.

Charlotte had a strange fascination with this play. She'd laugh at how quickly they fell in love, shouting things at the screen like, "Wait till you see her in the morning," and "You only love him because Daddy says you can't have him." But then she'd sigh in a sort of contented way when Friar Lawrence would marry them. She'd watch in horror as they took their own lives—desperate not to have to live without each other—fisting her hands and the blankets into knots and muttering, "That's not fate. That's—" But she never finished the thought.

"God help me," she whispered into the darkness of my room later that night after we'd watched every version we could find. "But I think I love being alive more than I love any person here on Earth. I must be a terrible sort of person if I'd choose living over loving."

It was still warm outside then, and I remember wishing that I had an extra blanket, extra weight to keep me grounded as I tried to think of something to say.

"Am I terrible?" Her voice was a ghost in the moonlight that snuck through the blinds.

"No." I rolled onto my side to look at her, small and pale on the inflatable mattress Mom had been so excited to buy so my new and only real friend could sleep over.

She wiped at her cheek and smiled at me. "Looks like I've got you fooled."

But she hadn't fooled me. I knew she was afraid of being alive—just like the rest of us. And I knew she was terrified of being in love.

Max gave me a flyer for the Sandstone production of *Romeo and Juliet*. Is that fate?

I dig in my bag to find my phone. I want so badly to talk to Charlotte, to tell her about Max and the flyer, *Romeo and Juliet*, and the strange tug I have in my heart to feel alive again.

With shaking fingers, I pull up my contacts. There are four: Mom, Dad, Charlie, and Charlotte. I scroll to my saved messages and hit play.

"Becca, when you come over this afternoon will you please, please, please bring me some coffee." Charlotte's voice washes over me with a warmth that makes me smile.

"Jo is being a caffeine Nazi, and I might have to maim her if I don't get something soon." Her magical laughter rings through the speaker of my phone, like a counter-curse for my lifetime of self-imposed loneliness. "You're the best. Thanks and hurry." The last word she draws out, long and loud.

I didn't know at the time that it would be my last message. It's a miracle I still have it. I probably shouldn't listen to it as much as I do.

I scroll back to my contacts and text Charlie.

***Me**: Met a boy. Put my face in his crotch.*

I glance at the clock and hope he's back from his last lab of the day. He can't have the phone out during labs and—my phone rings.

"Explain," Charlie says without waiting for my greeting. "What is going on?"

I chuckle and feel my face flush remembering it all. Telling Charlie makes it seem less horrifying—more hilarious. "I tripped."

"You have Dad to thank for that clumsiness. Genetics are a bitch."

"He was cute, too." I push the image of Max away, straightening a dog-eared crease in the *Romeo and Juliet* flyer I'm still holding.

"Nope. I'm not talking about this with you."

My whole body sighs with the relief of knowing I'm not really in this alone. Charlie is still here for me. Even if he's far away.

It wasn't always like this between us. We were like books on a shelf, each closed and self-contained. Charlotte opened us up, helped us learn to read each other.

"But this boy, Charlie, he was awfully cute. Tall, dark,

and handsome."

"Please, stop. This is me changing the subject. Tell me about your physics class."

I smirk. "He's got these long eyelashes and lithe muscles."

"Lithe? Is he a jaguar?"

I snarl into the phone. "Ass."

"He's a lithe jackass?"

"Moving on," I prompt. "My turn to change the subject. Tell me about your super smart school stuff." Charlie tells me about his week, and I relax into the sound of his voice. I glance over the flyer, noticing that the auditions start tomorrow. My finger taps the little box in the bottom corner that reads, SIGN UP FOR THE BACKSTAGE CREW BY FRIDAY.

"So do you have a plan, Bec?"

"Plan for what?" I ask, realizing I'd stopped listening to Charlie when he'd started going into detail about quantum something or another.

"A plan to keep Mom off your back," Charlie grumbles. "Exactly how long ago did you stop listening to me? What are you reading?"

"Nothing," I say, feeling like I should hide the flyer I'm holding.

"Becca Hanson, you are the worst liar."

"It's a flyer." I stand and stretch as I talk, walking toward my bookcase. "Sandstone is doing *Romeo and Juliet* for the winter play."

"You going to audition?"

I laugh, a mean snort like a bull.

"Fair enough," he says, returning the laugh. "But what about signing up to paint scenery or something? It'll give Mom hope that you aren't in fact going to waste away in your room. You've got to get out there again. Meet people."

"It's not that easy."

"I know." He sighs.

"No, you don't." My voice sounds too high, like when I was six. "You have Greta and James. You have MIT and classes that challenge you. You have—"

"A gaping hole where Charlotte used to be in my life." He pauses, and I hear him take a long, shaky breath. And I feel like a terrible, terrible person, but it makes me feel better knowing that I'm not the only one whose heart's been torn out. "It's not easy, but I keep trying because I'm pretty damn sure Charlotte would kick me in the balls if she thought I was giving in."

"I don't have balls."

Charlie chuckles and, despite my foul mood, a small smile tugs at my lips. "True," he says, "but she'd hate to see you like this."

"I don't know. A play?"

"It's not just any play. It's *Romeo and Juliet.* Charlotte loved that stupid play. It's got to be fate or something."

I wrinkle my nose. Hadn't I been feeling the same way? It's *Romeo and Juliet.*

"Think about it?" Charlie asks.

I agree to consider it. Mom did ask me to see Dr. Wallace at school. And, yeah, Charlotte said she was nice, but she also said she hated having to pour out her feelings for yet another doctor to analyze. I don't think I can handle anyone looking too closely at me right now. I don't want to be told what I already know—I'm less than whole without Charlotte. Maybe if I sign up for the backstage crew, Mom'll forget about my promise.

We say our good-byes. I take my copy of *Romeo and Juliet* from the bookshelf and snuggle into my nest of blankets to read it. I haven't read it since my freshman year, when we studied it in English.

Before going to bed I text Charlie.

> ***Me***: *I look good in black, don't I?*

> ***Charlie***: *I hear it's very slimming. What's your point?*

> ***Me***: *I'll need to wear black if I'm working backstage.*

There's a slight pause before he texts back. When he does, it's an image of a curtain rising.

> ***Me***: *Love you.*

> ***Charlie***: *You too.*

He texts again a minute later.

> ***Charlie***: *Keep your head up!*

> ***Me***: *Dork.*

Scene Four

[Sandstone High]

On my way to my first class the next morning, I make myself go down the theater hall. There's a big poster above a desk with a metal basket full of forms. I slow my gait as I pass it to read the sign.

WANT TO MAKE THE STARS SHINE?
JOIN THE SANDSTONE THEATER TECHNICAL CREW.
SIGN UP TODAY!

I stop and stare at the forms, my palms sweating. *Just reach out and take one, Bec.* It's not like they're laced with anthrax. I shake my head once and walk away.

I get halfway down the hallway before I work up the nerve to turn around. I fight my way upstream and snatch a form before the tide of students pushes me back down the hall. I'm still not sure if I'll fill it out, but when I get to class I snap a photo of it with my phone and send it to Charlie. He's got enough to worry about without adding me to the list.

At lunch, I slide the sign-up form out of my novel and

set it beside me on the cafeteria table. If nothing else, it's made a good bookmark today. I munch on trail mix and try to focus on my book. I can usually read at least twenty pages during lunch period.

I've just started reading when the light on the page before me darkens, and a hand grazes my shoulder. I yelp and jerk in my seat. Someone is squeezing behind me to sit in the vacant seat to my left—to sit in Charlotte's seat.

This is bad.

"Sorry," Max says, plopping down in the seat next to me. "I didn't mean to startle you."

I can feel my whole face explode red. "I don't like the cafeteria." My words tumble on the table like quarters and dimes.

Max smiles. His chapped lips are healing, and I can tell he's wearing lip balm. Beeswax, I bet. "No one likes the cafeteria."

I realize I'm staring at his mouth. I look away and nod at the rows of talking students. "They seem all right."

"They're faking it."

I hadn't thought of that. I study them again, careful not to look in any direction for too long.

"See how Kelli tugs her ponytail when she's listening to Amber?"

I don't know Kelli and Amber, but I follow his gaze and watch a bespectacled girl yank on her curly hair like she's ringing a church bell, while she pretends to listen to her table mate.

Max leans his head toward the left. "Notice Victor—he's my best friend—see his thumb?"

I look left. A boy with thick black hair is tapping his thumb in a staccato rhythm on his thigh. Another boy, with a broad back and reddish hair, is bent over a notebook, copying something.

"Is he copying his notes?"

"Homework."

"Oh." I watch as a teacher walks by a row away from Victor. His thumb beats double time. "Why doesn't he tell him to do his own work?"

Max laughs. "Because it's never that simple." He purses his lips and I want to touch them. I grab a lock of hair and twist it around my fingers to keep them still. His eyes dart to my book, open in front of me. He taps the page, saying, "Real stories are more complicated than stories in books."

I smile. It feels strange, but good. "Yeah, books are definitely easier for me."

Max grins. "Everyone has a tell. You know, like a nervous tic," he says, untangling my finger from my hair. "People's insides rarely match the outsides."

My stomach ties itself into a nice bow at the feel of his fingers on mine. "How do you know all this?" I fold my hands in my lap.

"I get bored in church." He shrugs and shifts to read the paper I had laid on the table. "Hey, tech crew." His voice sounds like he's wishing me a happy birthday or something. "I'm tech crew. So are Victor and Kelli. It's great." He taps the paper like it's a snare drum. "Does this mean you're signing up?"

I shrug and concentrate on keeping my hands trapped. They itch to tangle themselves in my hair, but I don't want to give myself away now that I know Max can read me like I'd read a book. "I told my brother I'd think about it."

Max nods at the crowd. "Brother, eh? Which one is he?"

"Oh, he's not here. He's in college. MIT," I say with my normal amount of pride.

"Fancy. My cousin went to Stanford."

"Greta's at Stanford. She's my brother Charlie's friend."

"It'd be hard to be so far away from your girlfriend."

I sit up straighter. "Greta's not his girlfriend," I say, the words clipped and cold-sounding.

Max leans back. He licks his lips. "Sorry, I—"

"No, it's not your fault," I say, feeling hopelessly stupid. Memories of Charlotte sitting where Max is now—humming as she sketched the people in the cafeteria—crowd around me, squeezing my chest and prickling my eyes. I snatch the crew form from the table, cramming it in my book before slamming it shut.

"Becca?"

I stand, gathering my things. "I need to go." My voice is too loud, and Max looks worried, and I should apologize, but instead I walk away as fast as I can.

I have to pull myself together. Why do I keep walking away from the only person at this school who's nice to me?

On the other hand, why is he being nice to me? How can he even see me? Has my *dead girl's friend* invisibility started to wear off?

I go directly to the girls' bathroom after leaving the cafeteria. I study myself in the smudged mirror. It's chipped in one corner. Someone's written "Mr. Dupree sucks!" in purple eyeliner across the bottom. But I can still see the redness rimming my eyes in the filmy reflection looking back at me. I will not cry.

Charlotte would be so pissed at me. She didn't have many friends at Sandstone, not once everyone found out about her cancer. She closed up like a pearl, hidden away from all the pitying looks and prying questions. Which was fine by me because I get the feeling that if it weren't for the cancer, Charlotte would have been the kind of girl everyone would want to hang out with. I'm just lucky she chose me.

She'd hate to see me like this. Haunting the girls' bathroom. Wanting to have a life, but afraid of living. It's not like I have cancer as an excuse to hide. I have to do one thing right this week. I don't want Charlotte kicking me in the balls.

I dig through my bag and find a pen.

I slink into English later that afternoon and sit behind Max. He's got his head down, reading the short story we're discussing today. I shift in my seat, scraping the feet of the chair against the tiles. His head twitches, but he doesn't look up. I clear my throat. He turns the page.

Ugh.

I fold my completed tech crew form and scribble on the outside.

Open me.

Then I draw an arrow down to the corner and immediately wish I'd used a pencil so I could erase it, because how old am I? This looks like the note of a ten-year-old. I consider tossing the whole thing in the trash, but it took all of my resolve just to pick up the form this morning, and then any I had in reserve to fill it out. There's no way I'd do it again. This is it. This is my chance.

I lean over my desk and poke him. His head jerks, his eyes wide but guarded.

I mouth, *sorry*, and pass him the note. My lungs feel like someone is pulling the strings of a girdle tight, tight, tight.

"To begin today," Mrs. Jonah says, taking her place at the front of the class. Max covers the note I've given him with one long-fingered hand. I might pass out from lack of oxygen. Mrs. Jonah continues. "I need to ask you all for a do-over."

There's shifting around me. Teachers don't often admit to making mistakes. The ones who do are a rare species, studied by students with intense scrutiny, like we're convinced we're being duped somehow.

"Yesterday, I asked you to get to know your critique partners, thinking that was a self-explanatory assignment." She pauses, pressing her perfectly lined lips together as she studies us, stopping a little too long on Darby's sulking face. Mrs. Jonah continues, "That was lazy of me."

Oh. I guess Mrs. Jonah is being real.

"So today, I'd like to try the assignment again, only this time, I'd like you to play a game of Would You Rather." The room hums with snickers and mumbling. She picks up a stack of papers from her desk. "I'll call one partner to come collect your prompts. Today, you'll go through the list of prompts together. Don't think too much. Instead, answer from your gut. You'll record your partner's response on your own sheet."

Mrs. Jonah walks toward her desk, opening up her planner to her list of critique pairs. "Okay, here we go." She looks up from her list at us. "Oh, and as incentive, the pair who gets through the most questions in eight minutes will earn free homework passes."

I peek at Darby and swallow the gross sludge of fear that's creeping up my throat. Her face looks like it's been carved from cold, hard marble.

Mrs. Jonah makes her way through the critique pairs. When she calls Max's name, he stands, smoothly palming my note—my possible future backstage—in one hand and shoving it in his back pocket. He sits with his critique partner, Brian, who has a new backpack today.

Just like yesterday, I'm left waiting until the very end. But Mrs. Jonah doesn't call my name to come collect the

Would You Rather worksheets. Probably an astute move, since I can't be allowed to ruin any more personal property (or introduce my face to any more personal property, either). Instead, she calls Darby Jones.

Darby stands, rolling her shoulders back and tipping her chin ever so slightly upward. She'll never beat Mrs. Jonah in height, but as she takes her first step forward with all eyes on her, I swear she grows taller.

Mrs. Jonah hands her the papers, holding on to them a beat longer than necessary as she and Darby stare each other down, each holding her ground. "Good luck," Mrs. Jonah finally says.

Darby turns away from Mrs. Jonah before rolling her eyes. Meggie snickers. Max shifts in his seat and watches as Darby walks, her boots clipping along the tile floor slowly, heel-toe, heel-toe, heel-toe. With each step closer, that imaginary girdle around my waist pulls tighter and tighter.

Darby drops our worksheets on my desk and sits in Max's vacated seat.

"Let's begin," Mrs. Jonah calls to the class.

Darby's whole body heaves with the weight of a colossal sigh. She turns to face me. "I don't give a crap about whether you'd rather have lobster claws for hands or beaver teeth, but I could use that homework pass, so let's go."

She snatches my pen from me. "So which is it?"

The edge of my vision is beginning to blur, and it's awfully hard to talk when you can't breathe, but I manage to sneak out a "what?"

"Lobster claws or beaver teeth." She points to her worksheet. "Which will it be?"

I glance around the room. Max is watching me out of the corner of his eye. "Uh..."

"Don't think. Just answer." She crosses her legs, and one boot starts to bob up and down.

Lobster claws would make turning a book page very difficult. "Beaver teeth?" Except as soon as I say it, I peek at Max again and wonder what things beaver teeth would make difficult.

"Lobster claws," Darby snaps at me. "Write it down."

I dig in my bag for another pen and scribble her answer as she reads the next question. "Would you rather eat breakfast for every meal or dinner?"

"Breakf—"

"Dinner." Darby looks like she's playing a game, like a cat toying with a mouse before it kills the poor little guy.

"Are you just picking the opposite of everything I say to prove some sort of point?" I wish I wouldn't do that, blurt out whatever's in my head. I blame my nerves. When I get nervous I ramble. "Because I already know you're not like me. You don't have to prove that."

Darby's boot stops swinging. Her nostrils flare just a bit, and I can tell she's fighting to keep her temper.

I look down at my worksheet and mumble, "Sorry. Dinner it is." I write her answer.

"Would you rather"—her jaw is stiff as she reads the next prompt—"change the past or design the future?"

It's like I've been punched in the gut, but the punch has thankfully loosened the strings on that blasted girdle, and when I recover I can breathe normally.

"Change the past." Then I wouldn't have to have lost Charlotte. Then I wouldn't be lost myself.

Darby looks me right in the eye, her gray eyes clear and flat like the horizon beyond the ocean. "Design my future."

We didn't get the homework passes. Meggie and her partner did, proving again that Mrs. Jonah hates me.

When Max finally reclaims his seat, I'm feeling like there is no way I'll make it through the rest of today. There's nothing I want to do right now more than open my book, fall into the pages, and quiet the chaos in my mind with a singular storyline that I'm not expected to control.

I'm staring blankly at my desk when my pathetic note is slid back toward me, the neat, square nails of Max's fingers tapping the corner where he's written *Turn me over*.

I peek up at him, noticing the way his sharp cheekbones angle upward when he smiles.

I hope he doesn't notice that my hand is shaking as I turn the folded technical crew form over and read his note, written in tiny capital letters that lean toward the right.

WELCOME TO THE CREW.

I bite back my smile and feel my cheeks flush warm, embarrassed that I kind of feel like crying.

He licks his lips. "So, not to be pushy, but do you think you could help me after school? We got new mics, and I want to hook them up and test them."

No. This is just too much. I begin to shake my head, but Max hurries to continue, "We can watch auditions from the booth. It'll be fun. And I'll give you a ride home. Please?" He punctuates his plea with another smile.

Not fair. How am I supposed to say no to a please like that?

I touch his written words and nod as an answer.

When I look up at him, he's beaming. Characters like

to beam in books. I've read that expression so many times, but you rarely get to see it in real life. It makes my face feel deliciously warm, like when you close your eyes and tilt your face up to the sun on the first warm day of spring. His smile feels like spring.

Scene Five

[The theater at Sandstone High]

The technical booth hums with electricity. A panel in front of us blinks like a distant constellation. Below us, the theater stretches out. Rows of darkened seats with garnet cushions radiate outward from the stage. The house lights are down, and a single spot illuminates the black painted wood of the stage floor. There's one small pool of light in the audience where the director and his student aide are sitting with small lights clipped to their notebooks.

Max explained that the whole backstage crew wasn't needed today since the theater arts teacher, Mr. Owens, prefers to do individual auditions without mics and by lighting the stage with only the giant spotlight. Max is all the crew he needs for auditions. Which means it's just Max and me in the booth, floating up here in what feels a little like a space capsule.

Onstage now, Darby stands in the spotlight. She's the last to audition. She's not wearing her purple boots and shorts. Instead, she's swapped them for a simple pair of black ballet flats and dark skinny jeans.

"Why'd she change?"

"Because she's smart," Max explains. "She's showing Owens that she can be a blank canvas. Darby's the Queen of Hearts of the drama club. She gets the roles she wants or it's—"

"Off with their heads."

Max nods. "Except, she and Owens haven't been seeing eye to eye lately. And since we lost the one-act competition last spring, things have been even rockier between them. She may be the Queen, but he can be a petty tyrant."

We listen to Darby's monologue. She's good.

"I can't find her tell."

Max leans closer. "It's because she never stops playing a role."

I think back to our exchange in class this afternoon. Was she just pretending to want lobster claws and medium-rare steaks? Perhaps she would prefer beaver teeth and pancakes? Even if that was part of an act, she was dead serious about her future.

She finishes her monologue and Owens's aide joins her onstage to read lines. In the ten seconds between playing one character and another, she slips back into Darby Jones mode—impatient toes tapping out a staccato rhythm on the wooden stage floor—and I realize that the girl we see every day in classes, domineering the drama club, wearing her purple boots, is an act. I have to admire her dedication.

"She's one hell of an actress," I whisper and Max nods. "It must be exhausting to be onstage all the time."

"Drammies live for that stuff, though."

"Drammies?"

Max grins. "That's what we call them." He nods toward the stage. "Those who live for the light and spectacle."

"Actors?"

"Yep. Egotists, all of them." Owens interrupts Darby and says something to her while gesturing wildly with his arms like a maestro conducting a full symphony. "And there's the biggest ego in the bunch," Max mutters as he fiddles with a dial on the panel in front of us.

Darby's audition wraps up, and I can tell the student aide is talking to Max through his headset in the way he tilts his head to the left and presses his lips together.

Turning to me, he says, "Time to test the new mics." He digs a handful of cords and gadgets out of one of the boxes pushed up against the back wall of the booth, and sets to work plugging things in and programming the computer and generally looking really competent around all this tech stuff.

By the time Max has set up everything, the theater is empty and dark, except the one spotlight still lighting the front of the stage. Max motions for me to follow him out of the booth. Mr. Owens and Darby are the last to leave. She eyes me as I follow Max but doesn't say anything. Instead, she pushes past everyone in a burst of speed, reaching the exit first.

"I'm heading out, Maximo," Owens calls. "I'll be in my office for a bit, if you need me." His voice is loud in the darkness, and I hurry to wait for Max at the bottom of the steps.

"Aye aye, captain." Max salutes. The back door closes as Max climbs the stairs to the stage.

I falter at the bottom, peering over my shoulder to be sure the place is truly empty. The seats are full of shadows and no one else.

"Come on," Max says, his voice buoyant like we're next in line for the roller coaster, not just stepping onto an empty stage.

I meet Max at the center of the stage. Looking out into a wall of light, it's like getting a glimpse of an event horizon. Charlie says that's the edge of a black hole, the rim between all the light of the universe and the deepest darkness. I can't see anything, and there's no one in the empty seats to see me. It's the safest place I've ever stood. Like I'm the only human who ever was.

Max stirs next to me, and the spell is broken. "Cool, huh?"

I nod, afraid the infinite depths of the black hole before me will swallow my voice if I speak.

"May I?" Max is holding the hands-free mic and earpiece toward me. His dark eyes reflect the light of the spotlight. I nod again.

He pushes a strand of hair away from my neck as he fits the earpiece in my left ear, and my skin prickles. His fingertips brush along my cheekbone as he straightens the small mic there. I focus on the event horizon, feeling weightless.

Max is wearing heavy black headphones with a mic. When he speaks, his voice is both solid and soft in my ear. "Test? Test? Can you hear me, Becca?"

I'm grounded again.

Max smiles. Not using his headset, he speaks to me. "I need you to say something."

I don't think I need to say anything. He has to be able to hear my heart pounding through the mic. But he's determined, coaxing me, gesturing with his hand like he can waft the words his way.

"Hi."

It's a small word, but the mic throws it into the black hole around us; even the farthest shadows can hear me.

"Perfect," Max says. "I'm going back to the booth to

check the levels. You stay here and keep talking."

"About what?"

"Lady's choice."

Within moments, the darkness swallows him. I watch the booth, waiting to see him appear in the window. I have to shield my eyes with one hand and squint. And then he's there. He waves. I smile.

"Tell me a story." His voice roots itself in my ear.

What to say? I grab a lock of my hair and whirl it around my index finger. "You remember that I had a friend, Charlotte," I begin, letting go of my hair and clasping my elbows behind my back. "Remember her? From history?"

"Yes."

His affirmation makes me stronger. "She had cancer—brain tumors that metastasized. You probably remember that, too. Anyway, she had this tattoo." I point to the spot where my neck meets my shoulder. "I loved that tattoo. I used to doodle it in my notebooks in class. Infinity and hope."

I'm surprised at how comfortable I am. Sharing Charlotte with the darkened theater is easy. It feels like the heaviness is leaching away from me with every word. I squint into the light toward the booth, but I can't make out Max's expression. "I was just an outline of a girl when Charlotte arrived. She filled in all the lines with color and life and, I don't know, good stuff."

I'm standing at the edge of the stage. Below me the orchestra pit is a gaping mouth. The music stands glint in the spotlight like braces on crooked teeth. "Now that she's gone, I feel unmade again."

Max has gone silent in my ear, but I've got nothing else I'd like to say, so I just breathe and feel the warmth of the light. I feel a little like I'm floating. I haven't felt this light in months, like telling the scary truth I've been holding has set it free.

"Becca?"

I look up. "Yes."

"Do you know any lines from *Romeo and Juliet*?" I nod. I don't tell him I read it last night. Don't tell him it's in my bag up in the booth right now. "Could you recite a few lines?"

"Um, yeah, I guess." I take a few steps back away from the edge and close my eyes, calling up the words on the pages in my memory.

"What's in a name? That which we call a rose by any other word would smell as sweet. So Romeo would, were he not Romeo called, retain that dear perfection which he owes without that title. Romeo, doff thy name, and for thy name, which is no part of thee, take all myself."

I open my eyes to the stillness around me. It's not crushing me like the quiet at home. It cushions me.

A door closes at the back of the theater. I look toward the booth.

"Max?"

"I'm here, Becca." He is leaning over the board, his hand pressed against the glass, and I can't help but think of Juliet up in her window waiting for Romeo.

Scene Six

[The cafeteria]

I read 681 pages over the weekend. Two and one-quarter books I finished. Three different characters reminded me of Max.

I'm halfway to my normal seat in the cafeteria on Monday when I glance up from my book and freeze. Am I early? Late? Why are there people sitting at my table?

The boy Max pointed out the other day, Victor, is there, along with the girl, Kelli. I actually recognize her from history, too. She wears funky, purple cat-eyed glasses that make me think of the Cheshire cat from *Alice in Wonderland*. There's another guy I recognize from my biology class last year, with hair the color of wet sand. As I watch, a third guy slides onto the bench beside the biology boy, swiping Biology's water bottle and taking a big swig from it.

I take a step backward, thinking of parallel universes and collapsing realities, and wonder if I somehow stepped through a wrinkle in time. Perhaps this is what lunch looks like for me in an alternate life?

Before I can retreat much farther, Max approaches the group carrying a tray from the lunch line. He sees me and waves me over. I notice my usual seat is still empty. Max slides into Charlotte's seat, smiling at me, waiting for me.

I could go over there, or I could go to the library and read. I'm not really all that hungry.

You're starving, Charlotte's voice whispers in my head.

She's right. As usual.

Max stands as I approach the table. "Everyone, this is Becca." He takes my books and sets them on the windowsill behind us. "Becca, these are some of the techies."

"The only ones worth knowing," Victor says, reaching across the table to shake my hand. The guy holding the stolen water sighs. Victor nods toward him. "That's Greg. You'll have to excuse him. He's in his angst phase."

The guy from biology snorts into his chips.

Greg's dark face flushes. "I'm not angst-y. I'm Victor-intolerant." He smiles at me. I like the way his deep-set eyes crinkle when he smiles.

"Well, we all suffer from bouts of that," Max says. "So Victor and Greg." He points to each as he introduces them. "That's Miles." *Miles from biology with the sandy hair*, I repeat in my head. "And this is Kelli," Max finishes, nodding to the girl from history who is sitting on his other side. She blushes right to her hairline where an abundance of curls cascade to her shoulders.

My insides feel like they've been run through a blender, but I smile and nod at them each in turn. "Nice to meet you all."

Those are the first words I've said out loud today.

The gang, as Max called them, quickly fall into their routine, telling stories, talking over each other, and joking. No one pays much attention to me, which is nice. I drift along in their current without having to paddle.

That is, until Darby comes storming over, churning up waves like a hurricane.

She stops nearly on top of me and fists her hands on her hips. "What are you playing at?" she asks, her expression needling me like icicles.

I look up at her, my mouth flapping open and closed, no words, no comprehension, no idea how I got here.

Max leans forward on his elbows. "What's the problem, Your Highness?"

A muscle in her jaw twitches before she unlocks it to answer him. "I just saw tomorrow's callback list for Juliet."

Max rolls a hand at her. "And?"

"And *her* name is on it." She spits out the word *her* as she juts a purple-nailed finger toward me. "Which I think is strange since *she* didn't even audition."

Max's face is a bit pale when I look at him. "Max?"

"Don't play stupid." She slaps her palms down on the table, leaning over me to get in Max's face. "Mr. Owens said he saw her when he stopped by the booth yesterday. He said you had her mic-ed, and she was blabbing about the cancer girl from last year. Said she looked perfectly vulnerable, just like he'd always envisioned Juliet might look."

Beside me Max inhales sharply, swearing under his breath. This is why Max had me recite those lines? It had nothing to do with mic levels, whatever the hell those are.

Victor's grinning so big I can barely see his eyes. "Owens wants *you* to play Juliet." He holds up a hand for me to high-five across the table. "This is awesome."

Darby curls her lip at Victor before turning her venom back to me. He pulls his waiting palm back, cradling it in his lap. "Watch yourself," Darby says, moving so her face is now a foot from mine. Her voice is quiet in the small space between us.

She turns and tromps away, bulldozing an unsuspecting bystander with her shoulder on her way out.

My whole body trembles, so much I'm sure Max and Kelli can feel the bench we're sitting on quake. I stand and face Max. "You lied?"

"What?" Max is on his feet beside me. "No."

"You were just checking out the new mics?"

"Yes, and then—" Max paces in the small area between tables. "Shit, Becca, I'm sorry." He stops pacing and starts wringing his hands. "Owens stopped by the booth on his way out. I didn't—"

I grab my books to go. I should be in the library right now. I should be turning a page in a book, not turning away from a table of kind faces.

Max stops me, his hand light on my shoulder. "Look, it's no big deal. Owens is probably trying to give Darby a scare. No one else even auditioned for Juliet. She could use the competition."

Max runs a hand through his hair, tugging it away from his face. "It's really no big deal. Just don't go to the callback, then there's no problem."

"The problem isn't whether I go to some callback or not." I hug my books to my chest to keep my arms from shaking. "The problem is that the Queen of Hearts wants my head on a platter. And the boy I thought might be a friend is keeping secrets from me."

"I wasn't keeping a secret," Max says, his voice one part anger and two parts dejection. "I didn't know there was anything to tell. Mr. Owens stopped in to remind me to lock up when we were done. I didn't know what he was thinking. I thought he just wanted to hear some lines over the mic. I thought he was impressed by the sound quality."

Victor snickers. "Dude, sound quality? No one gives a shit about *sound quality* but you."

"Shut up, Vic." Max rolls his shoulders, sloughing off the tension. "Look, I am sorry, Becca, but all I know is"—I can feel Max's eyes on me and, against my will, I look into them—"you were a natural on that stage."

His dark eyes are too intense, too easy to fall into, just like the comforting darkness of the theater. I look away, over at the table of faces watching us. Poor Kelli has gone white and stiff, like a starched sheet. Greg and Miles are sitting so close they could be getting ready to run a three-legged race. And Victor, well, Victor looks like he's trying with all his will to bridle his Labrador-like enthusiasm.

People, the real ones, are complicated, much more so than the ones in stories. There's no way to know them, all the bits of them. And it's the things deep inside people, the cancers growing in secret places, that will hurt a girl if she's not careful.

This boy is dangerous.

"I can't do this," I whisper. "Not again."

Without looking back, I retreat from the cafeteria, taking the same path Darby blazed just a minute before me.

Scene Seven

[The library at Sandstone High]

I have Spanish after lunch, and I immediately ask Señor Alvarado for a library pass. Once in the library, I slump in my favorite chair, hidden at the end of the long, narrow rows of book stacks. I don't want to deal with any more people today.

I know Max was trying to help by introducing me to his friends and making me feel comfortable. And he did honestly look as surprised as I felt when Darby told us—loudly—about my name on the callback list.

I pull my copy of *Jane Eyre* from my bag. But when I open it, the words all sort of swim on the page. I read the same sentence four times.

"I sometimes have a queer feeling with regard to you—especially when you are near me, as now…"

I take out a pen, determined to illustrate Rochester's words. He and Jane are sitting on a bench under the old chestnut tree, and he's explaining how he feels like there is a string connecting his heart to hers. He's afraid that should he lose Jane, should she go, that string would tug a hole in his heart and leave him to bleed out.

Perhaps if I can draw the feeling, if I give the sentiment shape and physical boundaries, I can move on to the next part of the book.

But I'm no artist, not like Charlotte, who illustrated her favorite novel in the margins of a paperback copy of *To Kill a Mockingbird*. I can't paint like Charlotte, who made me the most beautiful, original copy of my favorite story, *The Velveteen Rabbit*. I'm nothing like Charlotte, who was not afraid to make her mark on anything.

When I try to draw the old chestnut tree in the margin of *Jane Eyre*, it looks like a child's doodle. I won't even attempt to draw Rochester and Jane sitting on the bench at the foot of the tree. Instead, I press my pen to the page, my hand shaking, and draw a heart at the top of one page and another at the bottom of the facing page. I draw a string stretching across the pages from one heart to the other, but I don't connect the strings. They've been severed.

I close my eyes, willing my bleeding heart to keep going, to keep pumping despite the flood of loss in my chest.

If you were here, Charlotte, if you hadn't left, I would not have this hole in my heart.

There's a small commotion at the doors to the library, and I peek around the shelves of books, watching a troupe of toddlers walking in. Sandstone has an early childhood center, a preschool mostly populated by teachers' kids. The child development students from the high school volunteer as teachers' aides. We don't actually see the kids much, they usually stay in their classroom located near the front office, but it's apparently story time in the big library today.

I watch as they all sit, crisscross applesauce, on the carpet in front of the sunniest window. There's a row of rocking chairs there that usually face out toward the courtyard, but one rocker has been turned around to face the little kids, and who should take a seat there but Darby Jones.

My heart goes berserk, and I slouch even lower in my seat, peeking just the top of my face over the back of the overstuffed chair. Fight or flight is one crazy reflex.

Darby's purple boots are flat on the floor, toes pointed in a bit, and she's leaning forward talking to a little girl sitting in the front row of kids. I can't hear her, but her whole body looks relaxed, comfortable, and completely unlike the haughty despot of the drama club who verbally attacked me at lunch.

"Good afternoon, Busy Bees," the preschool teacher says, snapping everyone to attention. "Our favorite storyteller, Miss Darby, is here to share one of her favorite books with you."

Darby picks up the book she's been holding on her lap and shows it to the class of preschoolers, who cheer and clap and start wiggling like puppies. Their teacher quiets them down before Darby opens the familiar looking book and begins to read.

"Congratulations! Today is your day!" Darby says, her voice bright like the sunlight streaming in around her. She's reading from Dr. Seuss's *Oh, the Places You'll Go*.

My insides go haywire. I know this book. Too well.

I'm suddenly back in my bedroom with Charlotte, just minutes after midnight on my birthday last year. In my memory, I'm holding a newly unwrapped book identical to the one Darby is reading.

Well, not identical because my copy contains *The List*.

I curl up in my chair and listen to the story, slipping into memories just as the little kids are slipping into Dr.

Seuss's magical world.

"Do you ever write in your books, Becca?" Charlotte sits across from me as I flip through the pages of my new book.

I look up and shrug. "Why would I do that?"

Charlotte smiles, pulling the thin book onto her own lap. "To make your mark on the greatest pieces of literature ever written." She nudges my knee with her own. "To become part of the story."

"No. I never write in my books."

Charlotte nods once. "Want to start?" She leans over and reaches into her bag to pull out the tin she keeps there. It's full of pencils and pens, and rattles when she yanks it out.

My neck feels hot. "I don't know."

"Think about it," Charlotte says, handing me a purple felt-tipped pen. "When you die, your words live on in this book. Anyone who picks it up will get to know you—a piece of you. It makes you immortal."

My whole face feels hot now.

Charlotte sets the book so it is resting on both of our laps. "And it's fun." She opens the book to an illustration that covers two facing pages. The yellow pajama boy in the book is surrounded by a surreal landscape. The text at the bottom reads, "Oh! The places you'll go!"

"What do I write?"

"Start with a place you'd like to go."

"Like the library?"

Charlotte smiles. "Think bigger."

"The New York Public Library?"

Charlotte laughs and points at a space on the page. I take a deep breath and write the words.

Visit the New York Public Library.

Charlotte grabs a black pen from the tin and draws a tiny New York skyline above my words. When she's finished, she looks up at me and says, "Keep going."

We stare at each other for a moment, and it feels like she's reached in and unlocked a place inside of me where I'd hidden dreams I never knew I had. A slow smile spreads out across my face like warm syrup creeping across the dimples in waffles.

Charlotte adds a dream of her own before passing the book back to me.

Act in a Broadway play.

We stay up most of the night filling the book with dreams.

Build something with power tools.

See the Northern Lights.

Dance on a table.

Bury treasure.

Sleep under the stars.

Yodel from the top of a mountain.

Pet a wallaby.

Drive from one coast to the other.

Eat ice cream in the middle of the ocean.

On and on, our list grows.

Fall in love.

Find a cure.

Charlotte takes the pen from me and taps it back into its cap. "Let's see how many of these we can do before your next birthday."

Her smile was so fragile. I knew I'd screwed up. I'd hoped too big.

There's a sour taste at the back of my mouth from the lingering regret.

There's a small sound, like the rustling of dry leaves underfoot. I open my eyes and am looking into the face of a small boy with tight black curls and ears too big for his head. He's covering his mouth with one hand and snickering through his nose.

I sit up, surprised to see the boy, but more worried about Darby seeing me. A quick peek around the library reveals that she has finished reading to the group and is now sitting at a table not that far away, listening to a little boy in corduroy overalls read.

"You sleepin'?" The little boy's voice is too deep for his small body. He's like a tiny old man.

"I—uh—"

"Did Miss Darby's story make you sad?"

I wipe away a trail of tears I didn't realize was making its way down my cheek, unsure how to answer.

"It's okay," he says, patting my arm. "Sometimes I cry, too."

My heart warms with his simple show of solidarity. "Thanks. I was—"

"Oooooh," he coos, noticing *Jane Eyre* in my hands, jabbing one plump finger at the open page. "You're not supposed to color in books." He looks around, visibly relieved when he notices that his teachers and Darby are otherwise occupied. "You'll get in big trouble. Big."

I look down at my sad tree and broken heartstrings. "Big?"

"Big," he says, nodding with his whole body. "But I won't tell. Do you like to read?"

"Yes." I can't help but smile as his conversation continues to flit at hummingbird-like speed.

"Me, too. My favorite is *Where the Wild Things Are*. I like the wild rumpus." The boy puts his hands up, fingers curled like claws, and starts to growl and snarl.

He's cute, but loud, and of course, Darby looks over at the sound and sees us. The smile on her face crashes like a snowcap in an avalanche. Gone is sweet Darby, replaced by the scary She-Who-Must-Not-Be-Named Darby.

She stands and fists her hands on her hips and I think for sure I'm going to get it, but when she speaks, her voice isn't harsh. Instead, when she calls the boy, her voice is soft around his name like a giant marshmallow hug. It's weird, and I can't help but look around to see if anyone else is hearing this. "Marcel, what are you supposed to be doing right now, buddy?"

Marcel sighs. "Reading with Jeremiah."

To me he says, diplomatically, "I hafta go." He pats me one more time and takes a few steps away before he remembers something else he wants to say. He jogs back to me and levels me with his dark eyes that are too wise-looking for his gap-toothed smile. "If a story makes you sad, you shouldn't read it no more. Try *Where the Wild Things Are*. It's real good."

Would I feel better if I just never thought about Charlotte again? Am I trapping myself in my memories?

Marcel gives me one more smile before darting away. He joins the boy at Darby's table and challenges him to a game of rock-paper-scissors. Darby touches his dark curls with fingers so careful and light they could be butterflies, even while she glares at me with the weight of ten thousand pounds of hatred.

I start gathering my stuff, thinking I can make a quick escape, but when I stand Darby's beside me. "Look, let's not make this a big deal. I have, like, a ton of siblings at home, so child development is an easy *A* for me." She glances over her shoulder, checking on Marcel and his little friends. "It's not like I enjoy this or anything."

"Really?"

Darby's eyes squint like I'm some weird modern art she can't figure out. "Really."

"Because you're kind of good with them. You're less, I don't know, um, less terrifying."

Darby looks pleased—either with my saying that she's normally terrifying or that kids bring out the best in her—I don't know her well enough to say. But she quickly switches back into her sneer. "I'm an excellent actress."

She may as well have just shouted *Juliet is mine* in my face. "See you in class," she says, turning on her heel and rejoining the kids. Marcel gives me a thumbs-up just before he annihilates the other little boy's scissors with his rock fist.

When I leave the library, I don't go back to class. I go to the office and tell the nurse I don't feel well. No one questions me. It's a *dead girl's friend* perk. I lie down on the crinkly paper on the cot in her office and turn my face to the scuffed white wall.

I'm trapped by my sadness.

"Congratulations! Today is your day." I recite *Oh, the Places You'll Go* to myself. "You're off to Great Places! You're off and away!"

I haven't done a single thing on *The List* since Charlotte died. I haven't tried anything new.

I've done nothing.

Nothing.

Scene Eight

[The den in Becca's home]

The house expands around me as I step inside that afternoon. The only sound is the hum of the air conditioner, desperately trying to fight off the heat of early autumn. I look up the stairs, but the idea of climbing them to my empty room is exhausting. My skin prickles with an unnamed fear, like the house feels haunted, except it isn't. I'd never leave if Charlotte's ghost were hanging around.

I drop my bag on the couch and open the cabinet with the movies, rifling through them until I find the one I want. I pull out the cracked case with Charlotte's favorite version of *Romeo and Juliet*. It's a super old one directed by Franco Zeffirelli.

My favorite version is the animated movie *Gnomeo and Juliet*. I like the singing. And the happy ending.

I pop the movie in and flop onto the couch.

When Dad comes home from school, he joins me.

"Haven't seen this in a while," he says, reaching over and patting my leg in greeting. "Bad day?"

I shrug.

"Sad day?"

"They're all pretty sad, Dad, but time heals blah blah blah."

Dad scoots closer, and I lean in to him.

Mom arrives home just as Romeo croaks. "I've got Chinese," she calls from the kitchen.

"In a minute, hon," Dad answers.

Mom finds us and sits on my other side. I can see her cutting nervous glances at Dad and wonder if she's thinking about calling Dr. McCaulley for an emergency intervention. My stomach clenches thinking about how much Mom worries. I reach for her hand.

Poor Juliet wakes to find dead Romeo. I watch the emotions play over the actress's face, while I fantasize that Juliet is actually thinking, *damn, fool! This was not part of the plan. Didn't you get the freaking memo?* As usual, though, she offs herself.

Dad flinches as she jabs the dagger into her heart.

And I wonder, just as I did when I watched all these movies with Charlotte, why do they all have to die?

When it's over, my whole body feels numb. Mom turns to look at me and gets this determined expression on her face as she says, "Becca, I don't want you watching this stuff right now. I don't think it's good for you."

I nod. She's probably right. It's depressing as hell.

"I agree, but that may be a problem, Mom."

"Why?" she asks, squeezing my hand between hers.

I explain about Max and Darby and the gang of people sitting at my lunch table. I tell them about the comfort of the dark theater and fill them in on my talk with Charlie and how it would be a good idea to try to meet new people, get involved, not get committed to a psych ward.

"That's not funny," Mom mutters at the last part, but she's biting back a grin.

"Max thinks the idiot director may just be using me to prove some point to Darby, knock her off her pedestal, you know? But what if—?" Something about being onstage felt right. Like fate had drawn me there. "What if I'm sort of good at it? What if I could learn to be good at it?"

Mom tries to hide the way she wipes her eyes as she pulls me into a hug. Dad joins in, and they hold me and whisper how proud they are of me.

I breathe them in, pocketing this moment.

I'm going to try. I'm going to try to play Juliet. Probably. Maybe. I mean, what have I got to lose?

Scene Nine

[Sandstone High]

Last night I read 106 pages—exactly the number of pages in my copy of *Romeo and Juliet*. I realize the Sandstone High production of *Romeo and Juliet* is not the same as a Broadway play, but it's something. It's a small way to honor Charlotte—a way to cross something off *The List of Places to Go*. Maybe Charlie's right. Maybe this is fate giving me a hand.

I keep my face in a book at school today. Or at least, I try to. I do notice Miles and Greg at a locker in the morning when I first arrive. I'd never seen them there before. Or maybe I'd seen them, but not *seen* them, you know, the kind of seen that gets written in fancy italics.

Italics or no, I keep walking.

In history, Kelli tries to get my attention, but I read like my life depends on it—thirty-two pages, which is more than my average.

I go to the library for lunch.

But I can't read in Mrs. Jonah's class, and when I walk in it's obvious Max is waiting for me.

"Becca, look—"

I hold up a hand. I told myself I would go to the callbacks, even arranged for Dad to drop me off and pick me up after. But now, I can't seem to tell him. Maybe because I'd rather no one know when I fail. It's why I've been avoiding everyone today. Well, that and I made an ass of myself storming out of the cafeteria—again.

"You shouldn't be so nice to me, Max," I say, sitting in my seat. I try to ignore the invisible daggers of Darby's glaring gray eyes from across the classroom. "No one else is. Why are you trying so hard?"

His face goes from hard lines to soft curves. "Why are you trying so hard to hide?"

I press my lips together. "I don't have to hide. I'm the *dead girl's friend*. I'm invisible."

"Not to me."

I think my light grasp with reality has finally snapped. "What?" People don't really say that kind of stuff outside of books, do they?

Max swallows, his Adam's apple bobbing delicately at his throat. "What I mean is that I've lost someone, too, Becca."

I shake my head. I didn't know. Who has he lost? Why have I never paid attention to the living stories all around me?

Max continues, leaning forward with his elbows on my desk. "So I can see you. And just like you, I can see Thestrals, too."

Oh, I'm certain I've lost it now. There's no way he just—"Did you just make an allusion to a Harry Potter creature?"

He grins, and my insides go liquid. He can see Thestrals—fictional, skeletal, horselike creatures invisible to everyone but those who have known death—Max sees them, too.

I reach out to touch his left elbow. "I'm sorry for your loss." It feels so good to be on the other side of these words, to be doling them out instead of swallowing them like bitter pills.

Max's small smile is shaded with pain, tinted with understanding. "Thank you."

I take a deep breath, trying to slow everything down. Then I open my bag and pull out a small red book with a gold inlaid title. I set it on my desk between us. Max's smile is so large, I notice his right canine tooth is sort of crooked.

"Break a leg," Max whispers before Mrs. Jonah calls the class to order.

Darby and I wait in the hallway outside the theater. Most people have been dismissed for the day, but there are a few boys left to read for Romeo.

Darby is back in her audition costume, dark skinny jeans, ballet flats, and a plain black shirt. Too late, I look down at what I'm wearing and wish I'd paid more attention when getting ready this morning. I'm wearing faded jeans with a hole in the knee (and not the kind you pay extra money for, but the kind that comes from falling down when trying to learn to roller blade with Charlotte), an old mathlete shirt of Charlie's, and Charlotte's raven-wing shoes.

Darby's hair is in a ponytail, pulled away from her face. She has no blush on her sepia cheeks, but is wearing a deep burgundy-colored lipstick that draws attention to her mouth.

I can't do anything about my lack of makeup, but when Darby gets called into the theater, I quickly wrap my mop of brown hair up in a bun.

One, and then both, of the remaining guys are called in to read lines with Darby, and I'm left alone. My pulse throbs like a bass line in my temples. I stare at the pages of my book for a while, but none of the words are making sense.

There's a commotion at the theater doors as Victor comes barreling through. He crashes into the seat next to me, pulling both my hands into his.

"Are you ready? How are you feeling? Can I get you something?" His questions whiz by like meteors.

I try to smile when I answer. "No. Nauseous. An escape pod."

Victor's laugh echoes in the emptiness of the hallway. "Darby's almost done. I just wanted to warn you."

"Any advice?"

"Don't suck."

I nod, feeling like a bobblehead on a dashboard. "Right. That's good. You're very helpful."

Victor blushes. "It's why they keep me around."

The doors open as Darby steps out. Victor stands, folding his arms over his chest. "Got Owens warmed up for the real deal here, Darby? I hear he's looking to make a few changes in the drama club."

"Shut up, Vic." She stalks over to him, towering above his short, squatty frame. "We all know Owens won't actually cast a nobody as Juliet. Not when he's got local fame and fortune to garner." She sneers at me, but there is something in her posture—a rigidity in her spine, a tic in her jaw—that says she doesn't firmly believe it. Turning her attention back to Victor she says, "This is all a formality, techie." She makes the word "techie" sound like a swear word.

Victor bristles like a rabid ferret. Darby smiles this magnanimous smile and pats him on the head before she walks away from us. She doesn't even look back. She doesn't have to. She knows she's got a captive audience.

Once she's around the corner, I turn on Victor. "What the hell is going on?"

He grumbles, tapping his foot to no discernible beat. "Just the age-old struggle between the drammies and the techies." He faces me, placing his hands on my shoulders. "But none of that matters now, because you're here to shake everything up."

My eyes feel like tennis balls, like I have big, shocked Dobby eyes. "Shake what up? I'm not a shaker." My voice is climbing in octaves. "I'm not even a nudger." I'm about to bolt when we hear my name being called from the depths of the theater.

"Becca," Victor whisper-shouts. He's still holding my shoulders, and he has to duck his head this way and that to fully capture my attention. "Do not freak out, because if you freak out, then Max will freak out, and if Max freaks out, then he's going to be so pissed at me for freaking you out."

I focus on his small eyes, so dark I almost can't see where the iris ends and the pupil begins.

"Now, go get on that stage and break all the legs that ever were. Got it?"

I nod.

"Say it."

"Break all the legs."

"Good." He gives my shoulders a light shake before turning me and pushing me ahead of him into the theater.

Victor is a shadow following me down the aisle. A pushy, corporeal shadow that refuses to let me escape. He helps me with the mic and earpiece I'll use for this audition before giving me a thumbs-up and disappearing into the wings.

The two Romeos are sitting in folding chairs on the opposite side of the stage. It's strange, but the stage feels bigger now that I'm sharing it with other people. I'm suddenly lonesome.

"Welcome, Becca." Mr. Owens's voice floats up from his seat in the fourth row. The light on his clipboard reflects off his bald, round head, making me think of the moon. I can't find my voice.

Inside my ear, I hear Max's voice. "Say, 'Hello.'"

"Uh, h-hello."

Max chuckles and I glance around, but no one else responds to the sound of it. "That's right," he says. "Only you." I suddenly feel less solitary.

I have so many questions for Max, but Owens starts blathering on about wanting to grow the school's reputation ("His reputation," Max mutters) and produce only the finest shows with the freshest talent and on and on and on.

Max asks, "Doing okay? Still breathing? Tug your ear for 'yes.'"

I reach up and scratch my earlobe.

Finally, Owens instructs me to read with first one boy and then the other. They are both seniors, and I'm pretty sure I've never been in class with either of them.

The first guy is too good-looking. His whole face is symmetrical and perfect and kind of makes me want to color all over it with permanent markers just to make it easier to look at him. I don't do well reading with him. It's a little like I'm illiterate and have never seen letters on a page, let alone words.

When it's the second guy's turn to read, he comes to stand beside me and holds out a hand. "Thomas," he says as we shake. With a jolt, I realize it's the guy from the cafeteria, the one copying Victor's homework.

"Becca," I mumble.

"Nice to meet you."

I blush and nod and look away.

"Perfect," Owens shouts from his seat. "We haven't even started, and yet it's perfect chemistry."

Reading with Thomas goes much smoother. It's not that he's unattractive. He's as tall as Max, but with amber hair and the broad shoulders of a swimmer. It's that he reminds me a little of Ron Weasley, and that's comforting. Plus he's got this voice that is quiet and yet fills the dark spaces of the theater all at once.

"Humor me, kids." Owens says, standing from his seat. "Romeo, put your arms around Juliet."

All my muscles stiffen. "Easy, Becca," Max says in my ear. "Breathe."

Thomas closes the space between us and I watch our shadows on the stage floor merge in the light of the spot. He clasps his hands behind my lower back and gently pulls me toward him. His shirt smells like cut grass and chlorine. It's all so strange to be so close to a boy—I peek up at the booth—and so far away.

Owens claps his hands and makes a delighted noise, like a kid who's just caught the ice cream truck. "I give you," he says, holding up his arms. "Romeo and Juliet."

Scene Ten

[A parking lot outside Sandstone High]

Max insists he and Victor give me a ride home. I call my dad to let him know as we walk together toward the junior parking lot. As soon as we hit the asphalt, Victor shouts "shotgun," and sprints for Max's truck.

I'm not fluent in the rules of shotgun, but I'm pretty sure the point is that saying it reserves your space in the front seat, so that you don't have to sprint like a cheetah through the school parking lot.

When we arrive at Max's truck, Victor is bouncing on the balls of his feet, shadowboxing like a prizefighter and chanting, "Oh yeah, it's mine. I'm the shotgun champ. Oh yeah—"

"Dude, get in the back."

The back of the truck cab is a small compartment with these little bitty fold-down seats and questionable seat belts.

Victor stops, his arms frozen in a *V* over his head. "Why?"

"Because that's the polite thing to do."

"Polite? No. As the new girl, Becca needs to learn the curious customs of our little subculture."

Max's cheeks darken, but Victor ignores him and faces me. "If you want to ride in the front, Becca"—his voice lilts like a grandmotherly kindergarten teacher—"you have to—"

"Shut up, idiot," Max says, his voice low and rumbling.

"Dude. It's the rule. There's only one exception." Victor's sloppy grin is victorious. "And Becca does not meet that exception."

"What's the exception?" I ask.

They both look at me. Max licks his lips and shifts his weight away from me. Victor holds one finger up in the air, like he's quoting a famous speech. "The girlfriend exception."

"Well then," I say, trying to keep my voice steady. I fumble with the lever on the front seat until it flips forward. "I'll just take a seat back here."

I've got one foot in the car when we hear my name shouted across the parking lot. Darby, dreadlocks flying out behind her, is rushing toward us like a tidal wave. I'm reminded of Ursula from Disney's *The Little Mermaid* movie, and I suddenly feel like I'm drowning.

"*You*," she says, stopping inches from me, the toes of her purple boots grazing my sneakers.

My heart is going nuts, whapping around in my chest. I try to step away from her, but she's got me backed up to Max's truck.

"You backstabbing, poser, whore!"

"Hey," Max shouts.

Victor leans on the truck next to me, smirking at Darby. "Hey, Darby? I'm confused about the poser whore thing.

Do you mean that Becca actually is a whore, or that she's pretending to be a hooker?"

"Screw you, Vic."

"So that makes you the whore?"

Darby's whole body is trembling, her gray eyes feral. I'm afraid to speak, afraid my voice will push her over the edge, because it is very clear she is balancing some razor-fine line.

"You're going to ruin everything," she says, and there's more than anger in her expression. She's fighting back tears, biting her bottom lip, and I realize with a painful jolt that I've just stolen a peek behind the scenes. This Darby before me is no act.

Max asks, "Don't you think you're being a tad melodramatic, Darby? Owens hasn't posted a cast list."

She looks away from me, and the relief is physical, like her stare was a hand to my throat. The air I gulp burns.

The mask falls back into place on Darby's face as she fixes Max in her sight. "I just saw Thomas."

"Look," I blurt out, "it's not like I'm taking the role."

Darby recoils from me, like I've struck her. "What? Why wouldn't you?"

"Well, it's not like I know what I'm doing. I'd probably screw up."

"Oh, you'll definitely screw up, but that doesn't mean you walk away from the role of a lifetime." Darby's voice is strung out like a tightrope between us. "I don't want your leftovers." She whirls around, her hair swishing behind her, and disappears back into the school.

Victor drapes an arm over my shoulders. I'm breathless, and his arm feels like a life raft in a tempest. He tosses his other over Max's shoulders and hugs us to his sides. "So to clarify, Becca is going to play Juliet, and I'm riding shotgun?"

Max, who only a moment ago looked like he wanted to punch something, suddenly laughs. The sound is like a happy ending, making my chest ache in all the right ways.

A statue of the Virgin Mary looks at me from Max's dashboard.

"Mary, this is Becca," Max says as he slides in.

I wave at the figurine. Max's laugh fills the small cab of the truck, pressing the air out of my lungs.

"This was my cousin's truck when he was in high school," he says, by way of explanation. "Beni was always in trouble—too smart for his own good. My aunt superglued Mary in here to keep an eye on him."

"Oh, well, she's lovely."

Max's brow arches.

"I mean—" but I break off because I don't know what I mean. The figure has a close-lipped smile, and even though her eyes are painted on, I'd say the smile reaches them. She's comforting. Maybe that's the word?

"Mom and her sisters are old-school Catholic."

"I'm not religious." Why I explained that eludes me, so I tangle a lock of hair and try to keep any more dumb interjections from slipping out.

Victor turns around in his seat. "You'd better find God and fast if we're going to get home. Max's truck runs on miracles."

Max nods as he reaches for the keys where they dangle in the ignition. The truck hacks and sputters as the engine turns over and refuses to start. Max licks his lips, and I watch them moving as he silently pleads for the truck to cooperate. He jiggles the key, and the truck's complaining gets louder. Finally the engine catches with a growl. Max nods to the Mary figurine on the dash.

Victor mutters an "amen" and then begins fiddling with the radio dials, switching between one static-filled station to another.

"He does this every time," Max says. "Even though he knows the antenna is broken."

Victor grins. "I'm not looking for music. I'm looking for aliens."

They chuckle and talk about classes. I let their conversations and the warm breeze from the open windows roll over me.

"You okay back there?" Max asks.

I nod, pushing a stray hair behind my ear. "So what's Darby's story?"

They both look mildly surprised before shrugging. Victor says, "She's obnoxious," as Max says, "She's a natural."

"She's naturally obnoxious?"

They chuckle, but Max shakes his head. "No. She's a natural onstage. She's talented. She definitely wants in at the School of the Arts next year. The bitchiness is just a side effect."

"She doesn't just want in," Victor adds. He turns in his seat, facing me. "She wants to get out of here. Her dad started a construction company a few years back—the family that works together stays together and all that."

"Yeah, her brother was in Beni's class. He's working for his dad now."

Victor nods. "Darby won't come near the tech shop when we're building sets."

"Hates the smell of sawdust," Max says, smiling at me in

the rearview mirror.

Max turns into my neighborhood, and I suddenly take note of the construction trucks outside the third house in. It's not Darby's dad or anything, but it makes me wonder about the future and fate and what it'd be like to have a future already picked out for you. My parents have never even asked me about what I might do after graduation—like Charlie sucked that parental zeal out of them with his immense drive.

But plotting her own future is a priority for Darby. She told me so herself.

We're just around the corner from my house when Max pulls into a driveway. Victor's house looks like many others in our cookie cutter neighborhood, except for the enormous satellite dish in the yard. Victor sees me noticing it and explains in a voice that sounds like he's explained this a hundred times before that his dad uses it to watch television news programs from his hometown in South Korea.

"You guys want to come in?"

I disentangle a finger from my hair and try to smile. "No, thanks, but if you want to stay, Max, I can walk home from here." I point in the direction of my street.

"I'll take you home," Max says, hopping out and striding around the truck to the passenger side.

"Aw, dude, you're so sweet coming to open my door," Victor says.

Max flips Victor off before pulling him from the car. "Get out, Vic."

Victor grabs at his heart and feigns a swoon. "Ah, how quickly I've been replaced."

A laugh gurgles in my throat despite myself. Max arches an eyebrow at me. "Don't encourage him."

Victor bolts for his house calling out, "I don't have to take this from you, you heartless bastard." He's cackling like a madman as the front door closes behind him.

"What do you feed him?" I ask, unfolding from the cramped backseat of the truck.

"Puppy chow and candy bars."

I snort as Max closes the door behind me. When he gets back into the cab, silence wraps around us like fine spider webs. It feels like it should be so easy to break through them, but the words are trapped in my chest.

Max finally cuts through the quiet. "What are you going to do? About the play?"

"Not sure." I look away. "I guess I never thought Owens would actually pick me. I thought I could show up at the audition, do my best, feel better about myself, and then go back to my regular life."

"What does that look like? Regular life?"

"Books. It looks like a lot of books." I tangle a finger in my hair. "My brother thinks doing the play would've thrilled Charlotte."

Max smiles. "I'm sure."

"But if Charlotte were still alive"—I sigh—"I wouldn't be here right now."

Scene Eleven

[The cafeteria]

Max and Victor are in the cafeteria when I arrive the next day. It's still unnerving to see people at my lunch table, and I have to remind myself that there is no reason to run screaming from the room. These are nice people, not threats. They're not sharpening knives or lighting cigarettes with flamethrowers. They're studying stacks of drawings, harmless drawings, passing them back and forth, pointing and gesturing with their mouths full of food.

"What's all this?" I pick up a stack as I slide into the seat across from Max.

Victor answers. "Max's sketches for the sets."

My insides feel like they are being wrung out. Max is an artist. I glance at his fingertips, stained with ink today. An artist. Charlotte saw the world as shapes and color and chaos. What does Max see?

I study the first sketch in the stack. It's a football field, and it's raining as the two teams scuffle in the mud for the ball. I trace the pinpricks of rain as they drip off one player's helmet and into his determined face.

Before I can escape, I'm slipping in the mud of memories, falling back in time with Charlotte.

Charlotte's shoulder presses into mine as we sit side by side on my bedroom floor. She thinks I've been reading, but I've been watching her work on a sketch of a girl standing in the rain. The girl in the sketch has her back to us but is looking over her shoulder—except she has no face—not yet. Charlotte's frustrated because she can't see the girl's expression.

She tosses her pencil on the floor and groans. "Every time I think I'm getting close to her, she changes. I've always been able to see things so clearly."

"You'll figure it out," I say, leaning my head on her shoulder.

She rests her cheek on my head. "How do you see the world, Bec?"

I feel like that girl with no face as I answer, "I don't think I've ever really looked."

I blink away the tightness I can feel behind my eyes, refocusing on Max's sketches. Max is an artist. A damn good one, too.

"This is cool," I say, panic rising up my throat like bile, which is so dumb because it's not like there aren't plenty of artists in the world. *This* is not fate. I need to ask Charlie about the daily odds of meeting artists. They've got to be high, right?

I clear my throat. "Where's the balcony?"

A couple of pages are thrust at me. One depicts the football field I was just studying in the background, and in the foreground there's a girl standing on the top of the bleachers and a boy underneath them. Another page has a sketch of a stairwell with school spirit banners hung on the walls. Juliet is on the top step and Romeo looks up at her from the bottom floor. But my favorite is a sketch of the theater. Juliet is standing on the catwalk shining the spotlight on Romeo down onstage. The lines on each sketch are crisp—solid—inked with a sense of permanence.

Max's sketches ooze confidence, like he has no reason to question the world his pen is creating. Charlotte drew in short, static bursts, dragging her fingers back over the charcoal to solidify the lines. Using her flesh to make the pictures come to life. They are very different, Max and Charlotte.

I look up at Max, who's drumming his fingers on the table. "These are amazing," I say. His expression unfurls with a wide smile that makes my poor, wrung-out heart stutter.

Very different.

Victor takes the pages back and sorts them into piles. "Don't get too excited." He hands me another drawing. "This is the one he's turning in to Owens."

This drawing is beautiful, too, but the balcony in this sketch is like every other balcony Juliet has ever stood on.

"Why not this one?" I ask, pointing at the theater sketch.

Max's gaze slides over my shoulder, looking out the window behind me. I look at Victor.

"Owens is a traditionalist, and Max is a pansy."

Max flips Victor off.

"You have to show these to Mr. Owens, Max. They're brilliant." Max's eyes come back to mine. "You have to try."

"Oh, I do, do I?" Max leans forward, placing his hands over the drawings in front of me, our fingertips nearly touching. "What about you?"

"You want me to show him? Sure." I try to arch a brow

at him, but I feel like my face is made of plastic.

Victor laughs.

Max shakes his head. "You know what I mean. Are you playing Juliet?"

I am. Mom and Dad took me out to dinner to celebrate my decision last night. "Are you showing him these sketches?"

We narrow our eyes, sizing each other up over the table. My insides are on fire watching him this closely. I imagine sliding my fingers forward, locking them with his. But this isn't a story in a book. And that stuff doesn't happen in real life. So I stay firmly planted in my seat, staring at his mouth.

He must notice that my gaze is trapped on his lips, because instead of speaking out loud, he mouths the words *I'm in.*

Scene Twelve

[A classroom]

We stop by Mr. Owens's classroom on the way out of school. Max drums his thumb against the brown portfolio containing his sketches. I keep getting these punches of adrenaline that make me feel like my fingertips are electric, but I can't tell if I'm more nervous for myself or Max.

Max's jaw is set like stone as he holds the door open for me. Mr. Owens's classroom is darker than the hallway. The windows have thick curtains drawn over them, and the overhead fluorescent lights aren't on. Instead, he's got lamps spread around the room, each creating its own shallow pool of light.

Mr. Owens, sitting in one such puddle at his desk, smiles and waves us in. This is the first time I've seen him like this—up close, not hidden and mysterious as he sits far away in the audience and blinds me with a spotlight. He reminds me of a snowman, not because he's particularly jolly, but because he's so round. Round, balding head. Round torso. Even his hands look like he's wearing mittens.

"Maximo, you brought me my star," Mr. Owens says, his baritone voice so large it fills the dark corners of the room. "Come in. Sit. We have much to discuss."

I shrug at Max, who smirks and leads me to a loveseat framed by two floor lamps. We sit facing Mr. Owens, who comes around to the front of his desk and leans back on it. I get the feeling it is supposed to look like a natural position, but it seems rehearsed.

"My dear, Becca, I realize you being cast as Juliet was a surprise." Mr. Owens pauses and waggles his eyebrows at me. "But when I saw you on that stage and heard you speak, I knew, in a moment of divine inspiration, my prayers for the success of this play had been answered."

I blink, shifting in my seat.

"May I assume that you are here today to accept this most prodigious role?"

"Uh, sure," I say, looking down at the worn shag throw rug in front of the love seat.

"Good, good. Rehearsals begin tomorrow."

"Mr. Owens?" Max sits forward, tapping the portfolio on his knees. "I've got some preliminary sketches for set designs."

"Excellent, Maximo," Owens says, stretching a thick paw toward the folder. He opens it and sifts through the sketches, his whole face wriggling with a thousand expressions.

Beside me, Max has sucked in his lips and is biting on them. He'll need an extra slathering of ChapStick after this.

Owens's smile is broad and unnaturally white, as he holds up one page in particular. I lean forward to see which one it is, but the room is so dim I can't make it out.

"Perfect," Mr. Owens says in a breathy way. "She'll be

perfect standing here." He closes his eyes and leans back again, probably envisioning the scene in his mind. The paper falls forward in his hand and I can see it's the classic, *I've been standing on a balcony just like this for centuries now*, set piece. An angry wave crashes over me.

"Not that one," I say, standing and sifting through the drawings to find my favorite. Mr. Owens opens his eyes in surprise, and I shove the sketch of the catwalk at him. "This one. This is the one—the perfect balcony for Juliet."

Mr. Owens gives me a pitying look. "Going diva on me already," he says, chuckling.

Max stands beside me.

"A set like this will change the whole tone of the story. It'll make it possible to tell a whole new story."

"A new story?" Owens says, his deep voice tinged with shadows deeper than the ones falling across the floor. "What makes you think *Romeo and Juliet* needs meddling with?"

I step away, still holding Max's sketch. Pissing the director off before rehearsals start is probably not the best survival technique. I'm practically proving Darby's point. I'm going to fail.

"Sorry," I mumble. "Of course, you know best."

"Too often schools try to update this classic but, like a good pair of wingtip shoes, Shakespeare is never out of fashion."

Mr. Owens puts the sketches back in the portfolio and hands it to Max. "Get your crew building a traditional set, Maximo."

Max's thumb lies still against the portfolio. "Yes, sir."

"We're doing everything by the book. Traditional costumes. Traditional Shakespearean language. Traditional casting." Owens is making a frame around my face with his fingers, studying me through his lens.

"Traditional casting?" I ask. There is nothing traditional about casting me as Juliet. I don't know the first thing about theater. Sure I've read lots of plays, but until the other day, I'd never stood on a stage. I am an unconventional choice for Juliet at best.

"Yes, you will be perfect." Owens nods and circles back around to his desk seat. He smiles in what I'm sure he thinks is a grand and reassuring way, but it comes off more like he's constipated. "Becca, dear, you'll need to learn to trust me. I know what I'm doing. I'm a very successful director. Highly sought-after, even." He waves us off, turning his attention to the work on his desk. "Until tomorrow then."

I'm frozen, staring at the bald spot on the top of Mr. Owens's head as he reads. Max tugs at my elbow, directing me out of the room.

I have to blink in the bright light of the hallway. Max keeps pushing me along toward the doors to the parking lot, but I stop once we're on the sidewalk outside.

"That guy's crazy." The adrenaline from before drains away, leaving me feeling weak-kneed. "Seriously, Max. How is this a good idea?"

Max's smile barely lifts the corners of his mouth. "It's just how Owens is."

"An egomaniacal creep?"

"Well…" Max looks over my shoulder, studying the cars still in the parking lot. "Yes." He shrugs in an apologetic way.

"So why put up with him?"

He ticks off his answers on his fingers. "Because he's the director of the theater arts program here at Sandstone. Because no one at this school cares about the drama geeks anyway, and they care even less about us invisible techies. Because we have our ways of working around him. And in the end, because the play is the thing."

He sighs, a sound like leaden feathers. "Don't let Owens stand in your way. You'll be a bright spot in the production, Bec. I can feel it." His fist is clutched at his gut.

"Max— "

"Please?"

I look down at the sketch I've carried out with me. Working with Owens is obviously going to be a struggle, but working with Max? That may make all of Owens's dramatics worth it. "May I keep this?"

"Are you still in?"

His face is so earnest. "Yes."

"Then I'd be honored if you kept it, Juliet."

I make a face. "Don't call me that."

Max chuckles. "As you wish." I swat at him and he dodges. With a wink, he leads me off toward the parking lot.

I'm in. Deep.

Act Second
Scene One

[The theater]

Thursday evening is my first rehearsal as Juliet. At lunch, Max and the gang assured me it'd be fine. He said it'd be a read-through, no blocking (whatever that means), no props or light cues, and no need to have my lines memorized. The lines are the only things not worrying me.

I've always had a great memory for words. It's not exactly a photographic memory, but words have a way of sticking to me. It used to drive Charlie crazy. He's always said he could truly have been a mad genius if he'd been given half my memory. Up until now, I've only used my way with words to make it really, really easy to coast through school.

Dad drops me off before rehearsal. "Mom and I are excited for you, honey." He pats my knee. His half smile makes his mustache look like it's sliding off his lip.

"How did I get here, Dad?"

His mustache falls back into place. "I don't know. But you're here."

I lean over and kiss his cheek. "I am here." We exchange a quick smile and good-byes as I climb out of the car. A little over a year ago, I would never have thought to sign up for an after school club, let alone try out to be a freaking lead role in a play. I'm not the person I was before I met Charlotte, that's for sure. But I'm also not the girl I became when she was around.

The air conditioning hits me when I step inside the school atrium. My skin prickles, and I shrug off the shiver creeping down my spine. I'm not sure how long I stand outside the door to the theater, unable to command my arm to reach for the handle, unwilling to pull it open and step inside.

"Wasn't sure you'd show." Max comes around the corner, his hands shoved in the pockets of his dark jeans. "I'd hoped, but…"

I know. Sometimes that isn't enough.

Max stands beside me, his arm nearly brushing mine. "Whenever you're ready."

I inhale, feeling all the places inside where my breath catches. I am here. When I open this door, I will be there.

Here goes nothing, Charlotte.

You can do this, she whispers.

Max and I walk into the theater together. "This is me," Max says, pointing up the stairs to the booth. "Break a leg." He takes the steps two at a time, pausing halfway to turn back to me—like he's checking to see if I've already run away.

I wave and watch as he disappears into the dark booth.

Alone, I scan the theater, getting the lay of the battlefield before me. If I'm going to do this, survive this play, I need to know what I'm up against—besides Darby—and a crazed director—and my ability to sabotage myself—and why did I think I could do this?

I recognize some kids from my classes, which should be reassuring, except I'm not sure of anyone's name. Why do I never pay attention to these kinds of details?

I can see the circular bald spot on the back of Mr. Owens's head where he's sitting in the second row of seats. There are a handful of students around him, hanging on every word of the story he's telling.

I spot Victor and Kelli onstage setting up chairs in a circle. Victor chases Kelli around the circle singing in a horribly off-key way. He ends the song abruptly and dashes to a seat, pulling Kelli down with him in a bizarre game of musical chairs.

Thomas, my Romeo, is sitting at the edge of the stage, leaning back on his hands, a girl on either side of him. He's smiling and I can see dimples in his cheeks. He looks rakish and adorable at the same time, kind of how I imagine Puck from *A Midsummer Night's Dream*.

A door slams behind me and everyone stops to look up the aisle. Quick calculation of who is missing in the group and I know without turning around that there's a pair of pointy-toed, purple boots behind me.

"Wasn't sure you'd show," Darby snarls as she brushes past me up the wide center aisle. I'm amazed at how the same words can sound so different depending on how it's being said. When Max said those words, I felt reassured. When Darby says them, I want to climb under the last row of seats and hide.

Mr. Owens claps his hands. "Everyone take a seat onstage. Let's begin." He says this like he's in charge, but everyone glances at Darby before moving toward the seats.

Kelli and Victor are handing scripts to everyone. I'm the last one. Kelli gives me my script and a hug. I stiffen on instinct, not used to the casual physical contact. Kelli lets me go with a sheepish smile. "Sorry," she whispers. "I'm a hugger."

"It's okay." And I want to mean it, because she seems so nice, and it's not that I have anything against hugs, really. I'm just not used to them anymore.

Kelli points up to the booth. "We'll be in the booth rooting for you, so break a leg." She winks. "Preferably Darby's."

"Techies," Owens says, his voice playing at jovial, but dripping with disdain. "There is no need for you to be on our stage now." He opens his arms wide, indicating all the actors standing around him. "There are other, more suitable places for you to skulk."

Victor's face is suddenly beside Kelli's as he leans over her shoulder and whispers, "Owens would look good in a cast, too." He pulls Kelli with him offstage.

I hide my smile as I take an empty seat.

"No, that won't do," Mr. Owens says, bustling over. "Juliet must sit with her Romeo." He leads me across the circle and motions for everyone to slide down one seat. My stomach is a double knot of fear.

While Mr. Owens situates himself, everyone talks to the people around them. I stare at my script for a moment, but the words on the cover are blurry.

Meggie, Darby's short, curvy friend from English with long black ringlets of curls framing her face, is sitting on my right. She pushes her hair behind her shoulder and asks, "So, exactly what kind of acting experience do you have?"

I blink, not sure she's actually addressing me.

"None," Darby says, her voice flat.

My nerves are buzzing, and I know I should keep my mouth shut, but— "That's not true. When we were little, my brother wrote a play about a lonely electron, and he made me be the electron, because he said I was a natural for the part, and so we performed it for my parents, who said it was adorable, but I think that's just what parents say, because it was a pretty stupid play—the lonely electron just wandered around being depressed."

Meggie's mouth is open in a little *O*. Thomas has shifted closer to listen, and I catch a whiff of chlorine again. I've got one finger good and tangled in my hair. I tug on it as the verbal flood I've unleashed continues to wash over everyone.

"Electrons are like that, you know, because they can't ever hang out with other electrons. They repel one another. So the play sucked, because my brother was only good at science-y stuff then and didn't know about plot."

Not only are those closest to me staring, but the whole cast is stifling giggles. I can feel my face burning and realize I was a tad too enthusiastic in my retelling of the lonely electron story. And by enthusiastic, I mean loud.

Owens has stopped shuffling papers and is staring at me—a grim pallor on his cheeks.

"So, you see, I have some experience," I finish lamely.

A loud blast of music rocks the theater. Everyone jumps, and a few people scream, but no one is paying attention to me anymore. I look up toward the booth and can see Victor and Kelli dancing. Max is leaning forward, his hand on the glass, looking straight at me with a one-hundred-watt smile.

"Maximo," Owens shouts.

The music stops. "Sorry, Mr. O. My finger slipped." Max's warm voice, barely concealing his laughter, resounds through the theater like the voice of God.

Mr. Owens rolls his eyes, an expression you don't normally see on an adult's face.

I notice Victor and Kelli are still dancing. At this moment, I'd give my entire collection of Harry Potter books (Ron Weasley and all) to be up in that booth instead of here on this stage.

"Let's begin the read-through," Mr. Owens says, trilling his *R*s.

Thankfully, Juliet doesn't appear until the third scene, so I have a little time to convince my brain that no, this won't, in fact, kill me. No one is familiar with the lines, so all eyes are on the scripts in our hands. And since Shakespeare's beautiful language is like speaking in Pig Latin, where you have to pause and consider before each word, no one's really reading with any kind of emotion. Actually, that's not true. Darby reads her role as Tybalt with the exact amount of derision I might expect from both him and her. But everyone else is pretty flat.

As we get closer to my first line, my throat is filling with thick dread, and there's a slight tremor to my hands that makes the pages of my script tremble.

Meggie, playing the nurse, calls out, "What, Juliet!"

My stomach is like the fiery core of the Earth, heavy and hot. There's a gagging feeling in my throat from the heat of it. I know my line. It's four small words. But there's no way to fit them through my throat, so they have to scrape the sides painfully on their way out, sounding like rusty hinges. "How now! Who calls?"

Everyone's eyes look up from their scripts and right at me. Meggie and Darby exchange a look before Meggie asks, "What?"

Beside me, Thomas coughs to cover a laugh. Darby

eyes me like a hungry hawk spotting a lost bunny.

Mr. Owens sits forward in his chair. “Try again, Juliet.”

I peek up at the booth. Victor, Kelli, and Max are giving me three thumbs up. I clear some of the fire from my throat and say the line again, clearly this time, if not loudly, “How now! Who calls?” In the booth, I’m receiving a standing ovation.

My voice grows increasingly confident with each scene we read, and since I already know the play, I can sneak peeks at the booth. Every time I look up, the gang up there does something to make me smile. I’m feeling okay about the whole thing, until Romeo dies. As Thomas is saying his last few words, I glance up at the booth to find Victor’s tiny butt pressed up to the glass.

I can’t contain the laugh that sneaks out. Unfortunately, in trying to contain it, I end up snorting. Everyone looks up. Right at me.

I bury my face in the script, mumbling, “Sorry.” My insides are roiling with laughter, and my eyes water from holding it in.

Mr. Owens scrubs his face with a handkerchief. He would have a hankie.

Darby taps one boot like the rat-a-tat-tat from a machine gun.

The theater erupts again with music.

“Maximo,” Owens shouts, turning in his seat to face the booth. Thankfully, Victor has already holstered his butt, so Owens doesn’t see.

“Sorry, sir.”

Owens stands and shakes a finger at Max. “See that it doesn’t happen again, young man, or I’ll find a new tech captain.”

Darby snickers, and it’s my turn to shoot a look of

daggers at her. I don't think I scared her, though. Not if the smooth smile she tosses back at me is any indication.

"Go, get thee hence, for I will not away." I say my next line suddenly (and loudly) like I'm trying to be heard over the sound of a jet engine. It's the first line I've said with any kind of volume since The Lonely Electron debacle. Thomas chuckles beside me. He's shaking his head a bit, and I get a closeup view of those dimples.

"Yes," Owens says, lowering himself to his seat. He wipes his neck with his handkerchief. "Back to the play."

Thomas winks at me, and I'm not really sure what to do with that. My face contorts into a confused, smirky look that I'm sure is super attractive. This acting thing is going to be more difficult than I had imagined, and I had imagined it would be about as difficult as silently ripping off my fingernails, one by one.

Scene Two

[The library]

In English on Friday, Mrs. Jonah raps her knuckles on her desk to get our attention. "Today, people," she announces, "you're going to begin working with your critique partners on your latest writing piece." The latest piece is an essay, expanding our thoughts on the Would You Rather prompt from the other day. I wrote a thousand words about why I'd rather change the past than plan my future. About midway through the essay, I realized I'd chosen wrong. The idea of erasing Charlotte was worse than thinking I could play Juliet. I'd rather just plan a future where I know I'll never be in the position to lose someone like her again. I figure a future as an agoraphobic cat lady would be safe—provided I don't actually own any cats.

Mrs. Jonah is counting out stacks of papers for us to pass down the rows. "Here are the rubrics I will use to grade the pieces, but I encourage you all to come up with your own set of criteria for critique as well."

There's bustling and chatter as everyone pulls desks

together or moves to the quiet corners to work with their partners. Darby and I remain in our seats—a stalemate as to who will move first.

"Darby? Becca? My desk, please." Mrs. Jonah waves us over to her desk.

Darby stomps up the aisle. I follow in her wake, careful to avoid all backpacks.

"Why don't you girls use one of the group study rooms in the library today? Perhaps it would help if you worked together without an audience." She's looking at Darby when she says this, and her expression is complex, like she's both daring Darby and offering her a peace treaty all at once.

Darby leaves with a huff.

"Um, thanks, I guess," I tell Mrs. Jonah. She sighs, watching Darby, who's already in the hall, before nodding at me.

I scramble to catch up with Darby. We both look straight ahead as we walk past the sunny window of rockers where Darby read to the preschoolers. Once the door to the study room closes behind us, she flops in a chair and puts her head on the desk. The room is small and warm, with beige walls, a large wooden library table and chairs, and dark green industrial carpeting. I wrinkle my nose. It smells like dust and sweat in here.

I shift my weight, foot to foot, unsure what I'm supposed to do.

"You scare the crap out of me," I say, wishing I had better control over my inner monologue. Darby looks up, one brow arched. "Seriously. I don't know what—" I cut myself off, because her expression looks a little murderous.

I wish my voice were louder, but it sounds like a breeze through pine needles. "I didn't ask to be Juliet."

"Then why did you come to callbacks?"

I grab a lock of hair and twist it. "You'll think I'm nuts."

Darby sits up, a wicked smile twisting her face. "Oh, I already think much worse."

"There are lots of reasons, each one crazier than the next, but the craziest by far is this: I want my friend to be proud of me."

"Max?"

I shake my head. "Charlotte."

"The cancer girl?"

I clench my teeth. "Charlotte."

"Right, but the dead one?"

I step closer, my insides starting to bubble, like a slow boil. "Are you being obtuse on purpose?"

"Are we in geometry all of a sudden? I don't even know what that means." Darby holds her hands up, surrendering. "But whatever, we all have our motivations."

Without another word, she opens her notebook and starts reading Mrs. Jonah's rubric.

"We all have our—are you kidding me?" That slow boil in my stomach is starting to roll. "I just said I'm in this mess for a dead girl's approval. My mom has a shrink on speed dial in case I can't deal with my grief. I've never been on a stage before in my life. I'm terrified of people, not just crowds of people, individual people—even the nice ones like Max. And you're going to sit there and tell me we all have motivations? What's yours?"

Darby's face is painted with an expression of surprise. "Holy shit. That's a lot of words all at once. Did you think of them all yourself? Or are they from another one of your brother's little scripts? Maybe it's from the new musical *Whiny Girls?*"

"Oh, I get it. Your motivation is to be a bitch."

"Maybe." The word fires out of her like an arrow from a taut bow.

We've both leaned forward, hands pressed on the table between us. Mine are there to keep them from trembling. I think perhaps hers are pressed so firmly to keep from strangling me. I exhale a shaky breath and collapse into the seat across from her.

"Dammit," Darby says, pushing herself up from her chair. My legs tense, ready to jump up again and flee. "Juliet should have been mine. I've been working my ass off for two years for that jackass, Owens. But you—all you had to do was stand on that stage—and he fell in love with you. Do you know how crazy that makes me?"

"Crazier than a girl who's obsessed with a dead girl?"

Darby looks so pissed that I can feel the muscles of my face pulling away from her, preparing to be slapped. But instead, she does this strangled laugh thing—one loud syllable between us.

"Exactly," she says, her voice a barely contained Rottweiler on a short leash. "Now, please, let's just do our work."

I nod. "Okay. Anything you say, Your Highness."

Darby flops into her seat. "I hate that nickname, but at least I earned it."

Darby shoves her open notebook at me. "Now be useful and critique this. I need grades to get out of here."

I exchange my own notebook for hers. "For The School of the Arts?"

Her lip curls. "How do you— "

"Victor said something about it." I'm instantly sorry for mentioning Victor and make a mental note to tell him to hide—perhaps he should just move far away. I stick my nose in her notebook, determined not to look at her. "I'll do my best. I'm pretty experienced at, you know, reading."

Darby snorts. "I'll say."

We're quiet as we read. I want to make notes on Darby's draft, but I'm terrified to actually write on it. Instead, I scribble my thoughts all over the rubric. When we're done, I notice that Darby did not suffer from the same fear. She's written all over my paper in hot pink ink.

"You started off strong," she says, pointing to a relatively clean area of my draft. "But you fell apart in the middle, like you just lost all your conviction."

I nod. "Mm-hmm."

"Changing the past wasn't as easy as you thought, eh?"

The class bell rings. "I'll figure it out," I tell her, reaching for my notebook.

She pulls it back, out of reach. "Just like you'll figure out this whole acting thing?" She sits back in her seat, daring me with her steely gaze to take my own notebook. "Never pegged you as a hard worker. Figured you were more of a quitter."

I stand like my seat has been electrified. "Excuse me?"

She shrugs. "Unlike you, I'm observant. I've been watching you for years, nose stuck in a book, oblivious to everyone around you, coasting through school without applying any effort. I bet even your little friend last year didn't expect much from you—not really. Bet she was happy just to sit around with you and do nothing."

My stomach feels like a rock. She slides my notebook across the table, but her fingers linger. "There're no free passes with me."

I snatch the book off the table and leave without a response—not because that makes for a dramatic scene ending. I'm not that cool. There's nothing to say, because she's right.

Scene Three

[A Hallway at Sandstone High]

When I get to my locker, Max is waiting for me. His gaze runs over me from top to bottom, like a paramedic assessing a trauma patient.

"How'd it go?" He pushes himself off my locker as I reach for the combination lock. I don't immediately spin the dial. My hand freezes, and I stare at it like I can make it move with my mind. "That well, eh?"

I take a breath to clear my head and then unlock my locker. "Would you rather try at something and fail in a big, spectacular way or do the same thing every day?"

Max blinks, stepping backward as I open my locker door. "Um…"

"Don't think. Just answer." I drop my backpack at my feet.

"It's kind of a tough question."

"Answer." I'm not even sure why I'm asking, but it feels like every molecule in my body is holding its breath while waiting for him to answer.

He runs a hand through his choppy hair, tugging the longish fringes in the front away from his face. "I'll go with failure."

"Really?"

He shrugs. "I'm kind of an expert at it actually. I screw up lots of things. My mom says I have to break something before I can understand it."

I dig in my locker for nothing in particular, afraid that he'll see the tears that I can feel prickling at the corners of my eyes. Of course he's not afraid of failure. He's probably also totally fine with change. I bet he loves surprises. And my money is on his middle name being Spontaneous. Maximo Spontaneous Herrera.

"My turn now." Max shifts so his back is leaning against the locker next to mine. "Would you rather have telekinesis or super strength?"

"Telekinesis is the one where I can move stuff with just brain waves, right?" Victor asks, poking his head around the corner. "Hey, Becca."

I wave and finish loading my bag as Max answers. "Right."

"That'd be cool, but give me the big, rippling muscles, please." He flexes his arms and neck muscles in a way that makes him look like he's wrestling with a pickle jar. Despite myself, I smile.

Max chuckles. "Idiot."

"What?" Victor says, now shadowboxing and bobbing around us as we take off toward the parking lot.

Max replies, "If you have telekinesis you don't need super strength." I take this to mean that Max chooses telekinesis, which I agree sounds pretty awesome, but I'd worry that I'd start daydreaming in class and things might start flying around and it'd probably be safer for everyone involved if I had super strength instead. I could carry way more books home from the library without breaking a sweat.

Victor smacks Max's arm. "But without super strength you won't look hot at the beach sporting a Speedo."

"Dude, no one looks hot in a Speedo."

Victor looks to me for confirmation. I pinch my mouth and nose up to one side and nod. "It's never a good look."

He scowls at me, but then his expression flips and he's grinning again. "My turn?"

Max holds the door for us. "Just keep it clean. Okay, Hulk?"

Victor grabs his chest and gasps. "What are you implying, sir?"

But Max doesn't answer. He just arches one brow.

"Fine, fine, fine," Victor says in a sulk. "Would you rather be invisible or fly?"

Max and I answer at the same time.

"Invisible—"

"Fly—"

Huh. That's three for three. Max and I have about as much in common as Darby and me.

Victor laughs and then hollers, "Shotgun." Without another word, he's sprinting through the parking lot toward Max's truck.

"Man, he really hates the backseat, eh?"

Max's cheeks are like pennies again. "No," he grumbles. "He just really hates losing."

He shouldn't be so worried. I'm not exactly a tough competitor.

When Max and I reach the truck, Victor looks thoughtful. "Hey, Becca. Would you rather sit at home alone tonight or"—he reaches up to toss an arm over Max's shoulders—"hang out with the coolest techies in town."

"No," I blurt, my insides turning into jellyfish, stingy and squishy and not exactly the stuff you want your internal organs made out of.

Victor's smile is lopsided. "That's not how Would You Rather works."

Max avoids looking at me as he shrugs off Victor's arm. "Stop bothering her, Vic."

"Yeah, but it's not like twenty questions. It's not yes or no. She has to pick one." Victor holds the front seat forward for me to climb in back. "So which is it? Alone or cool kids?"

Max snorts. "We aren't exactly cool kids, man."

"Pishposh," Victor scoffs.

Max grins at me as I settle into the backseat. "Case in point. What kind of sixteen-year-old says pishposh?"

"Sixteen-and-a-half." Victor pushes his bottom lip out like a pouting toddler. "And maybe you should just shut up and let her answer."

Max's jaw tenses, and his brows pull down in a Muppet-like *V*. Victor smiles and bats his lashes at him.

Max sighs, but his lips curve upward. "He's right," he says, turning in his seat to face me. "I'm sorry. It would be awesome if you came."

I twist a lock of hair around my index finger. Max's grin widens. "You can get to know us better, then, I mean, since we'll all be working together in the play."

Maybe it's because Darby got under my skin, or maybe it's because I would like a night out of my room, but I nod. "Okay."

As we drive home I watch Max in the rearview mirror. Maybe I said yes because I'd like to get to know some of the techies.

Maybe it's because I want to get to know Max.

Scene Four

[Becca's room]

I text Mom when I get home from school to give her fair warning. I'd hate for her to pass out from surprise when she hears that I'm going to hang out with living, breathing people for the first time in over one hundred fifty thousand pages. The last time I went anywhere fun I was with Charlie and his friends. It was just before they left for college.

> ***Me***: *Got invited to hang out with people from the play. Is that cool?*
>
> ***Mom***: *OMG! So cool!*
>
> ***Me***: *Mom?*
>
> ***Mom***: *OMG is out?*
>
> ***Me***: *I wouldn't know.*
>
> ***Mom***: *We'll talk when I get home.*

Upstairs I sink into my reading nest, but I don't read.

Instead I stare into my open closet, trying to figure out what I'm supposed to wear tonight. Is this an occasion for dressier clothes? Trendier clothes? Clothes that say *I've got my crap together*? A trickling stream of panic starts to work its way down my spine. I don't know what else to do, so I call Charlie.

"I need advice."

"Want Greta's number?" Charlie laughs.

"This is serious."

"So am I. I suck at advice."

I'm silent while Charlie chuckles again. I imagine reaching through the phone and smacking him with it. Finally, he asks, "Okay, what's up?"

"Remember the play?"

"*Romeo and Juliet.*"

"Yep. Well I signed up for the technical crew that does the sets and lights and stuff, but accidentally auditioned for the role of Juliet. The director is insane, so he cast me—"

"As Juliet?" Charlie's voice jumps an octave in surprise.

"Yes."

"Whoa."

"Yeah, well, that's not why I'm calling. See, I'm sort of friends with some of the techies—"

"Trekkies?"

"No. Techies."

"What's a techie?"

"Someone on the backstage crew of a play. May I continue?"

Charlie grunts and I go on. "So one techie asked me to this get-together thing tonight, and I don't know what I'm supposed to wear."

There is silence on the line.

"Charlie?"

"Out of everything you just told me, you're worried about what you're wearing?"

"Yes."

More silence.

"My advice is to find a girlfriend, STAT."

"That's not helpful," I shriek.

"Yes, but I warned you before we began that I suck at advice. So my advice is to find a friend who's good at it. Preferably before the party."

"Bye, Charlie."

"Don't be mad, Bec."

I sigh. "Love you."

"Love you, too."

By the time Mom and Dad finally get home, I've declared my closet a useless waste of space. There is neither anything cool to wear nor a portal to Narnia inside it.

"Becca?" Mom calls.

"Coming," I shout back. I slam my closet doors. I should just toss out everything and fill the space with more bookshelves.

When I get downstairs, I find Mom and Dad are in rare spirits. Mom is humming while she takes raw chicken out of the package. She normally makes gagging sounds when she handles raw anything.

Dad bows before me and presents me with a bouquet of yellow daisies. "For you, Sunshine." He hasn't called me Sunshine since I was very small. It makes me feel like time is folding over itself, layering the past over the present.

"Th-thanks." I know my smile is a silly, lopsided thing, but I'm too stunned to straighten it. His mustache tickles when he kisses me on the forehead.

"Mom, look." I hold the flowers up to show her. "Aren't they pretty?"

"Not as pretty as my girl," Dad says as he pulls spices out from the cabinet. He shoos Mom away from the chicken so he can take over.

Mom holds her hands away from herself like they are radioactive. "So, tell us about tonight," she says as she washes up.

I find a vase as I tell them about Victor's invitation. I reassure them he lives close by—"Just around the corner, and Max said he'd pick me up at eight on his way over."

"Max is the one who asked you to help backstage?" Dad asks.

I nod, arranging the flowers in the vase.

"Looking forward to meeting him, then. I'd like to shake the hand of the young man who coaxed my Sunshine to come out."

Mom grimaces. "I love you, dear, but that was horrible."

"Too sappy?"

Mom shrugs, and Dad chuckles. "Good thing I'm so handsome."

I take the flowers up to my room, feeling a little like I'm walking on a foreign planet. It's been a long time since my parents have been so happy, so carefree. Probably since before they found out about Charlotte's diagnosis. They were absolutely giddy about my new friend last year until they saw the intense amount of baggage she carried.

I slide a stack of novels over on my desk to make room for the vase. I pick up the picture there of Charlie and Charlotte and me from my birthday last year. My stomach feels like it's floating up into my chest cavity, crowding everything. The gravity on my new planet is seriously messed up.

Scene Five

[A party]

I wear a pair of black pants and a soft gray shirt Charlie got me for Christmas that says *I read*. I'm not sure if it's the right choice, but at least I feel comfortable. Everyone is in some shade of black or gray when I get to Victor's. The only real color to be seen is the electric blue of Kelli's Pumas. I fit right in.

The lunchtime gang is all here, plus a few others whose names I'll need to ask Max to help me remember. After a while, people drift off. Miles and Greg are at the kitchen table discussing a movie they saw last weekend. Kelli and Victor are in the TV room with everyone else playing video games. Max and I are left at the kitchen island.

"I like your shirt," Max says. His own shirt says *Hyperboles are the best ever!*

"Yeah, well, I'll take that as a major compliment coming from a guy with the world's coolest T-shirt collection."

Max's face flushes as his dark eyes glance down at what he's wearing. He looks back up with a grin. "You like them?"

"It's one of the first things I noticed about you."

"Yeah?"

I nod.

"What else?"

My pulse ratchets up, and I feel my own face get hot. "Uh…" *Your lips*, I think, but the thought chokes me, and I sputter.

"I like your smile," Max says. "I noticed it last year. You don't do it all that often, but when you do"—my whole body is alight, sending alarms coursing through my veins—"it's like greatness is not just possible, but probable."

I blink, like I might start crying (*please don't let me start crying*). "I like your hair," I say, the words fighting their way out, the wrong ones winning and tumbling over one another.

Max blinks and runs a hand through his black hair.

"It's very shiny." Oh my God. That's not what I wanted to say, but I can't make myself stop saying stupid stuff.

"It's because I use conditioner. My aunt is a beautician. She gets the stuff by the gallon for us."

This is officially the lamest conversation ever, and it's all my fault. He said my smile makes him feel like good things are going to happen, and I compliment his shiny hair? Like he's a prize-winning shepherd in a dog show? I want to know all about him. Important stuff. Not what kind of conditioner he uses.

I take a deep breath, feeling it hitch on all the jagged pieces inside me. Max pushes a broken chip around on the counter.

"How long have you been drawing?"

He looks up from the chip. "Long as I can remember. My dad's an artist."

"What kind?"

"Kind of a Renaissance man. He draws, paints, and sculpts."

"Sculpts?"

"Metal works mostly. Cool stuff. You want to see?"

I swallow the lump in my throat and nod.

Max holds up a finger and leans toward the TV room. "Victor," he shouts. "Becca and I are leaving."

"Okay, but remember to use protection." Victor cackles, and then he swears. "You shot me. You freaking shot me, Kelli."

My face feels warm, but Max's looks volcanic. "I'm going to murder that little jackhole one day."

From the other room we hear video gunfire. "Not again, Kelli," Victor cries out.

"Looks like Kelli beat you to it."

Max only lives a few miles from our neighborhood, but he's far enough into the surrounding countryside that there is plenty of open land between houses. I sneak glimpses of him as we drive.

It is true. He does have shiny hair—so black it looks silver in the moonlight. But over and again, I'm drawn to his lips, their perfect shape and color. I'm sure if I pressed mine to them they would feel soft and taste so good.

I grab a lock of hair and begin to twist.

Max turns onto a long gravel drive, framed by pines. In the dark, they loom like shadowy sentinels, guarding the path to his home. Behind the pines, there is open land and then woods. But every so often, in the wide space between the trees, my eyes catch sight of creatures in the dark. I lean out the open window a little, squinting into the darkness. There on the right is an enormous silver tree, its limbs adorned with elaborate scrollwork.

"What's that?" I point.

Max's eyes flick over the metal tree. "Sculpture."

"Can we see it?"

Max nods. "There's more. We'll take a walk."

The sound of the truck on the gravel attracts attention from inside the small, neat, ranch-style house. The side door bursts open as a lively boy with a wide smile barrels out.

"Max," the boy calls breathlessly before flinging himself at Max.

Max introduces us. "Javi, this is my friend Becca. Becca, my little brother Javier."

Javier rolls his shoulders back and steps forward with his hand out. "Nice to meet you." He's got Max's eyes, but his build and face are much thicker than Max's, like he'll grow to be a football player.

"You, too," I say, shaking the boy's hand.

"Javi, tell Mom I'm going to show Becca the sculptures, okay?"

"Yep," he says, beaming as Max rubs his hand on Javier's cropped hair.

"And then, I think it's past your bedtime."

"I know, I know," Javier says, rolling his eyes at his big brother.

Max watches protectively as Javier goes back inside. "He's eight."

"He's adorable."

"Don't let him hear you say that," Max says, leading me toward a barn off to the side of the house. "You'll never shake him off."

The oversized barn door screeches on its rusty track as Max slides it open. "Alarm system," Max jokes. He flips a switch on the side, and the barn fills with the hum of fluorescent light.

"This is Dad's workshop."

In the center of the swept barn is a half-finished sculpture of a large horse. It is made from intricate scrolls of iron. Most of its ribcage is finished, but there are a few spots I imagine I could crawl inside like the Trojans of old, hiding away while I wait for the command to attack.

"This is a commissioned piece, so he has to stick within certain parameters. I like the ones he pulls out of his imagination the best." Max rummages in a box under a workbench, finding a flashlight. "I'll show you," he says, turning off the overhead lights.

For a moment we are lost in darkness. Max's hand finds mine. Surprisingly, I don't jump or flinch away. It'd be like trying to shrug out of my own skin.

The fragile beam of light from the flashlight illuminates a footpath through the fields around the barn. There are devils fighting dragons in these fields, a princess standing in the middle of a ring of great eagles, and a statue of a tall man, who reminds me of the grim reaper. When the wind blows, this last statue makes a faint whistling sound.

"Your dad has quite an imagination."

"He's a collector of stories," Max says as we stop at the base of the tree I'd glimpsed driving in, iron birds bursting into flight from its branches. "He likes to mix the old with the new."

I can see from here that there is a clockface in the trunk of the tree just under the spot where the branches split. The hands of the clock are both at twelve.

"Reminds me of Cinderella," I say, pointing at the clock.

Max nods, looking pleased. "My favorite."

"Princess?"

Max chuckles. "Sculpture."

It is beautiful, but it makes me wonder—what will

happen to me at midnight? I'll probably turn into a pumpkin. Then everyone will realize what a mistake they made thinking I could be anything other than a...uh, a well-read pumpkin.

"My dad keeps saying he's going to turn this into a working clock one day."

"But?"

"Well, time doesn't exactly stop and wait around for us." Max points the flashlight up at the clockface.

I think of Charlotte and those last months when we waited for something to happen while pretending nothing was about to happen. I think of how I prayed for time to stand still, or at least slow down a little, so we could all be together longer.

We walk back toward the barn. My hand is warm in Max's, and by some crazy miracle it isn't sweating like a damp fish. Do fish sweat? I don't know. This all feels unreal. Like I'm a character in a book, one of those cute romance books where no one dies and everyone lives happily ever after. I never pictured myself as a happily ever after kind of girl.

Max stops walking, tugging on the hand he's holding so that we're standing face-to-face. I try to keep my eyes off his lips, which I imagine would meld to fit perfectly against mine. Not helping. I look up at the night sky and take a deep breath. There's panic clambering up my spine, like a kid struggling up the rope in gym class. Could I deserve a happy ending?

"Maximo?" A voice cuts through the darkness, liquid, musical, accented in a way that tastes like hot cocoa and cinnamon. I didn't know sounds could have a taste, but there it is, sliding down my throat, soothing the rough edges.

Max looks over his shoulder, back toward the house. "My mother."

"Max?" his mother calls out again.

"Coming," he calls back, and I'm surprised to hear that same cocoa and cinnamon accent in his voice. His thick lips tug up into a warm smile as he turns and guides me back through the forest of his father's iron creations.

"Mom, meet Becca," Max says, as we step into the pool of light beside their home.

Max's mother is dressed in medical scrubs, her inky black hair braided down her back. She's shorter than me, but feels so much larger as she sweeps her own dark eyes over me.

"Evening, Mrs. Herrera," I say, impressed the words have found a way to work themselves around the knot of nerves in my throat.

Her dark face breaks into a bright, wide smile, showing off two dimples. She waves off my formality. "Esperanza will do." She comes forward and greets me with a quick, firm hug before turning to Max and wrapping him completely in her arms. "I'm off to the hospital and Papi is sketching, so would you mind checking on Javi one more time before you take Becca home?"

She lets him go, holding him at arm's length, awaiting her answer.

"Of course," Max says. "Anything for the lady of the house."

Esperanza's dimples deepen as she squeezes Max's arms once before slipping her purse straps back onto her shoulder. She winks at us before getting in her car.

Max nods toward the house. "Do you mind?"

I'm still feeling dazed from the brief interaction with his mom. She hugged me. "Why did she hug me?"

Max chuckles. "She hugs everyone."

I'm not sure if that makes me feel better or worse.

"My dad, on the other hand…" Max says, trailing off. "I'm guessing you've never been to Venezuela."

I snort. And then I blush and wonder exactly how far it'd be if I decided to run home right this second.

"Okay," Max says, laughing now. "It's customary to greet people a certain way." He steps toward me. The smell of cedar and honey makes my head spin. "Like this." Max brushes his cheek, rough like fine sandpaper, against mine, turning so his lips barely brush my skin, two soft kisses on one side, then the other.

I touch Max's shoulder, a feeble attempt to regain some balance.

"Sorry," Max whispers.

"No," I say, too forcefully, too loud for the small space we've made. "I can't wait to meet him."

Max's dad is buried in sketches when we walk into his studio at the back of the ranch house. He sits at an old drafting table with a crooked light clamped onto one side. There are charcoal sketches everywhere. He tells me to call him Dezi, and then he does indeed kiss me on both cheeks as a greeting.

I notice Max grinning as Dezi holds me at arm's length to study me. His deep-set eyes are heavily crinkled at the corners, his hair more salt than pepper. He points at a chair and pulls out a fresh piece of paper.

"Please?" He waves a charcoal pencil at the paper like a wand.

"Dad, no," Max says, but I wave him off. I'm excellent at sitting still.

So Max has gone to check on Javier as Dezi sketches me with fervor. I like the silence between us. He draws, and I breathe the familiar smell of the paper (and roses? Where are the—I spot a vase of flowers set up like a still life in one corner—roses), and I listen to the soothing scratching sound of the charcoal. The familiar smells pull me back in time. I close my eyes and imagine Charlotte beside me. I take a deep breath, and I'm back in a beautiful rose garden, Charlotte sketching at my side.

"Can I ask a personal question?" Charlotte asks, looking up from her sketchbook.

I mark my place in my book with the leathery leaf of a rose. "Of course." I peek at her sketch. It's the same girl she keeps drawing over and over again, but this time she has the beginnings of a face.

"Why don't you have friends? I mean other than me? Not that I'm complaining. I am a lot of work—high maintenance diva here." Charlotte pulls her sunglasses down from where she'd rested them on her head and tosses her short, black curls like a movie star.

I laugh. "I'm a teenage recluse. What can I say?"

"But why?"

I can't hold her intense stare, so I look down into the blue-green water of the fountain. The color changes as it ripples, reminding me of pictures of the Northern Lights. Finally, I answer.

"I don't know. I don't have some terrible trauma from my past or anything. I've just always felt strange, like an isolated species that didn't evolve quite like everyone else." I touch the water in the fountain, letting it lap at my fingertips like kittens.

"Mom and Dad used to try to do play dates and stuff for me, and one time it kind of stuck with this girl Trena, but

then she moved and I was like well, damn, I put all that effort into it and then poof—gone. I mean I was like eight, so I didn't really swear or anything. But you get the point."

Charlotte chuckles, and my heart swells. I love making her laugh. I continue explaining. "When I was ten my grandmother died. She was always baking cookies. That's kind of all I remember about her."

I wipe my hand off on my pants and lean back so my face is tipped toward the sun. "Gram's death shook me up. When people die in my books it's sad, but I get over it, because I can just flip back a few pages and they're alive again. It's a safer world—in books." I pluck a few rose petals from the flower beside me and set them like little boats in the water.

"Eventually everyone at school realized that no matter how hard they tried to be friendly, I wasn't going to let them in, so they stopped trying. And that made it harder for me to change my mind and say, 'Hey, everybody, now I'd like a friend, even though I've snubbed you since kindergarten.' It just became the norm. Becca the recluse. And I had my books, so it didn't bother me much."

Charlotte suddenly bites her bottom lip, like she's trying to keep herself from saying what's coming next. "What will you do after I'm gone?"

My eyes feel too full, and I blink up at the sun again. "Probably just go back to being a loner. I'm good at it."

"No," Charlotte says, her voice loud and jagged. "That's not acceptable. You're too sublime to be alone."

I smirk. "Ten points to Gryffindor for vocabulary."

"I mean it, Becca."

I nod. "I know." And when I drop my head onto her shoulder to look at the sketch she's been working on, I breathe deeply, holding on to the aroma of paper and roses and Charlotte's familiar vanilla scent.

I open my eyes and find myself back in a crowded art studio. Did Charlotte think I was a quitter, too? Am I quitting if I go back to being the person I always was before I met her?

I take a breath, trying to hold on to the memory of Charlotte in the garden, but Dezi Herrera's studio smells like turpentine and wood smoke.

"Not bad, old man," Max says, entering and strolling over to examine the picture. His thick lips curve into a smile as he studies the sketch. I accidentally imagine kissing the corners of that smile, which makes my whole neck erupt in red splotches of heat.

Dezi tilts his head and squints at his sketch. "Unfinished." He sighs, rubbing at a charcoal smudge on his thumb. "You'll come back, eh? Sit for me again?"

My left foot is asleep, and I stumble when I stand. "Um, okay." I wander the room, shaking out my foot and taking in all the work. There's a stack of oil paintings leaning against a wall in one corner. "May I?"

Dezi waves for me to search through them and goes back to his sketch work. The first canvas is a busy city street, packed with bodies and movement. Sound and color seem to leap from the painting. The second is a portrait of Esperanza holding a little girl. I glance at Max, and he comes closer to inspect it.

He smiles. "Mom and my cousin Soledad."

I flip to the third canvas, cradling the first two against my legs. This one is another portrait, and at first I think it's Max, but the forehead is too long and the cheeks are too soft. Again I look questioningly at Max. But he isn't smiling this time. His jaw is as tight as a prizefighter's fist, and his eyes look as though he's seeing something on the painting my eyes can't see. Some invisible message I can't read.

"Max?"

"My cousin, Benicio." His voice is sharp, scythe-like.

I glance at Dezi. He's no longer sketching. He's still looking at his work before him, but his eyes are unfocused.

I look back at the portrait, at the light captured in the young man's dark eyes—eyes very much like Max's. The grief hits me between my shoulder blades, knocking the wind out of me. "He's your Thestral?"

Max nods and looks away from the painting.

"I'm sorry—"

"No," Max says. "We've already done that. Let's not do it again—the whole *sorry your heart got blown to bits* thing."

But I want to know. I need to know, like a cancer that won't stop growing in me. Like being given a portion of his grief will somehow lessen mine, which makes no mathematical sense, because how do you add to something and get less? But Charlie's not here to ask, and I don't really care if it's logical or not. I just want to know that I'm not the only one who wakes every morning and wonders if this is the day I will stop hurting.

Max nudges the first two canvases back into place. "I should probably get you home." His hand hovers over my lower back without actually touching me. The phantom touch makes my spine tingle.

"Sure," I say, choking down all the questions I want to ask. "Just let me peek at my portrait."

Dezi's eyes refocus as I approach. He frames his sketch with his stained fingers. I take a long look, and I feel like I'm washing out to sea. "It's me." The tide tumbles me over and over. "I look—" But I don't want to say out loud what my look is. In a book my expression would be described as forlorn, lost, or maybe even condemned.

"When it is finished," Dezi says, his voice like a funeral hymn, "then you will not look so— "

We nod at each other, knowing but not saying it.

Hopeless. I look hopeless.

Scene Six

[Max's truck]

I read five hundred seventy-three pages this weekend. I helped Mom plant yellow and red mums and purple pansies for fall. I worked on revising my Would You Rather piece for Mrs. Jonah's class, too. It'd be easier to just rewrite the thing entirely. Scrap the idea of changing my past and orchestrate some kick-ass future for myself. But I don't want to give Darby the satisfaction. I may be afraid of failing in life, but right now, I'm more afraid of giving Darby any more ammunition.

Max said he'd pick me up before school today. It's a beautiful morning, warm but not humid, so I wait for him outside. I sit on the top step of the porch and stare at the empty curb in front of my house. I hear Max's truck around the bend in the road before I see it. The gears whine as he slows and pulls into the driveway.

As soon as he's stopped, Victor hops out on the passenger side. "Max says you get shotgun this morning, and if I argue, he'll drown me in hot tea."

I look confused.

"I hate hot tea."

"Got it." He hands me a Dunkin' Donuts cup. I thank him and hold the seat up for him as he climbs in the back. Then I slide into the front seat next to Max.

"I didn't know if you liked coffee," Max says, handing me a small bag, "but everyone likes doughnuts, right?"

I set my cup on the seat, securing it between my knees, and peek in the bag to find an old-fashioned cake doughnut. My favorite. "How'd you know?"

Max gives me a mysterious smile.

"Oh, please." Victor snorts. "Don't act like you just knew that shit. You agonized over that decision for five minutes." Max shoots Victor a look in the rearview mirror, but Victor doesn't slow down. "Seriously, Becky, the doughnut girl was ready to toss him out on his ass with the day-old doughnuts."

I take a bite of my treat to keep from laughing.

Max clears his throat. "I realized I didn't have your number, so I couldn't ask."

His phone is on the dash. "May I?" I ask, reaching for it. He nods. When I wake up the screen, there's a picture of Max and his cousin Benicio. I peek at Max. His focus on the road ahead seems laser-like. I feel all the questions I have crowding up, like traffic behind a horrible accident. And I feel guilt, hot and sticky in my gut, because I want so badly to see into his pain, to compare it to mine, to discover if maybe I'm not alone in all this grief.

I swipe the screen, and the photo disappears, just like my unasked questions. I add myself to his contacts, pretending not to notice that I'd have to scroll down to see all of them—way down.

When I'm done, I dig my phone out of my bag. I'm going to ask a boy for his phone number. I've never actually asked anyone for a number. Charlie set up my phone when we got it, and Charlotte entered herself into my contacts, like I just did for Max. I know it's a warm morning, but it suddenly feels too hot in the truck. "May I"—I clear my throat, thinking for the first time ever that old-fashioned doughnuts are really much too dry—"have yours?"

"I thought you'd never ask," Victor says. He leans forward and starts rattling off his phone number. Despite trying to look annoyed, Max laughs. "What?" Victor feigns innocence. "Oh, fine. I suppose you want Max's number, too." He gives me Max's number and adds me to his phone as well.

Then he tells me to add Kelli, Miles, and Greg. "Now you've got us all at your fingertips," he says leaning back to finish his breakfast. He hums to himself in the backseat as he eats his chocolate-frosted doughnut, careful not to spill any of his sprinkles.

I now have nine contacts. That's almost ten. My insides squeeze together, like they're in some happy group hug.

I put my phone away and pick up my coffee cup. I take an experimental sip of the coffee Max brought me.

"This is good," I say. I think it's better even than the Krispy Kreme coffee Charlotte and I drank last year.

"French Vanilla," Max says, when I take a second, much larger sip. "Cream and sugar."

"Thanks."

"And as much as I hate to admit it, the doughnut was just a lucky guess."

Scene Seven

[The theater]

Mr. Owens gives us the rehearsal schedule today. We have rehearsal after school every day from here until forever—at least that's what it feels like. Even if I'm not onstage, Mr. Owens wants me there to "breathe in the full power and majesty of the theatrical process." I could not make up a line like that if I wrote for ten years.

While Victor and Kelli set the stage for today's rehearsal, I lean back in one of the red cushioned theater seats. The velvet pile of the cushion is threadbare along the edge. It feels like satin as I run a finger back and forth across it while I study the schedule, trying to piece together the reasoning behind why each scene is rehearsed on each day. I didn't know this before, but scenes from plays aren't always rehearsed in order. I flip from the schedule to the script to see what scene we're doing today.

Act two, scene six is… I scan the pages until I find it. Act two, scene six is in Friar Laurence's room and—oh crap—it's the marriage scene.

I look to the stage where Thomas is leaning on a desk center stage. I swear that boy is always leaning. He's wearing a blue polo shirt that makes his eyes stand out, even in the dulling glare of the spotlights. I'm getting married today.

Beside Thomas sits a sophomore boy who is half his size. He's got soft brown curls and a deep dimple in his chin. I glance at my script where I've written everyone's names. Marcus Zimmerman—Friar Laurence.

"Juliet," Owens calls. I sink lower in my seat. "Where is the fair Juliet?" I worm my finger under the worn edge of the seat cushion and consider pretending I can't hear him bellowing like a water buffalo.

"Hiding, fair Juliet?" Max sits in the row behind me and drapes his arms over the back of the seat next to me.

"Maybe."

"Everyone has to start somewhere." He's holding an earpiece out to me. I pull my finger out, instantly feeling guilty about the hole I punctured in the fraying seat fabric. Max winks as he drops the earpiece in my open hand. "At least you'll start with a bit of an advantage. I'll be right here to help."

I fit the earpiece in just as Owens shouts, "Where is my Juliet?" He punctuates each word with a stamp of his foot on the stage. He shields his eyes as he looks out over the audience and spots me. "Becca, get up here," he says, dropping all pretense of grandeur.

Max squeezes my shoulder, and then he dashes off.

As soon as I step on the stage, Owens begins his directions. Thomas and Marcus mark up their scripts as Owens talks, and I try to follow their lead.

"Juliet, you will enter from stage right, cross to stage left, and sit in that chair there." He points to a plastic desk chair set on one side of a folding screen. Thomas and Marcus will be on the other side of the divider. Until the crew finishes the sets, it's meant to represent the confessional at the Friar's church where Romeo and Juliet meet.

Once he's finished, he takes his normal seat in the audience and then shouts in his biggest, most over-the-top theatrical voice, "And…scene." Everything inside me goes berserk.

Marcus and Thomas begin the scene. I remind myself to breathe while I wait in the wings for my cue.

"Therefore love moderately; long love doth so…" That's my cue to enter.

I release the lock of hair I'm tangling around my finger as I step into the warm circle of lights onstage.

"Here comes the lady; O, so light a foot," Marcus says.

But I'm not *light a foot.* I'm Becca Hanson. I take four steps out onto the stage and stumble forward, my footfalls on the wooden floorboards too loud. There's a ruffle of laughter from the wings. The ladies in Darby's court are sniggering.

I glance up at the booth. Max is standing, looking down at me from over the control board, and I think I can see him nod his head. Across the stage, Darby glares at me, daring me to screw up again, proving her point—casting me was a mistake.

I fumble my lines, and I'm not sure what to do with my hands or how to arrange my face or what the hell is going on over on the other side of the screen where Thomas and Marcus are standing.

Owens stops us. "No, no, no." He scratches the bald spot on top of his head with his stubby fingers. "Remove the screen," he barks at no one in particular. "I need you to see each other, know each other like true lovers before we can replace the screen."

Oh, dear Dark Lord, this is going to be unpleasant.

No one moves the screen. I guess that's techie work, so I grab it and heft it back. I jog back to my mark, ignoring the strange look Marcus Zimmerman is giving me, like I'm some mixed-breed dog with an overbite.

Meanwhile, Owens is hefting himself up onto the stage and motioning for Thomas and me to stand closer together.

"This is an old technique called mirroring," he says, positioning us so we're facing each other. I can feel heat at my cheeks and know my eyes are darting around like I'm some criminal brought in for questioning, but I can't figure out where to look. "As you say your lines, I want you to mirror each other's motions. So if Juliet raises her left arm, Romeo would raise his right just so." Owens flaps his arms, ballerina-like.

"But won't that look dumb?" I ask. Max chuckles in my earpiece.

Owens pushes us even closer together, so that we're standing only a foot apart. "It's an exercise to help you connect."

My back breaks out in a sweat.

"Begin with your line, Romeo. 'Ah, Juliet…'"

Thomas rolls his shoulders before he begins. I glance at Owens, who is standing beside us rolling his own shoulders and nodding at me to do the same. I try to pay attention to what Thomas is doing while he's speaking, but I can't focus. It's so unnatural to be standing this close to him, to be mimicking his every move. He's mostly waving his arms in ways that make his biceps flex into hard knots.

Ah, fair Romeo, thou dost slay my heart with your beefy muscles.

Any shred of concentration I was holding onto has slipped away. I snort at my own stupidity, which stalls

Thomas's speech. He looks stunned for a second, eyes wide, mouth open. I mimic his expression like I didn't just make a sound like a farm animal. He finishes his lines with his hands fisted by his sides.

But now that it's my turn to speak, I've got no idea what to do. I feel guilty for making fun of Thomas's stupid movements, because what the hell are you supposed to do with your hands when you speak in Shakespeare's convoluted tongue?

"Conceit, more rich in matter than in words," I begin, the words falling dead on the stage between us because I'm so wrapped up in thinking about movements.

In my earpiece, I hear, "Touch his face, Becca." My breath catches with the sound of Max's voice, only a whisper in my ear.

My fingers reach out, following Max's command of their own volition. They trace their way down the stubble of Thomas's jaw. His eyes widen, but his own hand reaches out and draws a line down my face. His fingertips are rough with calluses, and I wonder if he plays an instrument. The thought is distracting. I want to step away from his touch to remember the next line, but Max is back.

"Step closer. Wrap your arm around his waist." His voice frays on the words, like the edges have been hacked at with a rusty ax.

I glance at Thomas, who is studying my face intently now, waiting for my next move. Closing my eyes, I grab the fabric of his shirt at his waist and pull myself into his chest. I immediately feel Thomas's hand at my waist and have to fight to get my last line out.

"But my true love is grown to such excess I cannot sum up sum of half my wealth."

I feel Thomas's cheek resting on the top of my head,

his arms around me, and the warmth from his chest on my own cheek. I remind myself. This isn't real.

Loud clapping erupts from where Mr. Owens and Marcus are watching.

"Brilliant, dear Juliet," he says.

Thomas drops his arms and steps back, but he doesn't look away from my face.

Owens stands, still clapping, and says, "And to think, I discovered you, a hidden gem. Brilliant. Just brilliant."

I tangle a finger in my hair and look to the wings, catching only a fleeting glimpse of the back of Darby's purple boots as she slams open the backstage door. Looking up at the booth, I find Max's silhouette behind the glass.

When Owens dismisses us, I jog up the aisle and take the steps to the booth two at a time. Victor gives me a standing ovation. "Brilliant, dear Juliet," he says, his voice a horrible imitation of Owens.

I feel heat on my cheeks. "You should be applauding Max," I say to Victor and join in the applause. I flop in the chair beside Max. "Thank you."

He studies his hands, picking at his squared-off thumbnail. "I told you I'd help."

Victor claps him on the shoulder. "You're a good man, Maximo. Owens thought she was brilliant."

Max nods, but his chin droops down toward his chest, almost resting there.

Victor smiles at me as he backs out the door. "I'll see you guys at the truck." He waves and is about to disappear down the stairs when his head pops back in the doorway. "Oh, and Becky?"

"Yeah."

A wicked half grin settles over Victor's lips. "Shotgun."

Max snorts, his head bobbing once before his eyes

settle again on his knees. I smile and wave Victor off before swiveling my chair to face Max.

"Seriously, Max. Thanks."

He lifts his chin up from his chest. "Sure."

I try to unravel the language of his sloped shoulders, his guarded eyes, the way his fingers curl in toward his palms. I decide that if he were in a novel, the author would describe his posture as brooding. "Are you okay?"

He looks up at me, taking a deep breath that straightens his spine. His smile is so small, like the farthest star in the sky. "I'll be fine." He swivels back and forth in his chair. It's clear by the furrow in his brow that he's weighing his next words. "I just didn't expect to feel so crappy about seeing you in that douche's arms."

"Romeo?" I thumb toward the stage.

Max looks like he's eaten something sour. "His name is Thomas, and all the girls love him."

I lean forward in my seat, closing some of the gap between us. "My name is Becca, and I'm not a typical girl."

Max mirrors my posture and my instinct is to pull away, because now we are so close, too close. "You're right, Becca Hanson. Typical is not a word that applies to you."

His incisors, fully visible in the broad smile he's giving me, wink in the muted light of the booth. The crooked one on the right seems larger than it should. Something about it makes me want to run my tongue over his teeth, feel the uneven plane they make.

Oh God! Is that gross? That's gross. Except thinking about it makes my stomach flip and not in a vomit kind of way.

I turn back to the panel of controls behind me, hoping the glowing buttons will help hide the hot blush I feel pretty much everywhere.

Scene Eight

[A barn on the Herrera property]

The next Monday, after an only slightly rocky rehearsal (I didn't have to work with Thomas, so there was less sweating and stuttering and general idiocy on my part), Max and I find ourselves in his truck without Victor as a chaperone. Victor's staying late to help Kelli with costumes. His mom taught him to sew when he was in middle school. Kelli says he's actually even better than her at sewing, but his design skills are for shit. Her words.

We've got the windows down, and the wind buffering through the truck is the only music in the cab. To borrow Kelli's phrase, the truck's radio is for shit. But I don't mind. Sometimes, when Charlotte's music was blaring, I'd find my heart racing along with the beat and lose all focus. Music can be a distraction, and right now, I don't want to be distracted. Not from the warm silence between Max and me. Not from the way the wind blows his ebony hair into his eyes. Not from the way his fingers tap to the silent song playing in his mind.

"Do you have to go straight home?" Max asks. I shake my head. "Want to come do homework at my house? I want to show you something I made."

"Okay."

When we walk in the kitchen, Javier is at the table with a math worksheet in front of him. "Hey, man," Max says, dropping his bag on the seat next to his brother and peeking over his shoulder. "How's it going?"

Javier looks up with a glazed expression. "Math is dumb."

I laugh, pulling out the chair across the table. "My brother would have a heart attack if he heard you say that." Javier's cheeks flush, and I quickly add, "But I personally think you're right."

Max chuckles and pulls the paper in front of him. "Let's see what you're working on."

Dezi comes in from his studio in the back of the house. "Becca," he greets me with warm enthusiasm. "You're back." He studies my face a moment longer than is customary, but I'm used to it. Charlotte did it, too, taking her time to memorize features she'd sketch later. I've noticed Max doing it in the past few weeks. Although, when Max looks at me like that, my insides liquefy.

Dezi nods and fills a glass with water. "I'll take over on homework duty, Max," he says from the sink. "I know you wanted to show Becca what you've been working on in the barn."

"What's in the barn?" I ask.

Dezi looks like he can barely contain the secret. Max jumps up, holding a hand out to his dad. "No, don't tell." He looks at me with a crooked smile. "You'll have to wait and see for yourself."

The barn door squeals as Max slides it open. The

orange light from the setting sun falls in a brilliant shaft across the dirt floor. Max motions for me to step in, where I can see more trickles of light bleeding through the knots in the walls.

The center of the barn is filled with the enormous iron horse, now finished, with gleaming eyes and nostrils that I swear I can see moving. Its ribs seem to expand and contract, as if this metal beast were sharing the air with us.

I step closer, my hand reaching out to touch the horse's raised front leg and freezing mid-reach as my eyes adjust to the patchwork of light and catch sight of a new sculpture that wasn't here last time. I leave the horse and walk into a back corner of the barn where there is a set of stairs that lead nowhere. Max is standing beside it, his hand resting on one of the steps.

"What is this?" I ask.

"It will be a balcony of sorts. This took me all weekend."

"It's the catwalk from the theater. The one in the sketch you gave me."

Max shoves his hands in his back pockets and nods.

My eyes feel hot and full. "But why?" I walk around the structure, beautiful in its simplicity, touching the railing that leads up a set of four steps.

"I just wanted to see if I could do it." His voice has a smoky quality, like driftwood in a bonfire. "Dad's been teaching me to weld for a while, but this is my first solo project."

"May I?" I ask, pointing at the steps and placing my foot on the bottom one.

I can see the crooked canine I'm beginning to love when Max smiles at me. "Of course."

I climb the steps, stopping just shy of the top. From here, a streamer of golden sunlight falls across my face.

"Want to help?"

"Build it?" Max looks at me without answering. I smile. "I wouldn't know how."

His face is tilted up toward me, his black hair falling away from his eyes so I can see his entire face. "I'll teach you."

I think back to the list Charlotte and I made in *Oh, The Places You'll Go*. "Would I get to use power tools?"

"Does a blowtorch count?"

I laugh, a sound that feels good and right and free. It brings a smile to Max's face, wide and perfect in its imperfections. "In that case, I'm in."

I spend the rest of the week at Max's after rehearsals. We do homework with Javi (only his Sunday school teacher calls him Javier) and then go out to the barn to work on the catwalk balcony. Welding is sweaty, dirty, heart-pounding work—heart-pounding mostly because I feel like I'm one clumsy move away from incineration. By the time I get home each night, I shower, eat, and am so exhausted that I fall asleep within minutes.

On Thursday, I drag myself down to the kitchen for dinner. I grab the biggest cup we have and fill it with water, thirsty from sweating in the heat for two hours this afternoon. We've made great progress. The second set of stairs should be finished in a few more days.

"How's the set building going?" Dad asks, carrying plates of enchiladas to the table.

My stomach growls. "Good." When I told my parents about helping Max, they assumed it was for the play. I didn't correct them.

"We hardly see you anymore," Mom says, sitting down with a bowl of tortilla chips. "It's strange to come home to an empty house."

Dad swallows a bite of his enchilada and moans appreciatively. "Well, I'm glad you're getting more involved," he says before taking another large bite. I do the same, stuffing in an oozy, cheesy mouthful.

We're all quiet for a minute, and then Mom blurts out, "I wasn't implying it's a bad thing. I'm glad Becca's branching out."

I imagine branches sprouting from my head. It's a silly image, and I giggle. They both stop, Dad's fork midway to his mouth again, and look at me curiously, like maybe I really do have branches in my hair. "Sorry," I mumble, pushing enchilada sauce around on my plate.

"What's so funny?" Mom asks.

"Nothing." I take a big bite and chew. "I guess I'm just happy."

Scene Nine

[The barn]

Victor joins Max and me on Friday. He pushes himself up on the workbench against the wall and keeps up a steady stream of snarky witticisms and long-winded stories. I'm measuring the iron for the railing on the second set of steps, while Max is cutting the supports.

"Hey, Max, remember that time Beni almost destroyed this barn with that pumpkin chucker he made?"

At Beni's name, my head pops up, swiveling to gauge Max's reaction. His shoulders tense—the muscles in his neck straining above the collar of his gray T-shirt—but he also grins.

"He'd have been better off putting a hole in the barn than crushing Mom's vegetable garden."

"Oh, yeah. She was pissed." Victor's legs are swinging like crazy underneath him. He's looking at me when he explains. "Esperanza looks all sweet, but do not cross her. She'll start yelling shit at you in Spanish and shaking her fist in your face, and I swear she gets like three feet taller when she's mad." He's chuckling and shaking his head now, remembering the scene.

"What happened?" I ask, my curiosity crushing me.

Victor looks to Max to see if he wants to take over the story, but Max juts his chin at him, telling him to take the floor. Victor hops down from his perch and starts telling me about how smart Beni was and how his smarts were always getting him in trouble. I smile, thinking of the Virgin Mary glued to the dashboard of Max's truck.

"So one October, Beni made a catapult, only he had a fancy name for it. What'd he call it, Max?"

"It was a ballista," Max says, setting down the cutting torch. He grabs a rag from the bench behind Victor and wipes his hands. "It's like a crossbow, only for throwing stones or lead balls—"

"Or pumpkins," Victor says. He starts pacing and waving his arms around to illustrate the rest of the story about Beni building this medieval war contraption for fun. He'd dragged it way out into the field behind Max's house to launch a pumpkin. "But he'd gotten some calculations wrong, and so when he launched the pumpkin it went way farther than he expected."

I watch Max as he leans against the workbench, his smile so large his eyes are crinkled. He chimes in. "From where we were standing, we thought it'd hit the barn, but it sailed just to the left of it and crushed Mom's garden."

"Squashed the squash!" Victor laughs at his stupid joke.

I'm smiling, too. "That's crazy."

Max shakes his head. "Beni didn't get those calculations wrong." His look is far-off, remembering. "He was aiming for the barn. He wanted to see what would happen when an irresistible force collides with an unmovable object. I think he chickened out at the last second. I saw him nudge the ballista just before it launched."

"He sounds so amazing. What happened to him?" As soon as I've asked it, I want to weld my own mouth shut.

Victor freezes, looking at Max. Max's smile disappears as he tosses the rag back on the bench. "He wanted to see what would happen when an irresistible force collides with an unmovable object." He grabs his welding helmet and gloves and nods at the metal he's cut. "Better get back to work."

I look at Victor, who's wearing an expression that is one part grief, two parts protectiveness. I'm not about to ask anyone to explain.

Scene Ten

[The theater]

I read four hundred six pages this weekend. I also built a metal sculpture of a catwalk. Dezi complimented our work and pointed out places where the joints were too rough and needed finishing. Max looked crestfallen, but I didn't mind. It just means I'll need to spend more time in the barn studio working with Max.

I'm surprised at how comfortable I've become there. I never really left my house much before.

Near the end, when Charlotte was experiencing seizures and migraines big enough to take down a bull elephant, we spent more time at Charlotte's, where her sister could look after her, but not much—not enough.

Just yesterday, I went all by myself from the barn to the Herrera's kitchen to get water for Max and me. I made normal conversation with Dezi while he cooked dinner and even quizzed Javi on a few of his spelling words. And the whole time, my panic at being outside my comfort zone and with new people was barely palpable.

Today, Mrs. Jonah sets the class free to work with our

critique partners. We turned in our Would You Rather pieces on Monday. We've been working all week on what Mrs. Jonah calls genre bending, taking poems and writing them as either prose or dramas. I brought my Emily Dickinson collection from home. I'm thinking of writing "Because I Would Not Stop for Death" as a short story for my final project.

Max gives me a small wink before he joins his partner. I think he meant it to bolster me before working with Darby, but it pretty much makes my insides go mushy.

I gather my things and meet Darby by the classroom door. Since, according to Mrs. Jonah, we'd both come back unscathed from our last work session in the library, we are to conduct all of them there.

Unscathed? I marvel at people's inability to understand there are some scars that cannot be seen by the naked eye. I am terrified to be shut in a tiny study room with Darby again. What horrible realizations about my general ineptitude as a human will I have to face today?

When I follow Darby out, she makes a wrong turn at the end of the hallway, taking us away from the library.

"Where are we going?"

"A place to work."

"Does Mrs. Jonah know?" I ask, catching up to walk beside her.

Darby looks sidelong at me. "Why do you care?"

"Well, I just wonder if she'll know where to look for my body, or what's left of it, after you eat me alive." I hadn't meant to say it out loud, but then, I hadn't meant to audition for the school play, either.

Darby stops and turns to face me with this incredulous look on her face, all eyebrows up and mouth a bit open. "What?"

"Sorry."

She doesn't get mad. Instead she starts laughing. "Don't be," she says through her laughter. "That's the best thing you've ever said to me."

She leads us to the empty theater and then up the stairs to the booth. I feel suddenly possessive. This is Max's territory. "What are we doing up here?"

Darby leans over the control panel, searching for and immediately finding what she's looking for. The footlights come up, and she dims them so they are soft halos of light along the front of the stage. "Don't worry. I know what I'm doing." She sits back in Max's chair and stares out at the empty theater below. "Up here, I am the master of the universe."

I swallow a snicker. "You're He-man."

Darby freezes as she's pulling her notebook from her bag. "What?"

"Masters of the Universe is He-man. You know, She-ra, Skeletor, those big, weird cat things...any of this sounding familiar?"

Darby looks away, toying with the corner of her notebook.

My insides feel fluttery, watching her squirm. I should feel great, putting her in her place, but it feels hollow instead. "My brother is a dork. Adorable, loyal, kind, but a dork. He has the action figures."

I look out at the theater. It is beautiful from up here. I've always thought that. I guess I just figured someone like Darby would only like the view from center stage.

"You're really great down on that stage, Darby."

Darby rolls her eyes. "I know that."

I nod. "Of course."

We're silent in the dim booth. I get out my work,

figuring we're done talking. Time to get some writing done. I open my notebook and stare down at a blank page.

Darby sighs into the stillness. "You're not all that bad at it yourself." She glances at me. "Did you know that?"

I shake my head, afraid to look up from the blank page. There's no way I can make words. I'm too stunned.

"I mean, you've got plenty to learn, but the stage likes you, you know?"

"The stage what?"

She swivels her seat so she's looking at me. "Acting is a web of lies, but those lies are strung together with truths." She takes a deep breath, like it pains her to let me in on these secrets. Why is she being so decent? So human? "Obviously, you know nothing about boys and that kind of love." She pauses to give me a pointed look, allowing me a chance, maybe even begging me, to argue with her just so she can resort back to standard operating bitch procedure. I listen carefully instead.

"But it's not like you don't know what love is, right? I mean you were pretty wrecked without that friend of yours, Charlotte. You've got the pain and anger, confusion and passion inside of you—you've lived that truth—and all you have to do is channel it into Juliet. I think the stage knows, feels, the weight of all the crap you're carrying around. You're a medium, and the stage can use you to tell amazing stories."

"That's kind of creepy."

Darby smirks. "Do you want my help or not?"

"Of course. I need all the help I can get."

She nods like I've finally done something right. "Next time you're onstage and you see Thomas step into the light as Romeo, imagine how you'd feel if it were your friend, the girl from last year, walking out on that stage. Your heart would explode, right?"

My eyes fill instantly with tears, and I turn away from Darby, hoping she won't notice. I blink and focus on the glowing constellation of lights on stage. "It'd make me happier than anything."

"Exactly," Darby says. "That's exactly how Juliet would feel every time she sees Romeo. He is her everything. Her reason to exist."

We're quiet for another moment. "Why are you being nice to me?" I ask.

Darby leans back in Max's chair, and it squeaks in protest as she rocks. She's grinning a bit when she answers. "Just trying to butter you up before I eat you."

I laugh and Darby keeps grinning and it's like the universe is shifting and realigning all the planets in my galaxy. For a moment it does feel like I'm the master of the universe.

Scene Eleven

[The theater]

Owens glows with praise for my performance at rehearsal this afternoon, remarking how I was beginning to look like a natural on the stage.

"Which is a good thing, since I'm not staging a production of *The Bride of Frankenstein*," he says, laughing at his own joke. We're all sitting in the first few rows, waiting for notes and announcements. Owens snaps impatiently at his student director, who I've realized is really not allowed to do any directing, but is just a glorified gopher, and she hops up to pass out photocopies of a revised rehearsal schedule.

The first thing I notice when I glance over the new calendar is that we'll have three days off in the next few weeks due to "directorial personal commitments." I wonder briefly what that means, but don't have time to worry about it before I notice the next, and more important, change.

I have to kiss a boy. Onstage. Tomorrow.

I suddenly wish I *could* be a super strong, reanimated corpse, so I could smash through the cinderblock wall backstage and run and run and run.

I'm quiet on the way home. Maybe Victor and Max notice, but no one says anything. Instead, Victor plays a guessing game he calls, "Name that Directorial Personal Commitment." He and Max keep up a volley of ideas from fittings for a new Technicolor Dreamcoat to classes on clipboard smashing and being your own diva.

Once we drop off Victor, Max asks if I want to do homework at his house. Our balcony is essentially finished.

I shake my head, feeling a wave of anxiety pulling at my stomach. "I can't."

Max's brows dance up in surprise. I can't blame him. I never have anything to do. His expression is asking all sorts of questions, but I'm too embarrassed to answer. What am I supposed to say?

I've never kissed a guy, and Owens expects me to do it onstage tomorrow, so I'm going to try to cram for it like my brother might cram for a math exam. Don't suppose you'd like to be my study buddy?

Um. No.

Max licks his lips, and I can't sit here anymore with the crazy whirlwind of doubt and embarrassment swirling around in my head. "I'll see you in the morning?"

"Of course." His eyes flick over my face like he's trying to read me. "And if you need any help?"

Gah! No. Don't ask to help me. Not with this.

"Tomorrow," I say, loud and shrill like a fire alarm. I wave just before dashing off. "Thanks."

To prepare for my doom, I watch a lot of kissing. That sounds pervy. But since I've never kissed anyone, tomorrow will be like stepping on the moon for me. I've got no past experiences to hold me down; floating off into space is a real possibility, albeit an enticing one, since I'd implode in space and therefore wouldn't have to actually kiss Thomas in front of a theater full of people.

But even after studying a bunch of romantic movies, I can't figure out how the kisser and kissee know which way to tilt their faces, how hard to press their lips together, or what to do with their hands.

Patterns emerged from all the romantic scenes. Hands in hair, tilt face right, smash faces together like wrecking balls. Hands on face, barely tilt face at all, gentle brush of the lips. Hands on hips, tilt face left, open mouth, and—holy crap. I'm doomed.

I'm hiding in the stairwell down the hall from the theater after a sleepless night and trying to remember why I agreed to do this play. Could it really have been because of a list in a picture book? Because of fate? Fate, which I may or may not believe in? To say my stomach is in knots is an understatement. My stomach is crocheted into a heavy afghan that is making me want to vomit a rainbow of yarn. I pull out my phone and call Charlie for backup.

"Charlie, help," I whine before he can even say hello.

"A T-shirt and jeans is fine for a party, although some girls wear other, uh, fancier, types of clothes, but I think you should stick to the T-shirt and jeans look."

"What?"

"I asked around after your last call."

"That was weeks ago."

"I'm too late?"

"Yes."

"What did you wear?"

"Bustier and pleather miniskirt."

Silence.

"Kidding," I say, a smile unraveling a few rows of the anxiety afghan.

"Not funny."

"I have a bigger problem," I tell him. "I have to kiss a boy."

"Ew."

"I know, right?"

Charlie laughs. "No, I mean, ew, I'm your brother. I don't think it's legal for us to have this conversation."

"And I have to kiss him onstage."

"Pardon?"

"At rehearsal. *Romeo and Juliet*? Hello?"

"Oh," he says, exhaling with relief. "But it's a stage kiss, right? You guys aren't a couple or anything?"

"I'm invisible to him unless the spotlight is on me."

"Got it."

"What do I do? What did you do? How'd you figure it all out with Charlotte?"

Charlie sighs, and I feel bad for asking him to remember—for asking him to share those memories, but Charlotte was always very careful to keep her relationship with Charlie separate from our friendship, so I didn't get a lot of details—details I maybe could have used to figure out what I'm supposed to be doing here.

Charlie's quiet for a moment before answering. "I don't know, Bec. It was different because it was real. You're just pretending. So pretend you know what you're doing."

"I watched all the kissing scenes in all the romance movies I could find last night."

"And?"

"It was a lot of kissing."

"Close your eyes, pucker up, and let him do the work, then."

"Right. Good advice."

"Really?" He sounds so proud of himself.

"No. It's the worst advice ever—this isn't the 1950s—but I love you anyway."

I pocket my phone and take a shaky breath before pulling open the door to the theater. The shadows of the darkened seats surround me. Mr. Owens and Thomas are waiting onstage.

Close my eyes, pucker up, and let him do the work.

"Break a leg, Bec." Max's voice sneaks out of the darkness.

The ride to school this morning was, um, let's go with uncomfortable. Pulling my eyelashes out one by one would have been more comfortable. I guess Max spent a little time studying the new schedule last night and figured out my dilemma. Neither of us knew exactly what to say. Victor, on the other hand, slapped me on the back and told me to "Woman up and enjoy the ride."

Before Owens notices me, I slip into the seat next to Max.

"Any advice?"

He licks his bottom lip—a gesture I now know means he's nervous. Why is he nervous? It's not like he has to kiss a boy onstage. It's not like he has to embarrass himself in front of the drammies. Not like he'll have twenty sets of eyes critiquing his first kiss. Not like—my panic has just about crushed all of my reason when he finally says, "Remember it isn't real."

I fill my panicked lungs with a deep honey- and cedar-scented breath. Max. I feel a little more grounded. "That's what my brother said."

Max's eyebrow quirks. I want to run my finger along the high arched line of it. "He sounds like a wise brother."

"Well, he is a genius."

Max's smile lights up the small space between us. Onstage, Owens stamps his foot impatiently.

"Better not keep him waiting," Max says, patting my hand on the armrest between us. When I stand, my legs feel like they are made from overstretched rubber bands. I take a deep breath before making my way to the main aisle.

Close my eyes, pucker up, and let him do the work, because none of this is real. I repeat it to myself the whole walk down the darkened aisle to the stage. Once on the proscenium, I glance at the booth and see Max has taken his place there.

In the wings, Victor waves to get my attention and then pantomimes this weird and slightly obscene make-out session with an invisible partner. His tongue is waggling, and he's shaking his hips like the little dashboard hula girls for sale in gas stations. I use my middle finger to wipe an imaginary eyelash from my cheek. Victor cackles as he disappears backstage.

Thomas takes his mark beside me. Max centers the spot on us. I take a calming breath and look up at Thomas's face. I blink in shock. Thomas is nervous? His blue eyes are tight, his jaw even tighter. He is not comfortably leaning on anything right now. His spine is as rigid as one of Dezi's sculptures.

Thomas is nervous! Surely he's kissed girls before—loads of them if the drammie rumor mill runs true.

"Let us begin," Owens says, pausing dramatically between each word. Thomas and I run our lines a few times with Owens interrupting to place Thomas's hand on my face, or my hand at the back of Thomas's neck, or to entwine our fingers around each other. My whole body feels like my veins have been injected with shards of ice, making my motions stiff. When rehearsal comes to the kiss, I squeeze my eyes shut, pucker, and let Thomas do the work.

"No, no, no," Owens says, his sonorous voice huffing out each small word.

Thomas and I step apart.

"With feeling." Owens circles us. "You love him, Juliet. You want him." His voice is all around us. "You would die for him." He backs away, demanding, "Again, but with feeling."

Thomas sighs, rubbing the back of his neck. "Could you maybe try to act like you like me?" he asks, two flushed circles blooming on his cheeks. "Or, I mean, like Juliet likes Romeo?"

My brow furrows. The afghan inside me wraps itself around all my internal organs and squeezes. "I—"

"Again," Owens says, his voice a feral howl. "The kiss is everything."

This time when Thomas touches my face and says his line as Romeo, he leans in, his eyes wavering like a summer sky before a storm. I close my eyes and try to relax, try to call up some feeling I can use, like Darby said. Only Darby said to use my emotions about Charlotte, and while I loved Charlotte, I never wanted to make out with her, so that's not helping.

But then I remember the way Max's hands felt as he held my hand that first night at his house—the night we stood so close and he leaned even closer to brush my cheeks with his honey soft lips—but the calluses on Thomas's fingertips scratch along my cheeks, and his lips are hard and unyielding. Instead of melting together, I can feel my whole body tensing, from the pit of my rocky stomach to the tips of my wooden fingers, lying like dried twigs against his collarbone.

"Wrong. It's all wrong," Owens says, his voice a low-pitched moan. He points a finger in my face. "I didn't pull you from a life of obscurity to watch you screw up my entire play." He looks over his shoulder into the dark theater. "Darby?"

Darby steps out from the wings. Her jaw is tight as she looks from me to Owens.

"There you are." He waves his arms at Thomas and me, his voice imploring. "Fix this." He leaves the stage, muttering about ibuprofen for his headache. "I'll be back in five," he calls just before pushing his way through the side door.

Darby rolls her eyes in what I'm becoming to understand is a very Darby-esque way. She grabs my elbow and pulls me toward the back wall. She's not happy about having to help me, and I can see why. If Owens knows she can do this, why the hell didn't he just cast her?

Once we're at the back wall, partially hidden by a half-painted set piece, Darby faces me. "I thought we went over this. You've been making progress." She huffs and crosses her arms. "Regrettably." The word grates through her clenched teeth.

"This is different, though. This is kissing. You said draw on experience and—" I break off, too embarrassed to continue.

Darby groans. "You've got to be kidding me." She shakes her head at me like I'm in kindergarten and I've been caught eating crayons. "The moment your techie boyfriend turns that spot on you, you're no longer little miss I'm-so-pathetic-because-my-friend-died-so-I-have-an-excuse-to-be-a-loser, you're Juliet."

I flinch, and she scoffs. "What? It's true. You act like we should just excuse you for being this social oddity, but why should we? You could at least try to connect with people."

"But I am trying."

"Then try harder." Darby takes a breath to calm down. "Look, I get that you don't know Thomas. If Owens were doing his job, he'd have spent some time helping us all get to know one another and build, like, camaraderie or whatever."

She paces in front of me as she continues. "The truth is Thomas is a great guy. Nearly everyone in drama has a crush on him—girls and guys alike—because he's nice and mostly decent and not a pompous ass." She stops pacing and faces me. "So get over yourself and kiss him already."

She turns me around so I'm facing the stage, standing behind me with her hands on my shoulders. I can see Thomas, standing center stage, hands shoved in pockets, studying his shoes while he waits. Darby leans forward to speak into my ear. "You need to remember that on this stage, you are Juliet and Thomas is Romeo. And Juliet wants to make out with Romeo. As soon as the spot goes out, you can go back to your sad life, but when it's on, you are the star, and being the star comes with some responsibility."

She whirls me back around to face her. We stare at each other a moment. "Get it?"

I nod.

"You have to forget who *you* are on the stage."

"That why you love it?"

Darby narrows her eyes, sizing me up. "No. I like who I am. I like acting because *I* get to create my character's reality, instead of other people choosing it for me."

I step back, her honesty taking me by surprise.

Darby shoves me toward center stage. "Let's get this over with."

"He's not my boyfriend," I say, the words springing painfully from my chest as we cross the stage. "Max is just a friend."

Darby brushes past me. "Save the acting for the stage." She grabs Kelli's headset from her before joining Thomas and me center stage. She doesn't bother to put the headset on properly, but loops it around her neck and speaks into the mic. "Techie, I'm going to signal you when I want the spot on and off."

She positions me at center stage, and when Max speaks, I can hear his voice through the earphones. "What's the signal?"

Darby raises her middle finger. "On." She drops her hand. "And off."

Max's laugh sounds metallic through the headset.

"Let's go, Thomas." She snaps her fingers at him and he hustles to stand in front of me. "So right now we have Thomas and Loser onstage—"

"Hey," I interject.

"Whatever," Darby says, waving me off. "But now," she pauses and flips Max off. The spot blinds me as I look up toward the booth. Darby straightens my head so I'm looking at Thomas. "Now we have Romeo and Juliet."

She drops her hand. The spot goes out.

"Thomas and *Becca*," Darby says, drawing my name out. "Shake hands," she demands. We do as we're told.

The spot comes on.

"Romeo and Juliet." She repositions our handshake so we're holding hands. "Got it, kids?"

Thomas and I both nod. I stifle a smile. Thomas looks

worried he may be about to lose his head to the Queen of Hearts. The spot goes out just as Mr. Owens comes banging back into the theater.

"Good. Now do the scene." Darby takes three giant steps back before flipping Max off again.

When the spot comes up, I close my eyes for a moment. *I'm Juliet*, I tell myself. I take a deep breath. *I'm Juliet and this boy, holding my hand, is my sole reason for existing. There is nothing about my life that is good without him.* Despite the warmth of the spotlight, a chill runs down my spine. I'm Juliet, and this is my Romeo.

I open my eyes and study the boy before me, his curious eyes, the strong line of his jaw, the curve of his shoulders. This is my Romeo.

I part my lips—and speak. "Then, window, let day in, and let life out."

The boy steps closer, his hips pressing against mine, his breath in my face. "One kiss," he begs, "and I'll descend."

It's a plea, isn't it? Because Romeo can't live without Juliet, either. He needs the kiss like air to breathe.

I reach out and brush his wavy hair off his forehead. He cups my face.

He can't live without me.

The idea is intoxicating. I trace a finger across Thomas's lips. They are thinner than Max's. *This is my Romeo. I am Juliet. These lips are the only lips I want.* Thomas's eyes close, enjoying the sensation, as my fingers travel from his lips, across his jaw, and down his neck. It's a powerful feeling to make someone else feel good. *I choose this*, I think just before I raise myself up onto my toes and press our lips together. *I want this with Max.*

I break away from Thomas's lips to the sound of applause. Instantly, I'm back in my own skin—my own hot, blushing skin. I did it. I kissed a boy. I glance at Owens clapping in the audience with the other actors. I peek over my shoulder at Darby, not clapping, but shaking her head with the smallest grin I've ever seen.

They should have a name for that kind of look. I scan my memory, going over the thousands of words I've read in my life, looking for the right one, but I can't find it. It's almost a smirk, but not quite, because it's less *I told you so* and more *I made you so*.

Thomas is still holding me around the waist, and the spot is still on us, burning like an alien sun on a roasted planet. I can't make myself look up at the booth. Thomas clears his throat softly, and I glance up at him. "That was really good," he says.

I didn't think it was possible, but I'm about twelve degrees more embarrassed now. "Oh, uh, thanks." I squirm a bit, and he drops his arms.

"Sorry."

"No, I mean, Darby didn't tell us to move, so it's a risk."

He smiles, and it makes his blue eyes crinkle. "Well," he says, grabbing the back of his neck with one hand. "My middle name is Danger."

"Mine's Jane."

Thomas's mouth twists into a grin, but before he can say anything else, Owens swoops in, putting his arms around our shoulders.

"Brilliant. I knew it. I knew you two had something special." He squeezes us once and then drops us. "Now, do it again."

My stomach plummets. Again?

After rehearsal, Thomas touches my elbow as I'm leaving the stage. "I was thinking that maybe we should have lunch together sometime, you know, to get to know each other better. Maybe then the making out in front of a crowd thing would be a little easier."

A wave of self-consciousness washes over me. "Oh, well, I"—don't see how anything could make obligatory public displays of affection any easier—"Yeah, sure. Sometime."

He smiles and nods, running a hand through his hair. He seriously is adorable. But my whole body is aching to get away, to hide out in the comfort and safety of the booth, to see Max.

"Sometime," he says, waving at me as I turn away.

Scene Twelve

[The technical booth in the theater]

Up in the booth, I slide into the seat next to Max. We sit in the silent darkness watching the theater below. I feel like a bookshelf that's been overturned in an earthquake, like all my insides have been spilled across the stage for everyone to see, which is terrifying, but not as frightening as the powerful desire to choose my own fate that impaled me just before I kissed Thomas.

There's a tugging inside my chest, like I'm being pulled in too many directions. I want to step out of my books and explore, but I'm afraid. And it isn't just that I'm worried about death robbing me of another important person in my life. I'm petrified of losing my way—of losing myself in the midst of all these very real and terrifying emotions.

I can't let myself get too close to anyone. Not Max. Not anyone. Not again. And I don't care if that makes me a quitter. Real people are not dependable. They have annoying habits, like smiling with crooked canines, wearing cool T-shirts, and contracting deadly diseases that take them away in the middle of the night. That last one is a real bitch.

Max finally breaks the silence. "How're you doing?"

I shake my head, unable to piece together the answer. He sucks on his top lip, and my heart feels like it's groaning in my chest. Finally he says, "You did a great job for a first kiss."

Instantly, my body is buzzing with frustration. "Oh my God," I moan, hiding my face in my hands.

"No," Max says, swiveling to face me. "I didn't mean— "

"But you're right." I look up. "That was my first kiss, and I wasted it." My voice is too loud, and I want it to quiet the hell down, but it keeps rising instead. "And I wasted it on *him*," I flick my hand toward the stage. But Thomas has already left. Victor is standing center stage now, finishing setting up chairs at a long banquet table for tomorrow's rehearsal.

Max grins. "That *would* be a waste," he says, looking down at Victor.

Despite the ickiness inside me, I have to laugh. I lean back in my chair and grab a chunk of hair, tangling my finger until the tip feels numb. I glance at Max out of the corner of my eye and watch an internal conversation play across his facial expressions. He swivels our seats so we're facing each other, our knees woven together.

"That wasn't a first kiss," he says, "and I can prove it to you."

My fingers, even the numb one, are suddenly electric. "How?"

"When you kissed him, did your heart race?"

"It was racing before I kissed him, but mostly because Darby was looking kind of pissed and there were twenty sets of eyes watching me humiliate myself."

Max nods. "Okay, but when you kissed him, did your stomach feel swoopy? Were you consumed by it, by the kiss?"

I shake my head. I didn't do any of that. I thought of Max.

"Then that wasn't a real first kiss."

Max reaches out to unwind my finger from my hair and pushes the strand behind my ear. When he licks his lips, my skin erupts like a solar flare. I want to be the one licking those lips. A tremor slides down my spine.

Our breathing is too fast. His eyes flick from my eyes to my lips and back again. We're leaning toward each other, so close that I can see the light stubble across his jawline, even in the darkened booth. And I want to get closer, so much closer, but then the door to the booth flies open, flooding us with the light from the stairwell.

"Dude. Ride. Home."

Max and I fly apart like we've been shocked with an electrical current.

"Sorry," Victor says, swearing softly under his breath, as he backs into the hall again. "Sorry, man. I'll go hitchhike." He closes the door, and we're wrapped in darkness again.

I blink, resetting my eyes. And although our lips never touched, my stomach is swoopy, and I feel absolutely consumed by the sudden distance between us.

Max slumps over in his seat, his head in his hands, growling something about "Victor" and "murder" and "for the love of Pete," which makes me chuckle in a hysterical holy-shit-did-I-almost-kiss-Max? kind of way.

"Pete?" I ask, joking—trying to regain my balance around him.

Max looks up from between his fingers. His eyes are dark, but a smile twinges around his mouth. I want to capture his mouth with mine, but now that the moment has passed, and adrenaline is rocketing through my veins, I realize that may not be the best idea. It may be the worst idea. It may be the idea that destroys me. I hop up and reach for the door.

"Want me to go get Victor?"

"No." Max rubs his hands through his hair.

"We can't have him hitchhiking." My hand rests on the door lever. "He's liable to get kidnapped that way."

Max sighs, his fingers still scratching his head, buried in that inky black hair. "Becca, I— "

"There's nothing. It was nothing. Meet us outside, okay?" I open the door and back out of the booth. Max looks up at me, his dark eyes so full of everything I need—hope and want and life. His nod is microscopic, but I'll take it. "Okay," I say before I gallop down the stairs, running from the onslaught of emotions towering over me, ready to topple with the slightest touch.

I should stay the hell away from Max because he makes my stomach feel swoopy. Swoopy stomachs are the kinds of stomachs that get annihilated when trouble comes. And trouble always comes.

Scene Thirteen

[The cafeteria]

At lunch the next day, Victor and I debate the existence of love at first sight. Lately, lunch is filled with conversations sprung from *Romeo and Juliet*. Victor is surprisingly pro love at first sight. I say it takes more than three days to fall in love, which makes this play more farce than tragedy. Kelli chimes in on my side whenever I nudge her with my elbow, but she's more involved in finishing chemistry homework before next period than anything else.

Max is late—something about a meeting with Owens.

"Cynics," Victor cries, slapping his palm on the table with a laugh.

I nudge Kelli. "Two against one."

She looks up from her lab notes to reply, but the words get stuck in her mouth. She ends up spluttering and gulping like a carp in the shallows.

Thomas Harrison is standing behind Victor, a wide smile dimpling his cheeks and crinkling his blue eyes.

"Mind if I join you guys?"

Victor whirls around in his seat. His whole face flushes for a second. He swallows with some difficulty before clearing his throat and growling, "Lost?" He hitches his thumb in the direction of the table at which Thomas usually sits—the table from which Darby is flinging invisible arrows at me. "This is the techie table. Drammies sit over there."

Victor turns back toward us, rolling his eyes, but his whole face looks like he's broken out in hives.

Thomas's smile wavers. "But Becca's not a techie."

It was a simple statement. Thomas couldn't have known what he was saying. Not really. He couldn't have known he was pointing out the one thing I'd been hoping no one would notice. I don't fit, not really.

All eyes are on me. I decide to join Kelli, gulping wordlessly instead of speaking.

"Whatever," Thomas says, his voice strung tight with frustration. "Becca, if you ever want to sit with your own kind, you know where to find me." He turns quickly, his messenger bag swinging out and nicking Victor in the head.

"Asshole," Victor grumbles, fixing his hair where the bag grazed him. He stabs viciously at his mushy broccoli.

"Why can't Thomas sit here?"

They look at me like I just suggested we run through the cafeteria naked.

"He's not that bad. Is he? Darby said he was nice."

"No, you're right, he's not that bad," Kelli says quietly; she looks pointedly at Victor from behind her glasses.

Victor tosses down his fork, which ends up not being very dramatic since it's plastic and makes no noise when it hits the Styrofoam tray. "Yes, Becca. He's that bad. They all are."

"Why? What'd he do to you? What'd any of them do?"

"What'd he—?" Victor straightens to his full height in his seat. "They use us, Becca. They think they're better than us. They think the entire success of the play is due to their stupid acting and completely disregard all the work we do behind the scenes. We make them into gods, Becca, and they shit on us."

"But *you* think you're better than them, so how is that different?"

"No," Victor says, crossing his arms over his chest. "I *know* I'm better than them—smarter, more talented, harder working, and loyal."

Kelli snickers. "You sound like a Boy Scout."

Victor shoots her an evil look. "Look, Becca, you're new to our club, so we've made concessions." Kelli shakes her head, her mouth a stern line, but Victor continues. "Do us a favor and just follow the damn protocol. Drammies and techies do not mix."

"So why do you put up with me?"

Victor shrugs.

I'm not hungry. In fact, I'm regretting eating at all because it feels a little like my lunch is crawling up my throat. I stand, tossing my stuff in my bag, screaming obscenities in my head to keep myself from crying.

"Becca," Kelli says, putting her hand on my arm. "We are your friends. We all are. Victor just has this thing"—Victor slams his hand on the table and Kelli redirects—"Victor's just in a bad mood. Isn't that right?" She glares at Victor, but instead of looking at me, Victor stabs the piece of wilted broccoli that just slid off his plastic fork and studies it like it's alive.

I shake Kelli off. "Thanks, but I'm just…it's nothing. I've got to go." It's worse than I feared. It's pity. I'm their *pro bono* pity friend.

Kelli kicks Victor under the table. Victor yelps and stands. "Becca, wait."

"No," I shout. "And for your information, that is *my*

table. I was happily sitting here—ALONE—before you came and sat with *me*." My voice rises above the cafeteria din. I wave a choice finger in Victor's direction, as I weave through the tables toward the door. When I pass Thomas, he reaches out and takes my wrist.

"You okay?"

"Fuck okay." The ugly word ricochets around the cavernous cafeteria.

Thomas lets go, like his fingers have been singed. Darby sits back like she's watching her favorite show. Her expression is one part surprise and one part challenge. I can see a few teachers moving closer to the commotion I'm causing.

I know I should quietly slink away. I should go hide in the library—hide in the pages of a book. But there's something about the silent challenge in Darby's face. Like this is a test.

Walk away and disappear forever or stand up to be counted.

I guess I figure, what the hell, because I let it all go, and turn to scream, "Fuck you, too, Victor, you mewling, priggish maw." I cringe at the Shakespearean slant to my insult.

There's enormous pressure behind my eyes, and I just can't cry here in front of all these strangers. I turn to flee, but Mr. Dupree, the school disciplinary officer, holds up his hands to halt my progress.

"Let's take a walk to my office, shall we?" He ushers me away from the crowd.

When I glance back at the wake of my destruction, Kelli is gathering her things and muttering at Victor, who sits with his back to me, his head bent low over his stupid, soggy broccoli. Poor Thomas is looking completely bewildered. But Darby? I may have just won a few points with the Queen of Hearts.

Scene Fourteen

[The counselor's office]

Mr. Dupree's office is decorated in shades of white. From the scuffed tile floor to the painted cinderblock walls to the shelves full of books, and I wonder at how many of those even have white covers. The nameplate on his desk is white with black letters—Mr. Bradley Dupree, Discipline Officer.

For some reason, I keep picturing him as the Lone Ranger. I'm expecting him to stride back in here wearing white chaps, spurs a-jingle-jangling, and tip a gigantic cowboy hat at me before locking me in jail forever.

The red hands of his clock tick around, counting out endless minutes since he dumped me in here to cool down, but he still doesn't arrive. The whiteness of the room hurts my head. I close my eyes and lean forward, resting my forehead on the edge of his white desk.

I should not have lost it like that. All those eyes on me. All the whispering and pointing. That was no stage performance. That was lunch. I'm supposed to blend in at lunch. I'm supposed to blend in wherever I go. How have

I let myself get so sucked in to all of this? I rock my head from side to side, using the pressure of the hard, cool desk to massage my forehead.

"Miss Hanson," Mr. Dupree asks, pulling out his white desk chair, "are you okay?"

I can't even bear to look up at him.

Okay?

No. I'm not okay. I begin to cry. It's been so long. I'm not sure I know how to make it stop.

Mr. Dupree dumps a box of tissues in my lap and holds up a finger for me to wait here. He walks as quickly as he can, while still remaining impassively casual, out of his office. In other words, he's just shy of breaking the school's one-hundred-meter-dash record.

Five tissues later, he returns, ushering into the room a small woman with a long wispy skirt and dozens of bracelets clicking together on her wrists. I recognize her from last year. It's Dr. Wallace, the school counselor I'd promised my mother I'd go see. Looks like I can stop feeling crappy about breaking that promise.

Dr. Wallace is a few inches shorter than me, but she manages to pull me to my feet. Slinging her arm around my shoulders, she walks me down the hall to her office, where she sits me on a slouchy couch covered with jewel-toned pillows.

She murmurs shushing sounds as I shred tissue after tissue. There are only a few left in the box when I finally take a deep breath to staunch the flow of tears and snot and misery.

I look around Dr. Wallace's office. It's like she's trying to apologize for the sterile atmosphere of her colleague's room by cramming every color in the spectrum into her own space. Where Mr. Dupree's desk was clean, straight lines, hers is thick, with rounded edges and bulging stacks of papers on top. The shelves are crammed not only with books, but also with odd trinkets, pieces of driftwood, a collection of old bottles, a basket with wooden spools of thread.

Dr. Wallace is perched beside me on the couch, her head tilted as she studies me with dark, curious eyes. I'm reminded of a magpie, and for some reason, all the clutter relaxes me. Charlie's room felt like this. At least, it did before he moved out.

"I'm ready to listen whenever you feel ready to talk," Dr. Wallace says, her voice deeper than I'd expected from such a petite person.

I nod and wipe my eyes one more time. "I'm not sure what I'd talk about. I'm not sure exactly why I lost it."

Dr. Wallace pushes her bushy black curls behind her ear. "I remember you."

I sniffle.

"We've never really met, but I know you. Charlotte spoke of you all the time."

At the sound of her name, another sob lodges in my throat, but I'm just too tired to let it out. I dig my fingernails into my palm, focusing on the pinpricks of pain I can create there.

We sit in silence. Dr. Wallace's keen eyes are scanning me, collecting and categorizing information. She notices me squeezing my fist. I stuff my hands between my knees.

The silence swallows us. I begin to wonder why she's not asking me about my explosion in the cafeteria. "Am I in trouble?"

"No. Not trouble. Not this time." Her hands flutter around the hem of her embroidered tunic. "Not as long as you to come see me next Friday. Same time. Same place.

Just to check in." She catches my eye to be sure I've heard her before continuing. "And it'd be wise to refrain from using such vulgar language in school."

"Yes, ma'am."

She chuckles. "At the very least, don't shout it."

My mouth twitches in a grin, and the sob gripping my throat lets go. At least I don't have to tell Owens I can't make it to practice for a week because of detention. I imagine how red the top of his bald head would be.

Dr. Wallace stands and opens her door. "Like I said, I'm ready to listen."

I toss all my tissues in the trash and thank her. As I step out the door, her hand lands on my shoulder, the touch featherlight. "Becca, grief isn't something we can ever really leave behind. You'll learn to bear it, though."

I open my mouth, but there's nothing in me worth saying.

When I step into the hallway, Max and Victor are waiting for me, silhouetted against the light from the large windows across the hall. I'm painfully aware that my face must be all red and splotchy like I've been stung by a thousand angry bees.

Max grabs Victor. His fingers lock like pincers on the flesh just above Victor's elbow. "Victor has something to say."

Victor's face flushes. "Look, Becca, I'm sorry."

I cross my arms across my chest. "Yes. You are. A sorry, stupid ass."

Victor, who'd been about to continue, freezes with his

mouth open. It looks like he's trying not to smile, which infuriates me even more.

He closes his mouth and swallows his smile. "I was being an idiot. I was jealous, and that Thomas Harrison, he really bugs the hell out of me. He's so stupid handsome and perfect and gets everything he wants—anyone he wants. And for years now I've been watching him be all look-at-me-I'm-perfect and"—Victor looks lost for a second, but then picks up steam as he continues to rant—"and, I mean, he drives a freaking Escalade. Why does anyone our age need an Escalade? Shouldn't we all be doomed to bum rides with our friends in their crappy trucks? It's just not right. It's not natural."

Max pops Victor on the shoulder. "Right," Victor says, shaking his head like a wet dog. "Look, this is totally a case of it's-me-not-you. My reaction today wasn't really about you. Of course you're our friend, Becca. Max may have brought you into the group, but we all really like you. I mean"—he tangles his hands in the hem of his overlarge T-shirt—"I like you."

"But why? Why do you like me?" I realize it's unfair to expect Victor to answer this for all the people I've ever wondered it about, but Charlotte's not around to ask anymore, and I'm too afraid to ask Max. And Victor owes me.

"Why?" Victor blinks, like a mole adjusting to the sunlight. "Because you're actually kind of funny, and you know how to shut me up—a skill few possess—and you make Max happy."

I look from Victor to Max, whose face is now the color of a shiny penny. He's looking at his feet. He doesn't look happy. He looks like he'd love for the heavy glass window behind us to collapse on him in a catastrophic failure of structural engineering. It's kind of adorable.

I can feel my insides melting. "Are you just saying all of this because Max told you to?"

Victor's crooked grin answers me. "A little. But only because I'm immature and like to hold grudges, so I'd have preferred we drag this out and stare daggers at each other for a while, and maybe you'd make up some vicious rumor to get back at me, and then eventually, before we graduate, I'd ask for forgiveness."

I want to stay angry, but, I don't know, there's something about his honesty. "You really are an insufferable ass."

"And you are getting very proficient at the Shakespearean insults."

Scene Fifteen

[The woods]

"You know what we need to do tonight?" Victor asks from the back of Max's truck. "Ghost train."

I turn in my seat. "What?"

"Ghost train," Victor repeats. "It's cool and spooky." He smirks. Max is silent, focusing on the road ahead like we're driving through a blizzard. I may have forgiven Victor, but Max is taking a little longer to thaw out. "It'll be fun. Kelli, Miles, Greg, and I are all going out to dinner tonight, so we'll meet you two out there." Victor leans forward to look at Max. "Nine o'clock sound good?"

I try to read the look that passes between them, but I'm no expert at guy code so I'm not sure if Max thinks it sounds like a good plan or if he thinks a better plan would be to abandon Victor on the side of the road. When he doesn't say anything, Victor turns to me. "Looks like it's up to you then, Becky dearest. What do you say?"

I glance at Max. I'm not a fan of spooky (overactive imagination), but if it means I can spend some time with Max tonight, then—"I think it sounds great."

•••

The ghost train is way out in the country. Max and I hardly talk on the drive there, and the silence isn't comfortable like when we work together in the barn or do homework at his kitchen table. This silence is filled with ghosts and regret and unanswered questions.

We turn onto a road that isn't a road so much as a rut between the trees. The forest swallows us as we drive. When we get to the meet-up spot, a small clearing in the woods, Greg's giant blue Malibu is there, but it appears that they've gone on without us.

We walk down this nearly invisible dirt track. Max has a flashlight that illuminates our path with soft blue light. The night is loud with the rattling of pine needles in the breeze and chirping of crickets and toads. But the quiet between Max and me keeps growing and I feel like if I don't reach out to bridge the gap now, it'll grow too large, like Grand Canyon sized, and I'll be stranded on one side wondering *what if?*

I take a deep breath, screwing up all my courage, and whisper, "This is scary."

"It is a ghost train." His mouth pulls upward in a smirk. "It's supposed to be scary."

"Not this," I say, pointing at the dark forest around us. "Well, actually, maybe that, too, but I meant this." I point first to my chest and then to his.

"Me? I'm scary?" He tilts his head, watching me. It shouldn't be allowed—being so charming and handsome, funny and talented. There should be rules.

I link my arm in his. "Terrifying."

Max hugs his arm into his side, pulling me closer, and

the warm pressure of it all makes me dizzy. "You don't have to be afraid of me, Becca." He looks down at me as we walk again. "I'm not going to hurt you."

We look at each other for a few beats. I want to believe him. But Charlotte didn't mean to hurt me, either. I have to tell myself that. Every day. Otherwise, the fiery anger I feel when I think about her leaving would burn me from the inside out.

"So," I say, trying to breathe normally. "How do you know about this ghost train?"

"Beni." Max's voice sounds like he's farther away than the narrow trail would allow. I study his profile as we walk, listening as he elaborates. "He brought me out here when I turned thirteen. He had been talking it up for years."

I watch the beam of light wandering down the path ahead of us.

"The story goes that the engineer was behind schedule and was pushing the train as fast as it would go. He was in a hurry himself, because he was going to pick up his fiancée at the next station, and it was getting dark. Apparently some ne'er-do-wells—"

"Ne'er-do-whats?"

"You heard me," Max says. "Tricksters, shysters, rogues, flimflammers." He wiggles his dark brows, making me laugh.

"I see," I say, composing myself. Max leans closer, sending a wave of tingles down my spine. Is he smelling my hair? Oh thank you gods of cleanliness for suggesting I wash it twice when getting ready for tonight.

"So the ne'er-do-wells had accosted his fiancée while she waited at the station. They'd dragged her down the tracks, had their way with her, and left her for dead stuffed under some undergrowth beside the tracks."

"Geez, Max." I grab the flashlight from him and start

swinging it around into the leaves all around us.

"I didn't say it was a nice ghost story." He squeezes my hand before continuing. "They never are." A dry smile puckers his thick lips. "Do you want to turn around?"

I look behind us. We can't see the truck anymore, but ahead, in the slim beam of light, I can see an opening in the trees. "Please, finish."

"When the engineer reached the deserted station, he saw the louts stumbling up from the brush, covered in filth and blood. Long ghost story short, the engineer hopped off the train and went all ninja on the bad guys. He was near death, but dragged himself back the way he'd seen them coming, looking for his girl. They say that when she came to, she could see where he'd finally lay down in despair of never finding her—five feet from where she was hidden."

"Star-crossed."

Max nods. "Now, the engineer rides slowly along the tracks, back and forth, looking for his love."

"What about her? What about the girl?"

Max shrugs. "She lived."

He says this like it's supposed to make me feel better. "And?" The frustration in my voice scratches my throat.

"And it's a ghost story, so no one knows about her. We only know about the ghost."

We come to the edge of a long, narrow corridor cleared of trees. Here and there you can see large railroad ties still rotting in the ground, but the iron girders have been pulled up. Max leads me to the middle of what used to be the tracks and nods at the flashlight still in my hand. "You've got to signal him."

"What?"

"Signal the engineer. Flash the light three times."

For a long moment, I'm frozen, but I finally work up

the nerve to flick the light off and on three times. It's not like I expect a ghost train to come barreling down the forgotten tracks, but I do have the feeling in my chest that something is about to happen.

One breath, five, ten, twenty breaths later and still nothing.

I peek at Max and notice he's not looking down the tracks, but right at me. Everything in me flutters like the pages of a favorite book as I flip to the best part. His eyes, bright in the starlight as they look into mine, are becoming my most favorite passage in this story.

In the distance, we hear the whistle of a train. Suddenly, there's a flash of white light that washes through the corridor of trees, illuminating Max's whole face in its arc.

Shit. Eating. Grin. It's the only way to describe the look of glee on his face as I nearly hyperventilate.

He pulls me close so he can whisper in my ear. "Gotcha."

And, oh my God, he does. He's got me, all I have to do is give in, let him have me, whatever I've got left to give. I turn toward the light as it disappears in the darkness, and spy the outline of a lumbering train, about one hundred yards away, running perpendicular to where we stand. I can feel the clacking of the wheels inside my chest, matching, click for clack, the beating of my poor, broken heart.

"That's not a ghost." I am trying to keep my voice light, trying to rebury the thing inside me that keeps trying to get out, the thing that I need to stay dead if I'm going to survive. "That's a real train. How'd you know it'd come by?"

Max's laugh is loud and liquid; his mouth opens with the sound.

He's still holding me by the waist, and pieces of me are craving more, but I swat at his chest. I'm not mad, though.

Not really. I'm disappointed that his mouth is so close, so open, and not on me. Disappointed that I can so clearly see what I want, but am too afraid to take it.

"I didn't know. Sometimes you can stand out here all night and never catch a glimpse of anything. Just dumb luck."

Yes. Dumb luck.

The gang comes stumbling out of the underbrush moments later. Greg is in the lead with Miles and Kelli behind him. Victor steps into the clearing last. He looks like he's sulking.

"Where were you guys?" Max asks.

"We took a wrong turn," Miles says.

"Sev-er-al," Greg adds, drawing the word out.

Victor's scowl deepens. "How was I supposed to know?"

Greg shakes his head. "You said you knew where we were going, said you'd been here plenty, said you knew it like the back of your hand. That's how you were supposed to know."

"We know you know your own hand, Vic," Miles says, trying to choke back giggles, but it's no use. Everyone laughs—even Victor—and it sounds sweeter than all the frog songs in the night.

"You just missed the train."

They all groan. "Was it scary?" Kelli asks me.

Max snickers and I smack his shoulder. "Yeah, it was certainly unexpected."

"Maybe another one will come by."

Everyone starts plopping down in the clearing, settling in to wait for another train, lying side by side in the scratchy grass, watching the stars. They're clearer out here, away from the lights in town.

Max tips his head toward mine in the grass and

whispers, his lips almost touching my ear, "For the record, Becca, I'm scared, too."

When I turn my face to look at him, his eyes are fathomless in the darkness.

"You thought you got a scare tonight, Becky," Victor says. "But it's nothing compared to the first time Beni brought us out here. Remember, Max?"

Max tenses, a reflex like when a ball is thrown at you. I reach out and take his hand in mine. Maybe it's the darkness, maybe it's the stars, or maybe it's just that a piece of me knows that's where his hand belongs—in mine. He traces a pattern on my palm with his thumb. An owl screeches in the wood behind us.

"I remember," Max says, propping his head up on his other hand. He tells the story of his thirteenth birthday when Beni brought Victor and him out here. How Beni's buddies hid in the woods. How Max and Victor screamed. How Victor fell flat on the ground—"like he'd been shot in the chest"—when the guys jumped out at them.

That story melded into another and another, and before long I felt like I knew a little about Beni, but more importantly, I knew so much more about Max and his loyalty, kindness, and capacity for unwavering love.

And that I am a fool. I know that for sure now. I am a coward and a fool.

Max and I leave the clearing first, the others lingering behind, still telling stories, still waiting for the ghost train to reappear. When we reach the truck, I lean against my door so Max can't open it for me. Not yet.

He steps close; we're toe-to-toe in the trampled grass. "Thanks for bringing me," I say.

Max grins.

"I'm serious."

"You're seriously thanking me for dragging you out to the middle of nowhere and scaring the crap out of you?"

"No."

His brow and one side of his grin tic upward.

"I'm thanking you for sharing this with me."

This time his laugh is louder. "Yeah, the look on your face was pretty priceless."

I tug on the sleeve of his shirt. "I mean your friends, this place, the memories of Beni."

His laughing quiets, but his smile remains. "You're welcome." He takes a lock of my hair and twists it around his finger, studying the way the light reflects off it in the dim clearing before tucking it behind my ear.

"It was a stupid accident that took Beni away." Max swallows and I watch the shadow of his Adam's apple bob.

"Max, you don't—"

"I want to share this with you." His head is stooped so he can look me in the eye, and a lock of black hair falls over his forehead. I want to touch it, feel if it's as silvery smooth as it looks in the moonlight.

"He and his friends were drunk," Max says, looking up at the sky. The hair falls back from his forehead, and I feel angry that gravity has deprived me of the feel of it in my fingers.

"He'd been doing that a lot, getting drunk. Said it was no big deal, he was just blowing off steam. Said the pressure at Stanford was high, but he could handle it."

Max shifts, like he's going to move away from me, but I reach out and catch his hand.

His head shakes, like he's still in shock from the accident as he finishes speaking. "He stepped out in front of a moving car. They were playing chicken or something. He wanted to see what would happen when an irresistible force collides with an unmovable object."

I try to swallow the thickness in my throat. I should have swallowed my words along with it. "That doesn't make any sense. He could have moved. He did move, right into oncoming traffic."

Max nods, looking up at the treetops. "You're right. It makes no sense." I squeeze his hand and he looks at me with a mournful smile. "But tonight was good. I need to remember him more—the good stuff. Thank you."

"Do you ever worry that you'll run out?"

"Run out?"

I nod. "Sometimes, I'm afraid I don't have enough memories of Charlotte to sustain me. I keep playing the ones I have on repeat, but there's never anything new. I get angry that there are never any new ones. But I didn't know her as long or as well as you knew Beni, so it's probably different."

Max doesn't say anything. His eyes almost quiver with strain from how deeply he's trying to look into mine. He places his hands on the sides of my face, his long fingers at my temples and palms cupping my chin. "I do. Every day." His words are so quiet in the still clearing that I'm not even sure if they were said aloud or if I just felt them in my core.

I slide my hands around his waist and up his back to bury my face in his chest. His arms are around me, holding me safely like the straps of a parachute, breaking my fall.

Scene Sixteen

[Sandstone Library]

Before first period on Monday morning, I part ways with Max and Victor at the library to grab a new book. I'm on my way to the fiction stacks when I notice Darby sitting at one of the long tables to the left of the circulation desk. She's hunched over, scribbling furiously. *She even writes like a drama queen*, I think as I put my head down and make a break for the stacks.

Once I have a few books picked out, one new read and one old familiar one, I peek around the last shelf to see if the coast is clear. Darby's no longer writing furiously, but sitting with her head in her hands, which seems sad, but also means I can probably check out my books and leave without her noticing me.

But as I'm making my way to the self-checkout kiosk, my ears pick up a terrifying sound. Darby is crying.

Part of me thinks *good*! *Karma's a you-know-what.* And the other part of me, the part that has sat in this very library this year and cried, can't get behind that sentiment. And even though I know I'll probably get my faced ripped off for this, I stop at the side of her table and gently clear my throat.

"What?" Darby snaps, looking up and swiping at her eyes.

My pulse steps on the accelerator. "Can I help?" I look down at the paper she'd been working on. It looks like an essay that she's scribbled notes all over.

"No." She puts her elbows on the table, covering the essay as best she can.

I should walk away. At least I asked. I tried to do the nice thing. Mom would be proud of me. Charlotte would be proud of me. Charlie would be proud of me. Three gold stars for Becca! Instead, I pull out the chair across from her and sit down.

"Looks like you could use a fresh set of eyes." I point at her paper. "I am your critique partner, after all."

"This isn't for Jonah. You don't owe me anything."

I shake my head. "That's not true." Darby blinks and sits back in surprise. "I kind of owe you a lot. You've helped a bunch with drama stuff. And the fact that you simultaneously scare and irritate me has actually motivated me to, I don't know, put myself out there." I reach my hand forward so that my fingertips are an inch away from her work. "I think I'd like to help."

She's just about to give in and slide the paper forward when the bell rings. She swears under her breath and jumps up to start packing her stuff.

"Darby?"

"Maybe."

I smile, and I can't believe I'm smiling, but whatever. "We don't have practice after school. We could meet back here."

"No," Darby snaps. She cringes and takes a big breath.

"I have to be home. If I'm not at practice, I have to go home and help my mom. I have to watch the littles, my sisters and brother."

"Tomorrow?"

"Practice and then babysitting again."

Mr. Davenport, the media specialist, calls out a warning. The tardy bell is about to ring.

Darby rolls her eyes. "Can you come to my house? Today?"

My racing heart goes subsonic. "No, I—really?"

"It's the only way." Her voice is ragged, torn between hope and hostility.

"Okay." I nod as I answer. "Okay."

There's a flicker of something deep in her gray eyes, but I can't name it before she turns and leaves without another word.

Victor laughs at me as we walk toward Max's truck. "I cannot believe you volunteered." He chokes himself snickering and sputters, "Katniss Hanson."

"Shut up, Vic." I say. And then realize he's too busy making fun of me to call out—"SHOTGUN." I shout it in his face and then run the rest of the way to Max's truck.

I open the door for Victor, smiling with as much saccharine sweetness as I can muster, and hold the front seat up so he can climb in.

"Quit your grinning," he mumbles. "I may have lost this battle, but you're still going to war with the Queen of Hearts."

I'm maybe (definitely) not careful when pushing the

front seat back, and maybe (definitely) I smile a little when the seat smacks him in the face.

Max licks his lips. "It won't be that bad. Really, Becca."

"It'll be a disaster, but I said I'd help." I turn in my seat to look at both of them. "She looked super desperate."

"She's an actress," Victor says, throwing his hands up in the air. "She has a thousand desperate looks for every occasion. She's suckering you." He leans forward, resting his chin on my seat. "She's probably planning on kidnapping you and stashing you in a pit until after the play so she can be Juliet."

"Victor," Max says, his jaw clenching.

"I'm just saying there's no way I'd be caught dead helping Darby."

Heat is creeping up my neck, and I'm trying to breathe normally. "Well then, lucky for you that you aren't coming along. Max is just dropping me off."

Darby lives in one of the older homes just outside of town. It's not in a subdivision like mine, where all the houses look the same, but on a street of homes set way back from the road with lots of space between them. There are storage barns and odd collections of rusting cars, tidy gardens lined with cinderblock, and a full canopy of mature trees all down her street.

Max slows as we pull up to the address she gave me. He flicks his gaze between the house and me a few times, like he's trying to decide if it will be safe to leave me here. Maybe he's looking for a pit.

There are two storage barns behind Darby's squat gray ranch house. A large trailer parked outside of one barn reads JONES CONSTRUCTION COMPANY. The front yard is littered with bright plastic toys. As we pull down the long driveway, the front door opens and a little boy, maybe five years old, comes barreling out onto the lawn. He's not wearing pants—or rather he's not wearing pants in a traditional sense, since his pants are on his head.

I look at Max, and he's grinning his wide, crooked grin. He's got a little brother. He must understand what's going on.

Max parks the truck by the house. Inside, someone is shrieking. Darby comes through the front door with a wild look on her face.

"Been nice knowing you, Becca," Victor mutters from the backseat.

"Josh," Darby hollers. "Get back in here." Her face is a bright mahogany as she chases the boy around the yard. When she sees the truck, she stops in her tracks. Her mouth opens like she's going to say something snarky, but instead, she shakes her head and stalks back toward the stoop.

I get out of the truck, thanking Max for the ride.

"Good luck." He winks at me.

Victor crawls out from the back to sit up front now. He pats me on the shoulder as he climbs in. "You'll need it."

I watch them pull away. Standing in the drive, I look from Darby, who has lowered herself down to sit on the stoop, to her little brother, that snappy dresser, who is currently running in circles around a tree in the front yard. I make my way toward Darby.

She's barefoot. Her toenails are painted bright yellow. She's pulling at a loose string in the hem of her shorts, twisting it around one finger like I'd twist hair around one of my fingers.

"What's his name?" I ask, nodding toward her brother. He's now running back and forth between two trees. And he's barking like a dog. "Josh, you said?"

Darby grimaces. "He's four."

I nod a few times, but then frown. "I don't actually

know any four-year-olds. The whole pants-as-a-hat thing—is that a big preschool fashion trend?"

A smile—more like half a smile, but I'll take it—tugs at Darby's mouth. "No," she exhales in a loud sort of way. "He's a trendsetter."

Just then, Josh tips his head back and howls up into the sky. Darby gives a whistle, like she's calling the family dog. His head swivels toward us, the legs of his hat-pants swaying out like long, floppy ears. "Come on, boy," Darby calls. "Let's get you a doggie bone."

The boy comes loping toward Darby, screeching to a halt at her feet, his whole body wriggling with four-year-old excitement. Darby opens the door, and he scampers in. She motions for me to follow and, while I don't scamper, I walk right into the Queen of Hearts's castle with only the tiniest of heart attacks.

Charlotte, give me strength.

Josh refuses to take his puppy ears off, but does allow Darby to pull some shorts on over his Captain America underpants (but not until he'd explained, in detail, how he'd use Cap's shield to protect his family if bad guys came to their house). He grins at Darby, a dimple in his left cheek, as she hands him a bag of dog bone shaped crackers.

Her sisters, Mabel and Glory, come tumbling into the room as soon as they hear the wrinkle of snack packaging being ripped open. The smaller of the two girls screeches to a halt when she sees me and then quickly retreats to hide in the hallway.

Glory, who is six and who assures me that she can tie

her own shoes, snatches her snack and runs off. She has colored pencils poking out of the fuzzy bun on the top of her head. Mabel, Josh's twin, looks like a tiny replica of Darby. Except she's shy—painfully shy. She peeks around the doorframe with wide gray eyes.

"May-girl," Darby coos, crouching down and holding out Mabel's snack. "It's okay. This is Becca. You don't have to be afraid. You'll like her." Darby peeks at me over her shoulder. "She's a lot like you, Mabel. She's shy, too."

Mabel blinks, her long lashes touching her cheeks. She steps into the doorway, but doesn't come any closer. I step forward and squat next to Darby.

"Hi." I wave.

She waves, her hand down by her waist, eyes on the ground between us.

"Mabel has taught herself to read," Darby says to me.

I smile. "That's wonderful. Have you read *The Velveteen Rabbit*, Mabel? That was my favorite when I was little. It still is, actually."

She looks up at me, her eyes scanning my face, reading me, and I know exactly what she's doing, because how many times have I done it myself? She wants to let me in, but she thinks she needs to keep me out.

Finally, she nods.

"Yeah, it's a good one," I say, nodding, too.

Mabel takes another step forward and reaches out to take the snacks from her sister. I notice that her fingers brush Darby's when she takes the bag. She looks right in her big sister's eyes, and there is so much trust there that it takes my breath away.

Darby's smile is soft as Mabel walks away, peeking at us over her shoulder once she's far enough down the hall to feel safe. "We've got about ten minutes until Josh and

Glory get bored. We'd better get to work."

"What happens when they get bored?"

Darby purses her lips. "They get creative."

I follow her to the kitchen table, set in a bay window, where she quickly sweeps up crumbs and sippy cups to clear a space. I sit and take in the room while she digs in her backpack for the essay.

The cabinet doors have been removed, and half of the cabinetry has been sanded. One small section has been painted a buttery white. The countertops are littered with more plastic cups and lunchboxes, stacks of papers and mail—standard stuff. But there's also a plastic jug full of screws and a hefty cordless drill sitting beside the toaster.

"Ever heard the saying about the cobbler's kids?"

I pull my attention back to Darby, who is now holding her essay.

"The one about the cobbler's kids always having holes in their shoes?"

She nods, waving at the mess in the kitchen. "Same goes for the contractor's kids. We always have unfinished projects around the house. Dad means well, but the business comes first." She hands me the paper and flops in the seat beside me. "At least the pantry is full." She points at the pantry, its contents fully visible because the doors have also been taken down to refinish.

I don't know what to say, so I look at the essay. It's titled There's No Place Like Home. I scan the first paragraph, and my stomach does a jumpy, twisty thing like wringing out a sponge. "This is an application essay, isn't it?"

She nods.

"School of the Arts?"

"The early admissions deadline for the high school program is soon. The applications and stuff are due, at least, and then there are auditions and interviews."

"Ambitious—the early deadline stuff. My brother did that, too."

"If I get in, I'll need all the time I can get to convince my parents to let me go." She drums her fingers against the table and looks out the window behind us.

"Let's get to work, then."

Darby is a decent writer, but she's right to worry about this essay. There's something missing. It's about the place where she feels most at home. Unsurprisingly, it's about the theater at Sandstone. But as I peek up at her, she seems more at home here, pushing crumbs around on the tabletop, bare feet tapping out a rhythm on the dark wood floor, than at school. She's not being herself at school. She's playing the role of the Queen of the Drama Club. How can someone be at home in a pretend role?

My palms sweat as I try to find the words, words that are least likely to offend, to tell Darby she may need to start over on this essay.

Thankfully, Josh buys me more time. He enters the kitchen at a gallop and plops himself down at Darby's feet. He paws at her leg with one hand and whines like a puppy.

"What, Josh?" Darby strokes his head, and I wonder if she even realizes that she's petting her little brother like he's the family dog.

"Puppy palace." He begins to pant, his tongue lolling to one side.

"Not now."

He switches back to whining.

"What's puppy palace?" I ask, and then wish I could apparate to anywhere outside of this kitchen when Darby looks at me, her expression clearly trying to stab me in the face.

"Nothing," she says through clenched teeth. She looks down at Josh and points to the den where the TV is playing. "Go play."

But Josh is a persistent hound. "Puppy palace." He looks at me, his brown eyes huge in his little brown face. How can she say no to this face?

"Is it a TV show? Do you need me to change the channel?"

He shakes his head. Darby sighs as she pushes herself up from the table. "You keep working," she says to me. "I'll build the puppy palace, Josh. Let's go." She pats her thigh like she's calling a dog to heel and leads the way back into the den.

I go back to pondering what the hell I'm going to say to entice Darby to write about somewhere other than the theater. The sound of giggling coming from the other room distracts me. I investigate the strange sound.

Darby has built an enormous blanket fort, using at least three different blankets. From inside, I can hear them all laughing, and each of their laughs sounds similar, but also distinct. Darby's sounds like a church bell pealing in the distance.

I peek in an open flap. Darby's reading to her siblings. Glory is coloring while she listens, her pink tongue poking out as she works to stay in the lines in her coloring book. Josh is shaking his floppy pants-ears and belly laughing. Even Mabel laughs loudly, as Darby does a funny voice for one of the characters.

Glory sees me and pats the spot next to her. "You can read the next one, Darby's friend."

I glance at Darby. Her chest rises imperceptibly in a small sigh, and then she nods in the direction of the seat Glory is offering. "Her name is Becca, guys."

I sit next to Glory, and Josh immediately curls up next to me with a happy yip. We read book after book, Darby and I taking turns, until Darby's mom calls from the back door when she arrives home. The little ones rush out of the fort, squealing for their mom, and Darby and I are left alone.

I look around at the pastel walls of the blanket fort and the soft pillow floor. Darby is reclined, leaning back against a pile of pillows. She looks completely at ease.

"This is your home," I say, my voice soft like the fleece blankets around us. "You should write about this."

"How is this"—Darby points at the blanket ceiling—"going to get me into a drama program?"

I play with the corner of the book in my lap. "Imagine you're one of those admissions people. How many essays do you think they read from hopeful actors telling them that they are completely at home on the stage?"

Darby looks a little like I've slapped her. "A lot. Most of them, I guess."

"Is it the truth? Is that where you feel most at home?"

"The best I've ever felt was standing on a stage. I am powerful there. I'm heard. People see me. They—"

"They see a character. If anything, being onstage is like taking a vacation. It's not home." Darby wrinkles her nose, considering what I've said, which is huge and makes my neck feel prickly as I continue. "Be different. Be you."

I toss the book I was holding into her lap. "That's the essay they'll want to read. That's how you can stand out from the rest."

Darby sits up. "Let me get this straight. Your critique advice is to scrap the whole thing and start over?"

I nod. "You're not afraid of a little hard work, are you? I may have only just started paying attention, but I certainly wouldn't peg you as a quitter."

Darby snorts, which makes me laugh, too.

I crawl out from the puppy palace, but stick my head back in. "Thanks for this."

"For what?"

My brow wrinkles. "Um, I'm not actually sure."

Darby smiles. "You're a piece of work. You know that, right?"

"That." I point at her. "Thanks for that."

Darby may not like me much, but at least she's always honest with me. Then again, I did get to hang out in the puppy palace, so maybe she likes me a little.

Scene Seventeen

[The theater]

On Friday, when I walk onstage, the place has been transformed into an opulent party hall. The crew has nearly finished all the sets this week. And even though Owens made Max build the traditional sets, they truly are beautiful.

We're rehearsing the party scene and the Capulet house looks warm and inviting around us, draped in rich reds and purples, blues and golds. I run a finger down the lines of a finely painted tapestry and wish I could walk straight into the booth and tell Max how beautiful it is, how talented he is, and how much I'd like to grab a fistful of his T-shirt and kiss that crooked smile off his face. I wonder what his face would look like if I did that?

And then I realize that I'm thinking dangerous thoughts again. Thoughts that could get me in a position to have my heart annihilated, and that, I'm sure, is not what I want.

Owens calls us to our marks, and I push Max from my thoughts.

I take my spot onstage and close my eyes. I mentally

step out of my skin and put on Juliet. It's getting easier. In the two weeks since Thomas and I kissed, I've been able to more easily separate from Becca's world, full of doubt and guilt and possible annihilation, to Juliet's. And I have to say, that donning her singular mindset for a few hours each afternoon is easier than spending two minutes in my own chaotic one. When I'm Juliet, I can live by one simple precept: Romeo is my life.

Before we can begin, Kelli rushes onto the stage, her hands flapping, and drags Mr. Owens away to deal with what she calls "a costuming catastrophe."

"And you techies say you aren't into drama." He rolls his eyes, making the gesture even more melodramatic than Darby, and calls out to us, "At ease, soldiers. Your general shall return."

War metaphors? Today we're doing war metaphors? I catch Darby's eye before she retreats to the wings, her disgust with Owens's theatrics clear in her sour expression. She raises a brow and shrugs her shoulder. We haven't spoken much since Monday. I guess there's not much to say.

I shake my head and drop to the stage to sit cross-legged. Thomas joins me, his knee almost brushing mine. He's studying his script, even though he knows most of the lines by now. He glances at me, and I consider looking away, but I'm already busted, so I hold his gaze.

"It makes no sense," he says, holding out the script. "It's all nonsense."

I smile and take the script from him. "You get what they're doing here, though, right?"

Thomas looks wistfully at the script I've laid out of his reach. He runs a hand through his hair and cups the back of his neck. "No, Becca, I have no idea what they're doing."

"Flirting."

"That's supposed to be flirting." He flicks a hand at the script.

I nod.

"Romeo sucks." His pink lips pull into a half smile.

I laugh. "I'll admit, he needs a little work, but if we forget the words for a moment and focus on the emotion, maybe we can get it right."

"You want me to flirt with you?" He moves so he's sitting cross-legged in front of me, knee to knee.

"No," I say, kicking his foot. "I want Romeo to flirt with Juliet."

Thomas waggles a brow at me, his blue eyes cat-like in their mischievousness. "Heyyy," he drawls, "how's it going?" He's pointing his fingers, like guns, at me, the epitome of every bad pickup attempt I've ever seen in movies.

"Wow," I say, chuckling. "No wonder Rosalind ditched you."

He tries another line. "Say, can I borrow your phone? I promised to call God when I fell from heaven with an angel."

"That makes no sense."

Thomas's brow furrows for a second. "I think I may be confusing my lines." He grins. "It's a pickup line medley."

"It's terrible whatever it is." I'm smiling, too, surprised at how easy it is to talk to him.

"Wow. That's the first time you've actually smiled at me," Thomas says, tilting his head while he studies me.

I squirrel away my smile. There's a moment of silence before Thomas asks, "Why be stingy with the smiles?" He nudges my knee with his own.

I study the space between our knees. It's there, but so small it's hard to see. It's like it's only there because I imagine it that way. Like the lines that separate us all, the angles of our bodies, the skin that holds us in, is all unreal, all an illusion made to make us feel apart. Like my fear of connecting with others is unfounded since we're already all interconnected.

"Becca?"

"I once read this interview with a man who went blind later in life. He noticed that after going blind he stopped smiling, because he felt like an idiot not knowing if anyone was reciprocating the gesture. Smiles are like that, I guess. Maybe I've always been afraid I'd be the only one smiling."

I glance at Thomas's face, sure he's rolling his eyes at my stupidity, but instead he's looking at me with a goofy smile plastered all over his broad face.

"What?" I ask.

He doesn't answer—just keeps smiling—even his eyes crinkle up at the corners.

"Seriously, why are you smiling like that? Is this another acting technique like that mirroring thing?" My heart is skipping every third beat now, and I feel my face heating up.

His smile opens wider, revealing his teeth, straightened to perfection. And something in me snaps. A part of me wants to be angry because he shouldn't be making fun of me. I opened up. I told him about the blind dude who was scared to smile. That was personal. But from somewhere deep inside, an emotion bubbles to the surface. It feels light.

It starts as a grin that I try to stifle. Then grows into a smirk. And finally, I feel my own lips parting into a wide, toothy smile, coupled with a laugh.

"That's why we smile, Becca. Smiles beget smiles."

"Beget?"

"I thought it sounded very Romeo-ish."

The theater door slams, and we squint into the

darkness, watching Owens's figure roll through the shadows to his seat. “Okay, troops. Let's do this,” he orders, smacking his clipboard on the back of the seat in front of him.

Thomas stands and offers me his hand. I let him pull me up beside him.

He holds a palm out for me to place mine against. I am Juliet. Romeo is my life. When we say the lines, we exchange a constant volley of smiles.

I wait for Max at the stairs to the booth, but he doesn't come down. When I climb up there, I find only Victor.

“Where's Max?”

“He left a while ago to go work in the shop.”

I peer out the window at the empty stage.

“You and Thomas seem to be hitting it off, eh?”

I purse my lips. “As Romeo and Juliet? I hope so. That's kind of the point.”

“Well done, then. You guys were electric down there.” There's an edge to Victor's voice that makes my fingers tingle.

“Max is in the shop?”

He nods, his eyes studying me like I'm a circling hawk and he's trying to figure out my next move.

I turn to leave, but—

“Becca, wait.” Victor reaches out his hand but doesn't touch me. “Sit?”

I sit in Max's seat, swiveling it around to face Victor as he paces the back of the booth.

“What's going on?” I ask.

He stops pacing and clasps his hands behind his back. "I think I want to say something serious."

"You love me?"

Victor blinks. A lot. Rapidly. "What?"

I smirk. "So," I drawl. "*Not* what you wanted to say?"

He grins, a wary look about his face. He's not used to being on the other end of a quip. "No."

I shrug.

"I want to say something about Max." He's shaking his head while he says this. Maybe only part of him wants to say what he's about to say. "Max is my best friend."

I wait for more, but he just stands there. The silence between us is beginning to scratch at my skin. "I understand."

"Do you?"

But I do. I understand what it feels like to want to protect your friend, to know that you'd lay your own life down for them if it'd save them. "I do. I get it. I'm trying to stay away, you know. Trying to not hurt— "

"No," Victor says, the word like a grenade. "Staying away isn't the answer."

My neck breaks out in a sweat.

He starts pacing again. "I'm treading a fine line here, but I know Max, and he's so much— " He stops and sits in the chair beside me. "He's happier when you're around. Big goofy grins all the time, you know?"

I nod, thinking of the way Max's smile feels, like that first warm day after a long winter—like coming alive again.

"But you have to decide, okay? Don't drag him along behind you like a plaything."

"What?"

Victor flicks a hand toward the stage. "It kills him to watch you with him."

"Thomas isn't—I don't—"

Victor's hands wave me off. "That's not my business. Max is. He's family. Which is why I'm asking you to hurry up with the whole *do I like Max or don't I* crap. Either way you choose, you need to let him know. And soon."

I study his face, afraid for a moment that this is some elaborate joke. But there's nothing but sincerity in the look on Victor's face. It's off-putting to see him so serious.

It's not a matter of do I or don't I have feelings for Max. It's do I or don't I dare let myself feel them. And I've got to say, even that decision feels like it's being taken out of my hands with every minute I'm with him. There's no escaping what I feel. There's no more hiding in books, ducking into other people's lives to avoid my own, losing myself in words—because the only words I want to hear are those on Max's lips. And yet, what happens if those lips ever stop moving? "It's not as simple as do or don't," I tell Victor.

"Yeah, Becky. It really is." He stands and claps me on the shoulder like we're drinking buddies in a pub. "Now go tell him I'm tired of waiting for his sorry, love-sick ass, and I need him to take me home."

"He's in the shop?"

He nods.

"Anything for you, Vic."

But when we reach the bottom step, Darby is waiting.

"I'm giving you a ride home, Becca."

I shake my head, stepping toward the doors. "No, thanks. I'm off to get Max now."

Darby steps in front of me. Victor clears his throat. Darby sneers at him. "I'll bring her back in one piece. Cross my heart." She makes an *X* across her chest with one finger.

"No good, Queenie," Victor says, stepping up beside me. "Keep your blackhearted promises for someone who cares."

I swear they are about to start pulling each other's hair and hissing like feral cats. I'm getting tired of everyone around me acting like I'm incapable of taking care of myself or making up my own mind.

Except the Max thing. I guess it's fair to say I'm having trouble with that decision. But this, this is easy.

"Move, Darby," I say, pushing past her. She grabs my elbow.

"I don't think you want to walk away from me, Becca."

"Why wouldn't I?"

"Because my locker is down the hall from the guidance offices, and I may have overheard Dr. Wallace asking the secretary for your Mom's cell number."

I freeze. I totally forgot about going to see her for my weekly check-in. I helped Max in the shop instead. Darby sees the shock and fear in my eyes.

"I happen to be really good with parents. Bet I can get you out of this little scrape."

"But Max—"

"Would hate to see you get grounded all weekend, I'm sure."

Mom wouldn't ground me. Would she? Max and I have plans to take Javi to the Natural Science Museum tomorrow.

Victor is shaking his head, but I can't risk this. I've been looking forward to it all week. "Okay," I say. I shake off Darby's hand and stand straighter. "Victor, tell Max I'm not risking missing out on our da"—it's not actually a date, so I switch gears mid-word—"da-ay together. I'll call him later."

He sighs and recites Friar Laurence's line. "I'll go with speed to Mantua."

Darby rolls her eyes. "Now who's being the drama queen?"

...

In Darby's car, I ask, "Why are you doing this? Helping me?"

Darby hands me her phone. "Text my mom for me."

I wait for her dictation, but Darby chews on an eggplant-colored fingernail, staring at the road ahead. "What should I text?"

"I'm supposed to babysit the littles tonight—again. I need a great excuse to get out of it because Thomas is throwing a drammie party. You'll be my excuse. That's why I'm helping."

"Rehearsal is running late wouldn't work?"

"Ha." Darby coughs up the laugh like phlegm. "Not exactly. She and Dad already think the play takes up too much of my time—already think theater is a waste of time. Every afternoon I'm at rehearsal is just one more afternoon my mother has to divide her attention between the family business and the family itself."

Darby's voice takes on a strange quality, like she's repeating lines from another play, bitter lines she's sick of hearing. "It's time to be a little less selfish and a little more selfless, Darby."

I run my thumb along the teal case on her phone.

"Plus, Mom has weird superpowers and can smell a lie like a day old dirty diaper in a minivan."

I snort. "Day old what?"

Darby smiles. "You heard me." Her smile immediately fades, though, and she goes back to peeling the paint off one nail with her teeth.

I place my thumbs on the screen and type out a message.

> ***DARBY**: Friend in a bad way. Probably shouldn't leave her alone.*

I hit send without thinking.

"Hell'd you do?" Darby asks, trying to see my message.

"I told the truth."

The phone chimes in my hand.

> ***MOM**: What friend? How bad?*

> ***DARBY**: The one at the house the other day. Becca. Playing Juliet. Taking role too seriously. She missed an appointment w/school counselor today.*

We wait for Darby's mom to respond as I give Darby directions to my house. We're just turning on my street when her mom finally texts back.

> ***MOM**: OK but be home tomorrow by 8AM. I'm going w/Dad to job site.*

"You're free for the night," I tell Darby. "This is me." I point to my house, and Darby screeches up to the curb, scraping one wheel alongside it.

"She let me go?"

I hand her the phone, and she reads over the messages. I climb out of her car and can't help but study the way the side of her tire is smashed up against the curb. That's going to leave a scuff mark. And the old one had just worn away. "So thanks for the ride—"

"Wait," Darby calls, getting out, too. "Aren't you going to invite me in?"

"No." The response is a gut reaction. I can't let Darby in my house, just like I wouldn't allow a tiger, badger, or serial killer. Darby's face flinches, and in that tiny space, I get one of those rare glimpses of the girl behind all the masks, the girl in the blanket fort who does silly voices when she reads. "You really want to come in?"

She purses her lips. "I couldn't give a shit, but I said I'd help with your mom. If Dr. Wallace has busted you, you may need my skills." She's about to sit back down and drive away.

"Darby, wait." What am I doing? "Please come in."

She sniffs away a flicker of a smile. "If you insist, but I can't stay all night. I've got a party to get to."

I chuckle. "I insist. I really do."

Scene Eighteen

[Becca's room]

It seems strange to have Darby in my room, perusing each and every title on my bookshelves, studying the pictures pinned on my wall like works of art in a museum, running her fingers over the clothes hanging in my open closet. She'd make an excellent investigator, I decide, as she sniffs a bottle of perfume I bought because it reminded me of Charlotte.

Finally, she holds out the picture of Charlotte, Charlie, and me from my birthday. "This is your friend? The reason you stole my role as Juliet?"

"I didn't steal anything."

Darby raises a brow.

I sigh. "Yes, that's Charlotte."

"She was in my calculus class last year."

I raise my own brow, and with it a glimmer of a long dead feeling—hope. "You knew her?"

Darby shakes her head. "Just in the same class. I knew she was sick or something. And then one day, she wasn't there anymore."

I swallow my hope and sadness in one gulp. Because, yeah, that's how it went. One day, she was just gone. Charlie was there in her place.

I heard the car in the drive and ran out thinking it was Charlotte come to get me before school. Instead of her dented silver Honda, Charlie's ancient, crumbling car was in the drive, and my brother, sitting behind the wheel, looked older than his seventeen years. His eyes were red and there were these horrible creases in his forehead. His skin was so pale that he looked like a ghost himself. And I knew. I knew there was only one thing in this world that could make my brother look that way.

She was gone.

And so was I.

I try to staunch the tears and look away from Darby, but they're coming too fast, and my sleeves are too thin to wipe them all away.

Darby sits on the floor beside me, pulling up a corner of one of the blankets I'm cushioned in. She doesn't say anything, just hands it to me to help catch the stream of crappy sadness running down my face.

"Guess I shouldn't have missed that appointment with Dr. Wallace, huh?"

"That was true?"

I nod. "I was supposed to see her during lunch, but forgot. Helped Max instead."

"You like him a lot, huh?"

I suck in a hissing breath and hold it until my heart slows down a bit before exhaling. "I do, but I don't want to."

"Because of her?" Darby hands me the picture she's still holding.

I nod.

"I get that. I mean, that's why Juliet—" She pantomimes

jabbing a knife in her chest.

"I would never do that," I say, heat rushing to my cheeks.

Darby's quiet, studying the picture I've set in my lap. Finally she looks up at me and says, "There are lots of ways to stop living."

More tears slip down my cheeks. "I'm so confused."

"Aren't we all?" She waits without a word while I mop up my face, and then she takes a book from the stack on my floor.

"Why are you here, Darby? You're free for the whole night now. Why stay here?"

She opens the book in her hands. "I already told you. I'm going to smooth things over with your mom for you."

"But why? You don't exactly like me."

"You don't really know anything about me." She turns to the first chapter and starts to read.

I find my own book, sliding out the bookmark, but I can't focus on the words. I fiddle with the pages, stealing glances at Darby. Her whole face looks different, younger and maybe more, I don't know, free when we're away from school.

Minutes pass in silence before Darby snaps at me. "Just ask."

"Ask?"

"You're staring at me. Whatever it is you're thinking, just ask it. You're transparent, Becca. I can read you like—" She rattles her book in my face.

Transparent? Here I was thinking I'd gotten better at the whole acting thing.

"So spit it out because I'm getting to a good part in this story."

"Does it get easier—?"

"Yes."

"Wait. I didn't finish."

"You don't have to. It gets easier, playing the part gets to be second nature. Maybe even your first nature. It's safer." She picks at a chip in her nail polish. "Less disappointment."

"But don't you ever get lost in all of it?"

Darby looks at me, turns her whole face to meet mine. "Yes."

"I don't want to be lost anymore."

She shrugs, looking back at her book. "Then leave a trail of breadcrumbs."

We read silently until I hear the garage door opening.

"My parents," I say.

"Don't worry. I'm good with parents." Darby's face transforms before my eyes, from the quiet girl reading by my side into a teen girl you might see hanging with her pals in a Pottery Barn catalogue.

She wiggles her eyebrows at me, whispering, "Showtime."

The door into the kitchen slams, rattling the pipes in the walls. Darby and I freeze on the top step.

"Becca, get down here," Mom shouts, her voice cracking on the last word.

I swear under my breath. "Dr. Wallace definitely called," I whisper.

Darby cringes, but recovers quickly, holding a finger out to stop me from going down the stairs. "Follow my lead." Her voice is a whisper between us.

Before I can respond, she goes barreling down the stairs, her hair flying out behind her. I try to catch up, but by the time I get to the landing, she's made it all the way into the kitchen, smashing into Mom, who was about to come check on me.

"Oh, I'm so sorry," Darby says, her hands moving like moths around a porch light, trying to straighten Mom's scarf. "I'm just so sorry." The last bit of this is completely swallowed by a sob.

She's good.

I stop on the step behind Darby, my mom's shocked expression pleading for answers from me.

"Darby?" I reach out to touch her shoulder.

She whirls around and crashes into me, knocking me back a step before I can catch her. She's sobbing into my shoulder so hard it shakes my whole body. I pat her head. "Shhh. It'll be okay."

Mom rushes to grab the tissues off the counter, fumbling them in her hands as she thrusts them out at us.

"What is going on here?"

Still holding on to me, Darby takes a step farther into the kitchen. Like we've rehearsed the scene a thousand times, I suddenly know what to do. I lead her to the table and set her carefully in one of the wooden spindle-back chairs. Mom has followed us, holding the tissue box out like a beacon. I take the tissues, thanking Mom, and hand them to Darby before rushing to get her a drink of water.

Mom follows me to the sink.

"That's Darby, from the play. She had a fight with her—"

"Stupid boy," Darby mutters from the table. "Who does he think he is?"

"Boyfriend," I say. I watch my mother struggle. I can see her brain choosing sides and warring over the right thing to say.

What I'm doing is downright mean. I know how much Mom wants me to move on, to meet new friends. I know she won't tell Darby to go. But I also know she wants to ask about Dr. Wallace. Mom's smile is fractured as she takes the glass of water from my hand and turns back to the table.

"Well, Darby, you are welcome here," she says, setting the water down in front of Darby and pulling the chair out beside her. Mom puts a hand on Darby's shoulder. "You let me know if there's anything I can do to help."

Darby sniffles, mopping her face with a worn-looking tissue. "Thanks, Mrs. Hanson. I'm sorry to impose. It's just nice to have a good friend I can rely on, you know?"

Darby grabs both my hands in hers, struggling to keep her voice steady. "And, Becca, I'm so sorry about today, losing it at school and all."

I try to hide my surprise. "It's okay."

"No, I don't know what I would have done. Probably something dumb, like write some stupid stuff on his locker or something."

She turns back to my mom. It's such a carefully constructed scene I can hardly believe she's improvising. "I made Becca a little late for class after lunch today because I was so busy bawling in the bathroom."

Mom looks at me, lifting her brows in a question.

"I kind of missed my appointment with Dr. Wallace—she's the counselor you asked me to see at school—because I was with Darby. I'll apologize to Dr. Wallace on Monday."

Mom nods, still appraising me with her mom-vision.

I look away, back at Darby, whose gray eyes are looking glassy as she remembers back to the fake fiasco of her fake breakup with her fake boyfriend. In this moment, I kind of love this girl. She's brilliant. Shifty. But brilliant.

Scene Nineteen

[A party]

Darby's acting prowess did not end there. She somehow suckered me into coming with her tonight to Thomas's party. And she managed to make my mom and dad think it was their idea that we go out. The girl is scary good. I hope I don't run out of breadcrumbs so I can find my way home after all of this.

Thomas lives in a big house in a ginormous golf course neighborhood with humongous wrought iron gates that look like they could keep a tank out. Darby has dressed me in a pair of black leggings she found in the back of my closet, a long cardigan we found in Charlie's closet (why does my brother own a cardigan?), and a purple shirt that looks like it shrunk in the wash that Darby found in the trunk of her car, which is the only trunk in the history of trunks that is more disgustingly overflowing with crap than Charlie's.

At least I got to pick my own shoes—Charlotte's raven-winged ones.

Darby said to think of it as a costume. When wearing

the too-small shirt, I was not Becca Hanson, book nerd, but Rebecca Hanson, star of the high school stage, sweetheart to a line of waiting Romeos from here to the Mississippi. I'd eyed her like she'd lost it, but not for long, because she was coming at me, brandishing a mascara wand like the broadsword Greg taught her to wield onstage as Tybalt.

I head for the front door of Thomas's McMansion, but Darby pulls on my elbow. "This way, rookie," she says, leading me off toward the backyard. "And stop tugging on that sweater or I'll take it away." I'd been pinning the sweater shut with my arms hugging my middle, but I let them drop. It's only a costume. I'm only a character tonight. I repeat these mantras as Darby opens the gate.

There's a pool, of course, lit with tiki torches, and a patio with a dozen lounge chairs and—

"Is that a bar?"

Darby waggles her eyebrows at me. "But first we must find our host." Her voice is admonishing, like she's the queen of etiquette.

We weave through the crowd on the patio and enter through these giant doors that slide open to connect the pool deck to the finished basement (the size of my whole house, but way fancier with a TV the size of a frigging movie screen). Darby scans the crowd looking for Thomas, but before she spots him, her minions lock in on her.

"Darbilicious, where you been?" Meggie hip checks Darby, sloshing some of her drink on the floor.

"Oh, you know," Darby drawls, her face composed in a bored expression that I imagine would take me years to copy. "Be a doll and fetch me a drink, girls." Meggie and the other one—Peggy? No that can't be right? If it were, the tall one'd be Leggy?—I snort at my stupidity.

"What?" Darby asks.

"Don't you ever get tired?"

Darby blinks at me before her eyes crystallize, impermeable diamonds. "Camouflage is essential when"—her eyes slide away from me, looking just over my shoulder—"Thomas."

"Wow, Becca. I can't believe you're here." Thomas wraps an arm over my shoulders and pulls me into a side hug. I smell the pungent earthiness of beer on his breath.

I nod. "Me either."

He claps his hands, and everyone turns toward him. "Guys," he shouts, and I want so badly to run away, but Darby is blocking any escape on the other side. "The fair Juliet has arrived."

The crowd cheers, and I'm crushed with hugs and high fives and—my, these drama folks sure are a happy bunch.

Darby claps her hands like she's dusting them off, before slipping away in the crowd to join her harpies on the leather sectional sofa that's bigger than my kitchen counter.

Marcus Zimmerman (the benevolent Friar Laurence) and Terrell Donovan, who plays Benvolio to Darby's Tybalt, are playing something on a video system, and the competition must be fierce because everyone's gathering around and cheering. It reminds me of being at Victor's house, listening to Kelli and him trash talking as they play. Victor can't sit still when he plays, though. He dances around with his remote, like moving his body helps his poor avatar escape Kelli's sharpshooting.

Marcus Zimmerman wails as Terrell's sleek car nudges him off the road into a fiery explosion. Everyone goes wild.

How did I get here? I'm feeling trembly, like my bones have gone to gelatin, so I clench my fists by my sides, forcing the stillness to spread from my muscles there to the rest of my body.

Thomas leans down to whisper in my ear, "You okay?"

I shake my head. I suck at acting. Why can't I just pretend to be *girl having fun at a party*? "I need to get some air."

Thomas grabs my hand and pulls me away from the crowd, back out to the patio. "Come on then," Thomas says. "Let's get you a drink."

Outside, the last vestiges of autumn warmth drape around my shoulders. Thomas grabs two beers from behind the outdoor bar and leads the way to a pair of lounge chairs on the far side of the pool. We sit in silence and watch the others from across the pool.

"Where are your parents?" I take the beer Thomas is holding out for me.

Thomas shrugs. "Out. They had to attend the something society of something or other's charity ball of do-gooderness."

"Ah," I say, weighing the heavy sarcasm behind his words. "I've heard of them. They do plenty of gooderness."

He's just about to take a sip of beer, and does a laugh-snort kind of thing into the can that makes a funny woofing sound. "You're kind of funny, Becca."

"Well, thanks, kind of."

We clink cans. I take a sip, and he takes a long gulp before leaning back in his chair with his face turned toward me, his eyes earnest. "Can I ask a personal question?"

My heart speeds up. "Um…okay."

"I can't read you like I can read other girls."

"We're not books."

His lips quirk in a half grin. "Do you…I mean"—he takes a big breath—"is it serious? With you and that techie guy, Max. Are you dating?"

I clench my hands around the beer can in my lap to keep from twisting a chunk of hair right off my head.

"Too personal?" Thomas asks.

"No. I just don't like my answer."

"Why?"

"I don't know exactly what's going on."

Thomas sits up, swinging his long legs into the space between our chairs. "Because you're blind?" When I peek up at him, he shakes his head and continues. "That guy's got it bad for you. Romeo bad."

"And we all know how well that worked out."

Thomas chuckles, his eyes shining in the light from a nearby tiki torch. "Okay, yes. Bad example. But you know what I mean. If you like him, too, I don't get what's holding you back."

"Soul-crushing fear."

"Oh, sure," he says, grinning at me. "I can see how getting everything your heart desires could be terrifying."

Everything my heart desires. What do I desire? I want to sit and read while Max works in his dad's barn on sketches and sculptures, bending iron with his bare hands. I want to take him to my favorite section in the library downtown and show him my favorite books, and if we were to kiss there in the stacks, well, that'd be okay, too. I want to tell Max how special he is to me and that I want to be with him even though I'm afraid to be with anyone I care about because what if—

What if, Max?

I'm staring up at the stars, lost in thought, when Thomas continues. "But hey, that all works out for me. You should definitely not date that guy when there are plenty of other young Romeos around." He nudges my hand with his fingertips, drawing me back into this reality. I take a long sip of beer and blow out a lungful of stale air.

"All the world's a stage," he quotes.

"And all the men and women merely players," I continue.

He finishes. "They have their exits and their entrances."

Yes. Yes, they do. And I can't take any more unsanctioned exits. My life. My terms. I say who comes into my life. I say when they leave.

"Let's rejoin the party." I want to get back to pretending I'm playing the role of *girl at a party*, not reprise my most famous role *girl who frequently fails at life*.

Standing, I reach out my hand to pull Thomas up after me. We have to stand very close in the small space between the lounge chairs. I can hear music, a familiar song, playing from inside. "I want to dance."

Charlotte taught me to dance. I've just never had anyone dance with me. I push away the second beer Thomas offers me and join Darby and some others at the center of the makeshift dance floor, a wide-open space between the foosball table and pool table in Thomas's fancy basement.

The music is everywhere now, wild with a thick bass line that moves you from deep inside. Thomas joins the crowd, slowly moving closer to me. One song ends and another plays and we keep dancing. We can hardly move where we stand at the heart of the crowd. I slide toward the pool table, climbing up to get away from the pressing bodies. Thomas joins me. I close my eyes and sway my hips like Charlotte used to. Thomas's right hand perches on my hip. I don't open my eyes.

For a fleeting moment, I think of *Oh, The Places You'll Go. I am dancing on a table. Charlotte, look! I am dancing on a table.* But then Thomas moves closer. His hand slides around to the small of my back, under my cardigan, to the slip of skin Darby's too-small T-shirt fails to cover. His fingers play the bones of my lower spine like chords on a guitar.

Thomas gets a peculiar, determined look before he leans in to my ear, his stubble brushing against my cheek, to whisper one of Romeo's lines. "There lies more peril in thine eye than twenty of their swords."

There are catcalls from below as he presses his lips to mine. Someone cries out, "Go, Romeo." But this is no stage kiss—not for him. There is no holding back, no timidity, no show for the audience around us. And most importantly, there is no Max in a booth shining a spotlight on us. I immediately break away, leveraging my hands against his chest.

"Thomas—" I'm interrupted by applause from below as the crowd cheers, but even their cheers are different than those in the theater. This is unscripted. This is life off book.

"This is a mistake," I say.

"Wait," Thomas pleads, his hands slipping from my waist as I pull away. Just before I climb off the table I catch Darby's eye. She looks a little too pleased, and I feel like such an ass for thinking any of this was a good idea—trusting Darby, coming here, dancing with Thomas, pretending to be someone I'm not.

She's pushed her way through the crowd to meet me when I hop off the pool table. "Let me guess," she says, taking my elbow to lead me out, "you want to go?"

I shake her off. "Not with you."

I push my own way through the crowd, conscious that both Darby and Thomas are following me. I make my way to the pool deck and gulp the fresh air before whirling to face them.

"Is this some kind of joke?" They both freeze in their tracks. "Because I'm not laughing."

"Becca," Thomas pleads, taking a wobbly step toward me. "I'm sorry. I thought you—"

"Were Juliet? Well, I'm not. I'm Rebecca Jane Hanson. I sit in my room and read. I especially do not kiss boys in front of an audience. I am not Juliet."

Thomas recoils.

"And you," I say, pointing at Darby. "Acting like my friend. Helping me with my mother. Playing with me like I'm a paper doll." I tug on the shirt she's loaned me.

"Hey," Darby says, reflexively.

"Why did you bring me here?"

That same smug smile returns to her lips. "Well I was hoping you'd screw up royally, of course. So thanks for coming through."

"Jesus," Thomas swears, stepping away from Darby.

All the words in my vocabulary have evaporated. I stand there gaping at her.

Darby gets closer, her face in mine. "I did this for your own good, Becca."

"My own good?" Words! Finally! Okay, so I just repeated hers, but it's a start.

"I am sorry, Thomas, that I had to use you to prove my point, though." Darby shrugs.

"Use me?"

"Becca's determined to throw away a good thing, the thing she really wants, because of some screwed-up idea that the worst thing in life is to lose what you love."

Thomas shakes his head. I still don't get what's going on, so I mirror him.

"There is worse shit out there than loss. Regret. That's a real bitch, and you'll have no one but yourself to blame."

"But now I'm going to regret this," I say, motioning to the space between Thomas and myself.

Darby's face contorts into a small apology. "Yeah, well, so my plan wasn't perfect."

"Perfect?" Thomas asks.

"I said I was sorry," Darby snipes. "I didn't expect you to kiss her. I just wanted her to come here and have a crappy time and realize that she needs to take a damn chance."

I pinch the bridge of my nose, trying to squeeze out the headache blooming there. "Thomas, I'm sorry." I turn toward him. "I didn't know—I mean, I thought—"

"No, Becca. It's fine." He holds his hands, palms out, between us, warding me off like I'm rabid. "Darby's got a warped point. At least I know I won't regret walking away from you." Shaking his head again, he backs away a few paces before turning and striding back inside.

When he's gone, I turn on Darby. "Don't ever meddle in my life again."

Darby crosses her arms over her chest and shrugs. "But that's what friends are for."

I growl deep in my throat as I walk toward the back gate. When I pass Darby, I don't regret reaching out and shoving her in the shoulder. She loses her balance and topples with a giant splash and a loud shriek into the pool.

"Oops," I grumble. "Sorry, friend."

I walk around front, pulling out my phone. I'm so angry I'm shaking. Screw you, Charlotte, for leaving me all alone with this giant mess. And damn you, Darby Jones, for making sense in your own twisted fashion. And fuck me for not getting out of my own way sooner.

I'm done with regret. My life. My terms. I flip to my contacts and listen to the ringing on the other side.

As soon as Max picks up I start talking. "I'm going to kiss you."

"What? Becca? Are you okay?"

"It's the only way. I think about it all the time—kissing you. And so if we just get it over with, then, you know, I'll know."

"Know what?"

"Whether or not you're worth risking my life over."

"Risking?"

"Yes. Because if I fall for you, Max, and then something happens like—" I don't explain. I don't have to. "Well, I wouldn't survive that—not again."

"Where are you?"

I sigh. "Thomas Harrison's house."

There is a heavy silence on the other end of the line. I imagine the string between the two tin cans Charlie and I used as phones in the fort in the backyard one summer—we pulled so hard it snapped.

"To be more specific, I'm walking down the street in his fancy neighborhood, away from his house. He's drunk, and I think he forgot that we weren't actually rehearsing the play."

"Did he—"

"He kissed me. But, Max, I don't want to kiss Thomas. I want to kiss you."

There's a beat of silence that drags on for what feels like years before he asks, "Are you okay—you're not hurt, are you?"

"I'm fine. I'm just pissed at myself and embarrassed, and there may be a reward for my head since I kind of pushed Darby in the pool on my way out."

Max laughs, and I can hear his truck coughing to life. "I'm on my way, but stay on the phone, okay?"

I nod, which is dumb, but my throat is too full of apologies and regret and longing, so I can't say anything. "Wait, Max." My voice shakes with the weight of a new realization. "Do you want me to kiss you?"

"Becca, I said I'm on my way, didn't I?"

The grin on my face is the stuff of romantic legends. It's downright Arthurian.

I'm sitting on the curb outside the gates of Thomas's neighborhood when Max pulls up.

He stops the truck and gets out, meeting me around the front, the headlights blinding us like twin spotlights.

His hair is a rumpled mess, and his shirt is tucked up in his jeans on one side, and in the bright lights, I notice that he's got a long purple splatter of paint running up one leg and across his T-shirt.

He's perfect.

I don't stop walking, but collide into him—giving in to the irresistible force of my emotions. I erase any space between us. I slide my fingers through the inky hair at the nape of his neck and pull his face down toward mine. When my lips finally find his, all the tumbling, crashing chaos inside me stills on impact. This moment, this one right here, is worth my life.

Act Third
Scene One

[Becca's house]

Max holds my hand as we walk up the steps to my porch. The street is mostly dark, but my parents have left our porch lights on. I'm smiling on the inside because this feels like fiction, but it's not. I squeeze Max's hand, and he gently returns the pressure. That's real. He's real. Which means I'm real, too.

"You there, Bec?"

"Huh?" I blink and pull myself back from wandering further into my thoughts. Max chuckles.

"You kind of spaced out on me."

"Sorry, I was thinking of a book." He gives me a wry smile and steps closer. "*The Velveteen Rabbit*."

"One of your top three," Max says, showing off his impeccable listening skills. We spent an hour sitting in Max's truck outside Thomas's fancy neighborhood and talking about silly little things. Things that don't feel like much on their own, but when you add them up, they give a relationship weight and heft—substance to keep it standing. Like the heavy pincushion bottom of the Velveteen Rabbit, filled with sawdust to keep him upright.

"Mom would read it to me when I was little and tell me I was like the little rabbit. She said one day I'd look up from my books and find that someone had made me real. And that always scared me because the Skin Horse says it's painful, becoming real, and I believed him. And he's right because love is…messy."

Max smiles at me, a half grin, like I've said something that may be amusing, but he's not sure. And then it hits me. I'm talking about Charlotte and how loving her, her fierce friendship, made me real, but maybe that's not what he thinks I'm talking about and—"Not that we're in love."

I want to open the door and get as far away from this sudden embarrassment. I can feel a verbal onslaught building in my chest; it's not going to make this situation any better. "I'm not saying that we're in love because that'd be crazy. I mean we've only just, and I don't know the first thing, really." Max's eyes and his smile have been growing larger with every stupid word I utter. I can't look at his beautiful face any longer, so I drop my gaze to his chest and focus on the flickering flames of his *Fahrenheit 451* shirt.

"Finished?"

"Yes."

"Good," he says, tipping up my chin so he can look me in the eye. His laugh is a low note on a cello. "I'm going to kiss you now. It's the only way to know."

"You probably should have done it fifteen seconds ago. Would have spared us both."

"No. I like your book recommendations," he says, his crooked smile hovering above my lips. His eyelids slide closed, and I should close mine, but his lips look so wonderful. I watch them until I'm about to go cross-eyed, then close mine.

Max's fingers tangle in my hair as he cradles my head. He hugs me so tightly that I can imagine those burning red flames from his shirt spreading across my own chest, engulfing us both. I pull him tighter, afraid I can no longer breathe on my own, and if he takes his mouth from mine, I will surely suffocate with want.

There's a knocking, and I think for a second it's my racing heart, but Max pulls away and cocks his head, looking at the front door. "I think someone's knocking."

"But we're outside."

There's another series of rapid-fire knocks. I reach out and open the door. Dad is standing in the foyer looking sheepish.

"We heard a car and I looked out the window and"—Dad clears his throat—"your mother wants to know if you two would like to come in and have some ice cream."

"Why'd you knock?"

"Well..." Dad's mouth twitches. "I didn't want to interrupt."

Please let the warped wood of the floorboards swallow me alive.

Dad looks at Max. "Good to see you again, Max. I'm trying really hard to be cool right now."

Max shakes his hand. "You're doing an excellent job." They nod at each other, and, yes, this is all very civil but—

"Tell Mom I said, 'We're not hungry for ice cream.'" I step between them and grab the doorknob.

Dad's eyebrow curls. "Right. Will do." He's about to turn away when he adds, "But she's got toppings."

"Bye, Dad," I say, closing the door.

Max is chuckling, his hands shoved in his pockets. I lean the crown of my head against the shut door, staring down at my shoes.

Max whirls me toward him, wrapping his arms around my waist. "Your dad is a good guy. He seems very"—he pinches his face up, searching for the right word—"hip?"

I lace my arms around him, laughing as I look up at his face. He schools his expression into one of mock seriousness. "But, Becca, next time someone asks if we want ice cream, remember the answer is always, 'Yes, please.' Who doesn't love ice cream?"

I let go of him and step back to swat him. "Fine," I say, laughing. "Go enjoy some ice cream with my parents."

Max's crooked canine shows in his wide smile as he gathers me up in his arms and squeezes me in a giant hug that takes my breath away. "I'm going to go," he whispers, dropping kisses along my jaw before letting me go. "We're still on for the museum tomorrow?"

"Yes."

"Good. Enjoy your dessert." He draws his lips across mine, and everything in me melts.

Inside I find Mom leaning on the kitchen island scooping bowls of ice cream. Dad drowns his in chocolate syrup.

"Not cool, guys," I say, pulling one of the bowls toward me. Dad hands me a spoon and gives me an apologetic kiss on my forehead.

Mom feigns innocence, her voice lilting in all the wrong places. "What? It was a legitimate question. Who doesn't love ice cream?"

I snort and reach for a spoon.

Dad takes his ice cream into the family room. Mom passes me the caramel syrup as a peace offering. We each take a bite before she apologizes. "I am sorry, Becca. I didn't mean to interru—"

"Stop. Please, just don't." Mom's blonde hair is pulled up in a ponytail with wisps falling around her face. It makes her look younger. I shrug. "It's fine. I guess it's your parental responsibility to embarrass the crap out of me."

She nods. "True, and given your reclusive nature, we've never really been given an opportunity to fulfill that responsibility. There was talk of stripping us of our official membership cards."

I roll my eyes at her.

"More and more like a real teen every day." She mutters this with a mouthful of ice cream. "So what happened with Darby?"

The huge bite of ice cream I take does nothing to cool the anger pooling in my stomach. "Oh, she was too depressed for a party, a real wet blanket," I say, remembering the way her dreads stuck to her forehead when she emerged from the water. "She didn't want to hang out anymore, so I got a ride from Max."

"A ride, eh?"

"Mom, I swear—" She giggles. "Is there real rum in your Rum Ripple ice cream? Are you drunk?"

"Sor-ry," she mumbles, but she's still smirking.

"It's not like that with Max." My throat clenches, and I struggle to swallow. All my old panic is flooding back in. "I really like him, Mom."

Her eyes soften, and she reaches out to cover one of my hands with hers. "I know."

"But what if something happens?"

She looks pensive, her face pinching up on one side. "Well, what if something doesn't happen?"

The storm of crazy whirling thoughts that were threatening to pull me under just moments ago burns out. She's right. I take a deep breath and release it. Flipping my hand so I'm holding hers, I squeeze. "You are seriously out to win some parenting points tonight, aren't you?"

Mom squeezes back. "You know it."

Scene Two

[Becca's room]

Mom and Dad are on the back porch stargazing. They'd invited me to join them, but I'd rather relive my night with Max up in my room. I flop into my bed, remembering the way my lips tingled from Max's kisses. A real kiss feels so much better than I imagined—so much better than any of the writers said. A part of me longs to try to find the words for the way his lips brushed along my jaw like feathers and the zing of powerful energy that coursed through my body when he pressed them to mine.

I don't know if there are enough words, or the right words, but I crave a way to capture it. Without thinking I pull out my phone and open my messages. I'm about to open a new text message when my fingers freeze.

I was about to text Charlotte.

I want to tell her about my first kiss.

I want her to squeal and be happy for me.

I got a part in a play. I got the meanest girl in drama to be a little less of a bitch—okay so she may have stabbed me in the back, but I think it may have been partially accidental—she did look sort of contrite just before I pushed her in the pool.

I kissed a boy—a beautiful, kind, adorable boy who really seems to like me. Me. Becca Hanson.

Why, Charlotte? Why aren't you here for any of this?

And then I realize how long it's been since I've missed her. I think about her often, but this sinking, clawing, heart-shredding sensation of missing her has been gone from my life for a few weeks now. What kind of a crappy friend am I? I'm worse than Darby.

I throw the phone at the wall, hoping it'll shatter into a thousand satisfying pieces. Thanks to the superhero-powered strength of the protective case Charlie got me, it thuds into the wall and flops to the floor.

I'm so tired. So tired of wrestling with this feeling, this grief left over from Charlotte's death. It's always there—even when I don't notice it. Every day. Every hour. Every breath. It's there for the bad stuff and worse yet, it's there for the good stuff. It taints everything. It consumes me.

This grief has stolen the happiness right out of the moment. I heave my pillows at my closet, knocking some of the hanging clothes off the rack. Not enough. I want to destroy something the way heartache is destroying me. With great, heaving, sobbing sweeps of my arms, I knock the books off my bookshelf. I rip everything off the stupid bulletin board mocking me with memories of Charlotte. All the while, there is a shrieking in my head, like the wail of a siren. I toss the picture frame from my desk onto the floor and stomp on it with the heel of my shoe, smashing the glass.

The sound of the glass crunching, like the hollow bones of a finch being crushed, stops me. I slowly lift my heel, and a whole new wave of guilt and grief washes over me. I bend to pick up the framed picture from my birthday last year. Charlotte smiles from the middle as Charlie and I flank her, moons to her planet. A shard of glass cuts my hand as I grab the broken frame.

The pain is exquisite. Red, hot, and real, the pain flares and drips over my hand like the blood pooling in my palm. I toss the picture aside and squeeze my hand, gasping as the pain bites deeper. Tears prick at my eyes, but don't fall.

The cut isn't deep, but it bleeds, and while it bleeds the screaming in my head gets quiet.

My phone beeps from the floor. A text from Max. I stand over it to read the message.

> ***MAX****: Miss you.*

As I'm reading, another one comes through.

> ***MAX****: That was lame. Sorry. I was just thinking of you and*

And what? And what, Max? I grab a wad of tissues, clenching them in my cut hand. I hold it above my head—I've read about first aid—and stop to grab my phone.

> ***MAX****: Sorry. Again. Meant to delete but hit send instead. I should stop now. I just wanted you to know that I was thinking of you. But not in a creepy way. Just happy thoughts, you know?*

He's having happy thoughts. I look around my room, at my clothes spilling out of my closet and the floor full of books and debris. Why can't I have happy thoughts?

> ***ME****: I know.*

I pocket my phone and pick up—carefully—the smashed picture. I wiggle the photo out from under the broken glass. One corner is creased, but otherwise it's okay. I turn it over and read Charlotte's loopy script written on the back. "The gang," it says in blue ink along the bottom right corner.

I look from the picture to my cut, the bleeding already slowing.

I'm struck by how time passes and we're moved along in its current, sometimes so slowly that we don't even realize we're moving until we look around one day and don't recognize the shore.

My life is repairing itself around the hole where Charlotte was, just as the skin of my hand will seal up my cut. If I'm lucky I'll have a scar—something to mark the trauma long after it's gone. But I can't stop the process of healing. Not if I'm living.

Maybe that's what Juliet was thinking. Maybe she just really didn't want any more scars.

Scene Three

[Max's truck]

Max picks me up Monday morning as promised. There's a surge of adrenaline spiking through my chest when I slide into my seat next to him. I wonder how it's possible that Elizabeth Bennet only ever suffers mild flutters when she sees Mr. Darcy. I feel like my body is about to explode. What's wrong with me?

Oh God! I'm the ridiculous Bennet sister. I'm Lydia!

Max's eyes look sleepy, and his hair is pushed up in the front in a way that makes me want to run my fingers through it. He gives me a quick grin that makes my breath hitch.

Victor pats my head when I get settled. "Hello, Becky dearest."

I reach for my coffee in the cardboard drink box balanced on the seat between Max and me. "Hello," I say, taking a sip.

"Max told me you two had a good weekend. Little rendezvous Friday *(lots of kissing,* I think to myself*)*, little fun family trip to the museum Saturday *(the hall* *of dinosaurs is dark and there's this corner behind the triceratops...)*, little studying on Sunday *(I'm going to flunk my calculus quiz today).*"

My mouth is on fire, and I can't lay the blame on the coffee alone. My eyes are huge in my head, like the spooky dogs in Hans Christian Andersen's *The Tinder Box*. I bet I look like the dog with the eyes the size of saucers. But I'm nothing compared to Max, who whirls to swat at Victor with eyes as wide and round as the tower of Copenhagen. "Jesus, Vic. Not helpful."

Victor ducks, snickering. "Helpful? You're right. I'm not very helpful. But I bet Becca is very helpful. She's your new study buddy, after all."

The heat on my neck feels like an inferno, but I guess I should have prepared for this. I think back to all the times Charlie gave Greta and James crap for dating each other. So. Many. Times. This is what having friends is like. I have friend-s. That "s" makes a big difference. Victor can't fool me any longer. I sit with the techies because they are my friends. And to be a friend, sometimes you've got to—

"Sorry to have replaced you so easily, Victor. But really, can you blame Max? I've got brains and boobs."

Victor chokes on his coffee, spraying it all over the back of Max's headrest. Max swerves, coffee spit and the word "boobs" still ricocheting around his truck. He pulls over to the side of the street, his face a deep copper, and covers the ears on the Mary statuette on the dash. "Becca," he says, and I'm so glad he's biting back laughter. "You can't say b-o-o-b-s in front of the Virgin."

"Oh," I say, pulling my face in an exaggerated expression of guilt. I turn and look seriously at Victor. "Sorry, Vic."

Victor is still wiping coffee off his face, but stops mid-swipe, mouth agape. Laughter spills across the front seat as Max lets go of the statue to take in Victor's shocked face.

"Well done, Becca. Bravo," Victor says, raising his coffee cup in a toast.

"And don't you forget it," I say, clinking mine against his before taking a satisfying gulp.

Scene Four

[The guidance counselor's office]

At lunch, I knock on Dr. Wallace's door to apologize for missing Friday's appointment. I decided to stick with the story Darby and I had used on my mom. It'll be easier than juggling multiple lies. "Oh what a tangled web we weave" and all that stuff.

Mrs. Wallace welcomes me in, carefully trying to hide her annoyance with me behind a big, gap-toothed smile. She whirls her long curls up and jabs a few pencils in to hold it in place before motioning for me to join her at the little sitting area in a corner of her office. She folds her legs up under her long skirt as she sits, crossing her hands in her lap and waiting for me to begin.

"I'm sorry about Friday. My friend had some boy trouble. I found her crying in the bathroom and just couldn't leave her."

Mrs. Wallace's face flickers with disbelief, but she settles it quickly. "A friend?"

"Darby. She's in the play."

"Darby Jones? I didn't realize you were friends."

"Only since the play," I say, nodding for emphasis, remembering the way Darby shrieked just before she hit the water.

"Well, I'm glad you made it today."

We sit in silence, and I'm aware she's waiting for me to say something, like I keep epiphanies up my sleeves and can pull them out on a whim. But I've got nothing.

"I've got nothing," I say.

She chuckles once.

"No, seriously. We'll be waiting here a long time if you think I've got some sort of amazing discovery about myself to disclose. I thought maybe doing the play would help me figure out my life, but I'm just as confused now as I was when I agreed to do it."

"That's impressive."

"I know, right?" I shift forward. "Sometimes I feel like I've got it figured out." I think back to my amazing kiss with Max, the way I felt whole again for just a moment. "But then, I don't know, it's like I'm back where I started—missing Charlotte so much that it hurts. My chest aches and my stomach burns and my head is a mess. Plot twists in real life suck."

Dr. Wallace leans toward me. "A little like taking a step forward only to stumble and slip backward again. Right?"

"Yeah. It's frustrating. I just want to get better." I drop my head into my hands.

"Becca?"

I groan in response.

"You're not broken."

I peek at her between my fingers. "I feel broken." Pressure like a thousand boulders thunders through my skull, piling up behind my eyes until I think they may burst from my head in a flash flood of tears. I push the heels of my hands into my eyes, trying to hold myself together with an unraveling thread.

I hear the tinkling of Mrs. Wallace's bracelets as she stands and places her hand on my shoulder. "You're not broken. You're grieving."

"But for how much longer?"

Dr. Wallace lowers herself to sit on the edge of the coffee table in front of me. "Forever."

Looking up, I count four deep lines in her forehead. I wipe my eyes with the cuff of my sleeve. "That's really depressing."

She nods.

"You kind of suck at this."

The wrinkles on her forehead shift upward as she grins. "I'm a work in progress—same as you."

The bell for next class sounds out in the hallway. Dr. Wallace sucks in her lips and then releases them as she exhales messily. "Well, thank you for coming to see me today. I'm not going to require you to come back, but remember that I'm here to listen."

I stand. "Maybe I can stop by or something, I don't know, sometime."

She cocks her head to one side and her smile goes lopsided. "That'd be lovely."

Scene Five

[The theater]

In the week since the party at Thomas's, Darby has reverted to growling at me instead of talking to me (which is fine by me because that girl has no idea what the word *friend* really means). And poor Thomas. He's civil to me, but a lot of our spark as Romeo and Juliet has died. Owens has noticed. He stomps around wailing about how this play will be the death of him.

The one bright spot in all of this is that Thomas's sparring with Darby when Romeo kills Tybalt is explosive. My heart races watching them hack at each other. Thomas is definitely putting his anger to good use.

Today Owens has us rehearsing what Victor has dubbed *the postcoital scene*. Romeo and Juliet have spent their ill-fated wedding night together, and Romeo must now get the hell out of town before someone finds him and kills him.

I follow Thomas over to a long, low futon. Victor swears the bed will be made to look historically accurate by opening night. His face got all red and sweaty when I joked I'd read somewhere that Shakespeare had a futon. I was informed that I am most definitely not funny. Victor takes stage dressing seriously.

This scene is a major test for Thomas and me right now because there's like a million kisses and tender looks and all that stuff. That's right, one million kisses in sixty lines of iambic pentameter. Shakespeare isn't the only one who can write hyperbole.

I glance up at the booth where Max is working. "Yes," he says, his voice sweet in my ear. "This will be weird."

I smile, placing a hand over my earpiece, like I can hug him through it.

"Tell him if he gets fresh, I'll drop a Leko on him."

"What's a Leko?" I ask.

"Huh?" Thomas says turning toward me, still adjusting his own mic.

"A Leko?"

"Oh." He points up at the giant light fixtures that hang from the catwalk above us.

I look up at the booth and burst out laughing.

At Owens's instruction, Thomas and I lie back on the futon. When we blocked this scene a few weeks ago, I lay beside him rigid and untouchable, exactly the same as I lie in the corpse scene. But today when Owens calls the scene to action and that spotlight burns over me, I curl into Thomas's side. I trace lazy circles on Thomas's chest with soft fingers, remembering the way Max's kisses feel along my neck.

"Hmm…" Max's voice is a soft buzz in my ear. "I think you're getting too good at this acting thing." I hide a smile, burying my face in Thomas's neck.

Thomas's intake of breath is sharp as he turns his head to look at me. But the spotlight is on, and I'm not Becca

Hanson. When he turns, I'm Juliet, and he's the man of my dreams. I stamp out the little voice that is crying bullshit at the back of my skull.

"Wilt thou be gone? It is not yet near day," I say, making my voice liquid like syrup on Sunday morning pancakes. Thomas pushes himself up on one elbow, a finger sweeping my hair from my face as he listens to me speak. "Believe me, love," I say, sliding my hand from his chest to cup the back of his neck.

There's chuckling in my ear. "By the way, I totally saw him eating the fish sandwich at lunch today. Enjoy that."

Ewww. It takes all my willpower to keep from wrinkling my nose in disgust. I pull Thomas's face to mine and breathe a light kiss on his lips before finishing my line. "It was the nightingale."

"I hate him." Max sighs, and it sends tingles down my spine.

Once we've finished the scene, Mr. Owens claps his broad hands in a way that echoes across the empty seats in the back of the theater. His Cheshire cat smile is bright white in the glare from the spotlight. "Bravo, Juliet. And thank goodness, too, because I thought for sure we were going to have to cancel the whole show the way you two have been acting lately. Bravo, indeed." He's trumpeting like a drunk elephant.

Max cuts the spot.

Mr. Owens blinks a few times and calls out, "Light, Maximo. I need the light. I have a grand announcement to make."

I glance up at the booth and smile. Without the light on I can see Max, but as soon as he throws the switch, he becomes a shadow puppet along the back wall.

Mr. Owens claps three more times and then clasps his

hands together in front of his heart. It looks a little like he's going to burst into an operatic aria.

"My young actors, I have wonderful news for you, and for me." He beams at us, motioning for the kids in the first few rows of seats to come closer. Darby and her court step out of the wings. "I have been speaking with a dear friend at the School of the Arts—"

There's an audible gasp. Mr. Owens pauses. It looks like he really enjoyed that reaction. People whisper to one another, a few high fives are thrown, and Darby's minions are doing a squealy group hug thing behind her.

"Yes," continues Owens, "you heard me correctly. I have invited a Mrs. Natorini to be our most special guest on opening night. Mrs. Natorini is one of the talent scouts in the admissions department."

There's another explosion of excitement. Thomas snatches me up in a huge bear hug, whirling me around twice before setting me back down. He rubs a hand through his hair with an apologetic expression once he's returned to his senses.

Mr. Owens watches us with a proprietary look in his eye. "Yes, a reason to celebrate, especially since Juliet has continued to grow under *my* tutelage." Owens slides himself over so he's standing beside me, waving his arms around me like a spokesmodel at a car show.

I glance at Darby out of the corner of my eye. The knuckles of her right hand are white where they wrap around her broadsword. As much as I hate to admit it, most of my progress is due to Darby's help—not Owens.

"I know many of you have your sights set on The School of the Arts. This may be your opportunity," Owens says. "The play is the thing. In the next few weeks, I expect each of you to eat, drink, sleep, and breathe this play. Our futures may depend on it." He opens his arms wide and takes a small bow before exiting the stage.

Bedlam. It's the only way to describe the frenetic energy that explodes in the theater once he's gone. Thomas is about to hug me again, but the spotlight cuts out quickly, and he glances up, losing momentum, stunned by the ordinariness of the lighting. I step back a few paces.

"So, this is good news?" I ask.

"This is amazing news. Auditions are hard to come by, and if a scout picks you out, there's a great chance you can get some scholarship money, too. Plus, for juniors like you, if you get into the high school program as a senior, you're practically guaranteed a spot in the undergrad school."

I pan the crowd, taking in their excitement, stopping briefly where Darby's girlfriends have engulfed her in their group hug. This play just became the most important thing on Darby's agenda—the boost she needs to realize her future. I wonder if that makes her more dangerous now. What will she do to get what she wants?

I look back at Thomas to ask, "But not everyone wants to go to The School of the Arts, right?"

Thomas raises an amber eyebrow. "The only ones who say they don't are the ones who fear they can't afford it." He opens his hands at his sides, indicating the stage we're standing on. "This is the dream, Becca."

It is? I enjoy slipping into the role of Juliet, taking a time out from being Becca, but I don't dream about it.

Scene Six

[The woodshop]

Owens caught Max on our way out of the theater and demanded a few new panels for the Capulet ballroom. He insisted that if we were going to have a scout at the play, everything needed to be beyond perfect—as if perfection weren't hard enough to achieve on its own.

The shop has tall ceilings and cinderblock walls painted that jaundice yellow public schools are so fond of. The windows are all near the ceiling and with the lateness of the afternoon and the angle of the setting sun, the western wall of windows is lit like the world outside is on fire. The room reminds me of Dezi's barn studio, full of open space and smelling faintly of straw, wood, and dust, with maybe a twinge of barnyard animal, which makes no sense, but there you have it. It's a comforting place to be.

I drop my bag on a long, dusty table in the shop and then pull myself up, too. My legs swing. Max drops his bag next to me, but moves off to the workbenches along one wall, gathering a long power cord, a T square, and a few other things. He shoves a pencil behind his ear before setting everything by a large board propped up on sawhorses. Then he begins sketching long lines and soft curves onto the board.

"Max?"

He glances at me but doesn't stop working. "Yeah."

I can't squelch the strange new nervousness in my stomach. "Is the scout coming to the play a big deal for you?"

He shrugs, smudging a line and redrawing it. "Why?"

"Well, it's a big deal for the actors. It's obviously vital to Darby, and even Thomas says it's what everyone wants—the stage."

He cocks a brow at me. "That's what Thomas says, eh?"

I purse my lips and slide off the table to come closer to where he's working. "I guess I just didn't realize. I mean I thought it was just for fun. I didn't think any of it mattered."

Max puts the pencil behind his ear and straightens to face me. "It is for fun, Bec. Don't let it get to you." He runs his hand down my arm, making the hairs there stand on end.

"Fine, but it made me think." I can't help but twist a long strand of hair. "I worry because"—a sigh escapes me—"I don't know."

"Don't know what?"

"I don't know what I want to do."

"When you grow up?" He chuckles, and I can see that twisted canine when he grins at me.

I roll my eyes and snatch his pencil, pointing it at him as I speak. "Don't mock me."

His face becomes serious. "I'm not mocking. I'm just suggesting that perhaps you don't have to worry about when you grow up just yet."

"Everyone else does."

He shrugs and steals his pencil back. Turning back to his work, he says, "Yeah, but I bet they don't really know. I bet they're just faking it."

"So what about you? What do you want to do?"

I notice he's bearing down on the pencil harder so that this line is heavier than the others before. "Mom says I'd make a great structural engineer. Dad says artist, of course."

"Of course."

"I say, we'll see."

"But what about college?"

"I'll go wherever I can get a scholarship."

"Wherever?"

He shrugs again.

"How can you not care?"

"I don't have the luxury of caring, Becca." He's pressing so hard on the pencil that I can see a groove in the board. I think back to our game of Would You Rather and the choice between failing or doing the same thing every day. Max chose failure, but perhaps he's still afraid—afraid of caring too much about a future he may have no control over.

He peeks up at me from his work. "I just want to go to college."

"Sorry. I shouldn't be saying anything, right? I mean, I haven't even thought about going anywhere. It's just that Charlie always knew where he wanted to be. I don't think he even applied anywhere other than MIT."

"Risky."

"Not if you knew my brother. He was made for MIT. Or maybe MIT was made for him, just biding its time until he was old enough to attend." But then I remember how Charlie almost let it all go. How he almost said, "screw it"—

would have left it behind for the chance to spend more time with Charlotte. He'd had a new dream. One filled with Charlotte.

Max is finished with the sketch and has plugged in the power cord for the jigsaw. He secures a long, slim blade into place. The metal teeth catch the fiery sunlight and sparkle like prisms on a chandelier.

"I need a dream." My voice is jagged like the blade's edges. I feel like I'm wasting space on this planet, like Charlotte would have one hundred dreams if she'd been allowed them, and I can't come up with one.

Max looks up, setting the saw to the side. He places his hands on my shoulders, running his fingers down the length of my arms until he tangles them in my mine. "I hope when you find one, it makes you happy." He squeezes my hands before letting go and reaching back to present me with a pair of fluorescent orange safety glasses. He fits them over my ears, setting them on the bridge of my nose, dragging his thumb down my cheek and under my jaw when he's done. "And I hope there's room for me."

He destroys me with a gallant smile before he puts on his own ugly glasses.

When we're finished, I sweep the floor as Max stores the tools. "So I was thinking," he says, grabbing the dustpan and bringing it to where I've swept up a pile of shavings. "We should go out, just the two of us." He squats with the dustpan and looks up at me. "No Victors. No little brothers. No homework. No interrupting fathers. No ice cream."

"No ice cream?" I carefully move the pile into the dustpan.

Max chuckles as he empties the dustpan into the trash. "You're right. What was I thinking?"

"Ice cream is essential," I say, holding a finger into the

air like I'm making an official proclamation.

"Victor is not."

We finish up and grab our bags. Max takes my hand on the way out. "So Friday? Just you and me?"

I nod before I remember. "No."

Max freezes mid-step. "What?"

"We're going to see Charlie this weekend. It's family weekend at MIT." I tug on Max's hand and turn so I can rest my forehead on his shoulder. "I can't this weekend." Looking up at his face, into his bottomless dark eyes, I smile. "But my birthday is next weekend."

"It is?" His smile is perfectly devilish. "What would you be wishing for?"

I glance at his lips. He leans forward and gently brushes a kiss across mine. Behind my closed lids I see a kaleidoscope of possibility when we touch.

Scene Seven

[Boston]

Dad and Mom take turns driving Friday evening. We go north through big cities like Washington, D.C. And past rural towns with cow pastures that butt up to car lots. We get to our hotel after midnight and fall into our beds exhausted.

"Tell your brother we made it safely," Mom says, before pulling the covers up around her chin. Dad is already softly snoring.

> ***Me**: We made it. See you in the AM.*
>
> ***Charlie**: I have a surprise for you.*

My stomach flutters.

Charlie greets us in the morning with a huge smile. His hair is shaggy and he's wearing a T-shirt I've never seen before. There's a picture of a blue bicycle and a quote, written in German and attributed to his personal god, Einstein.

"What's that mean?" I ask, pointing at his chest and

stopping him mid-hug.

He smiles. "Life is like riding a bike. In order to keep your balance, you have to keep moving."

He smells of foreign laundry detergent when he hugs me.

His school is enormous. There are people everywhere. He shows us some of his labs and the projects he's working on. We meet professors and lab partners and roommates. We see dining halls and study halls and really big lecture halls.

Charlie fits perfectly here. He's surrounded by people very much like him—driven and determined—and I wonder what would have happened if Charlotte hadn't died. He still would have come to MIT. Charlotte would have made him. But his attention would have been divided between here and her.

Suddenly, my whole body feels heavy, and I struggle to keep up. We're forgetting her too often. Our lives are going on without her, and I know that's how it's supposed to be, but it feels wrong. It feels like betrayal.

"Becca?" Charlie looks at me over his shoulder. I've stopped walking, and he doubles back to me. "You okay?"

I shake my head and stare at the blue bicycle on his shirt.

Charlie waves Mom and Dad on, telling them we'll meet them in the student union. "What's going on?"

I open my mouth to answer, but close it soundlessly. Standing is suddenly too much work, so I sit on the sidewalk in the middle of a busy quad. It's much colder here than home. November in New England is a different creature than down south, but the cement is warm from the sun. I close my eyes and will my legs to drink in the warmth, wick it up through my bones, and thaw me out.

"Becca, you can't just sit in the—" But Charlie cuts himself off. He sits down beside me. After a few minutes, I open my eyes and look at him. "Feeling better?" he asks.

My face pinches in thought, and I sigh, "Not sure." I point at his shirt. "I want to keep moving, but then just when I build up momentum, I feel like I'm abandoning Charlotte, and I panic, which makes everything screech to a halt."

Charlie takes a look at the shirt he's wearing, pulling at the hem to straighten out the wrinkles. "It doesn't say anything about life being a sprint, Bec. It just says keep moving."

"I'm afraid I'll get too far away from Charlotte. I'm afraid I'll lose her."

Charlie smiles a wistful half smile. "See, that's funny, because I'm afraid of the opposite. I'm afraid I'll never get over her." His eyes fill up, and he shields them, pretending it's the wind that's making them water. "I'm afraid I'll be alone forever without her."

That would break Charlotte's heart. If it weren't already stopped cold in the ground.

After lunch, Mom and Dad decide to attend a seminar on financial aid. Charlie has scholarships and a grant, but "every little bit helps," says Mom. Charlie drags me to the T, Boston's public transit train system, to show me the surprise he'd promised last night.

Two trains later, we get off at Boston Public Garden. We grab two coffees from a vendor and sip them as we walk through the fallen leaves on the pathways.

"Look," Charlie says, pointing ahead of us. There, frozen in bronze, are Mrs. Mallard and her ducklings, characters from a beautiful children's book Gram used to read to us, *Make Way for Ducklings*.

I jog up the path to get a closer look, patting each of their little heads. "Is this my surprise?"

Charlie shakes his head. "Nope."

Charlie takes my picture with the ducklings, and I text it to Max. I add, "Making friends in Boston," after the photo.

Soon we're headed out of the park into the busy streets of Boston. I do a lot of looking up and gaping. We come to another park, this one much smaller. There's an old church with a plaque dating it to the 1870s butted up against a modern glass skyscraper. The two are such unlikely neighbors, but something about it works, the old and the new, the past and the present living and working together in this city.

"It's amazing," I tell Charlie, but he doesn't stop walking.

"It gets even better." He tugs my hand, pulling me across the square to a giant stone building with a red tiled roof.

"This is your surprise," he says, holding out his hands to the imposing building.

Etched into the facade just under the roofline, I read, "Boston Public Library Built by the People and Dedicated to the Advancement of Learning."

"A library?"

Charlie walks toward it with long strides. "You're gonna flip out when you see inside."

But I can't make my feet move. "You brought me to a library?"

Charlie stops and fists his hands on his hips. "Not just

any library. According to the nice research librarian who helped me, this library has the second largest collection of books in the entire United States."

"Even bigger than New York?"

"Library of Congress is the only one bigger." Charlie's grin is so wide the corners of his eyes wrinkle. "Aren't you surprised?"

"That you know all this? Yes."

He chuckles and walks behind me to shove me forward a little. "Come on."

He's impatient to get inside the library. My brother, who until last year refused to read anything that wasn't in comic book form or covered in numbers and scientific notations, is rushing me to get to a library. Not just any library. A giant library.

What a strange world.

We step inside and everything roiling inside me—doubt, anxiety, insecurity—stills to a peaceful hush. It's a feeling a little like kissing Max, and I'm glad the lobby is cool and dim so Charlie won't notice me blush. But seriously, this library is so beautiful I'd like to make out with it a little.

We climb the marble staircase, passing between twin lion statues on pedestals. Each gallery is more beautiful than the last. Stepping into the reading room, long and wide with high arched ceilings and windows that capture all the light of the city, makes me weak in the knees. And the smell! Paper, leather, wood, and ink—sweet and smoldering scents that blend together to make the best smell on earth. Holy crap. I think I'm in love with a building.

Charlie is grinning beside me, bouncing on the balls of his feet. "You like it, huh?" He nudges me. "I did good, right?"

I nod, and he wraps an arm around my shoulders. "How

did you know?" And I'm thinking about *The List of Places You'll Go* that Charlotte and I made. I don't think Charlie's ever seen that list.

This isn't the New York Public Library. It's bigger, though, according to Charlie and his research librarian friend. And it's more than I could have dreamed a library could be.

"You like books," he answers with shrug. "I haven't even shown you the books yet." With that, he tugs on my hand again and pulls me along to see the rest of the library. As we wind through the stacks, I begin to wonder if there isn't a way for me to be a little more like this big city, marrying the past me with a present me. One that reads and gets lost in stories, but who also lives to write her own? Maybe that's a thing I could do. Maybe that's the start of my very own dream—my future.

Scene Eight

[An MIT banquet hall]

When we get back to campus, we meet up with Mom and Dad for a special dinner and lecture the university has organized. I texted Max on the T, telling him about the amazing library, but I haven't heard anything back from him. When my phone rings at dinner, I excuse myself, thinking it's him. But when I get out into the hallway and glance at the phone, it's Victor.

"Hey," I say, answering. "What's up?" I'm trying to keep breathing normally. There are plenty of reasons for Victor to call me. Just because I can't think of one isn't proof they don't exist.

"Um, hey, Becca." Victor's voice is too deep, too calm. "Are you somewhere where you can talk?"

"Is everything okay?"

"Everything will be okay, but there's been an accident."

My vision goes splotchy, and I lean back on a column in the corridor outside the banquet hall. It feels irredeemably cold now that the sun has gone down. I think Victor is waiting for me to say something, but my throat is too swollen with fear to speak.

"Max was in an accident. He's kind of beat up, concussion, broken bones and stuff, but nothing too serious." He pauses, again, to give me a chance to say something, but remembering how to breathe is taking too much effort. Words escape me. "So, I just wanted to let you know. He's at Memorial if you want to see him when you get back in town. I'll text you the room number and stuff."

Charlie finds me sitting on the ground with my head between my knees sometime later. I think maybe I said good-bye to Victor. I can't be sure.

"What's up?" Charlie asks, sliding down the wall to sit beside me.

"There was an accident," I say to my heels.

"Is everyone okay?"

I pick up my head, and it feels like heaving a boulder up a hill. And since my boulder head is solid, there's no way to process thoughts and make words and say all the heavy things weighing me down.

"Jesus, Bec," Charlie says, grabbing my arm. "Did someone—" But he can't say the word because we don't say that word. We know how much that one hurts, how much it costs to say it out loud and make it real. That word we walk around like someone else's garbage on the street.

I hand him my phone with the text message from Victor telling me where Max is.

Charlie mutters a "thank God" as he flicks to my contacts and pulls up Max's number. "Call him," he says, thrusting the phone at me. "Maybe he can talk. Or at least you can leave him a message."

I nod and take the phone, but the voice that picks up isn't Max.

"Victor?"

"Hey, Becca. Again."

"Sorry, I— "

"I should have told you. I've got his phone, at least until he, you know, wakes up."

I nod into the phone, which is dumb, but it's all I can do. Charlie gently takes the phone from me and introduces himself to Victor. He asks lots of questions about the accident and Max's status at the hospital. He asks all the things I should have asked, but don't want to know.

I don't want to know how another truck ran a red light and T-boned Max. I don't want to think about the sound of metal crunching or the bones in Max's arm, either. But I can hear Victor's voice over the phone as he explains it all—the swelling in Max's brain, the medicine to make him sleep while it subsides, the cast on his arm.

I can't hold my ginormous rock head up anymore. I rest it on my knees and look away from Charlie, who is thanking Victor and exchanging numbers with him in case of emergency. I close my eyes and think what a strange world it is when Charlie and Victor become emergency buddies.

When he's done, Charlie places my phone beside me. "I'm going to go talk to Mom and Dad. Will you be okay out here by yourself?"

I turn my head so I'm facing him. "Yes." I watch his face relax with the one little word. Such powerful things—words. Powerful, but deceptive.

Yes, I'll be okay by myself. Of this I'm sure. It's the *letting people in* part that gets tricky. I'm not sure I'll ever be okay again if I lose one more person I love.

Scene Nine

[A hospital room]

Max is sleeping. That's what they call it. Sleeping. The euphemism makes me want to vomit. He's not sleeping. He's drugged. The left side of his body is made of plaster and bandages. There are machines to monitor his vitals. With my eyes, I trace the tubes from the IV pole to the blue-black vein of his arm. I wonder if I scream, would he wake up?

Outside, the waiting room is filled with people. Dezi is napping in a corner. Greg, Kelli, and Victor are spread out on the floor with Javi playing a board game. Miles is reading. Esperanza is buzzing about in her scrubs. Every once in a while she whispers prayers in Spanish. Prayers the stupid Mary statue on the now-mangled dashboard of Max's truck obviously didn't hear.

Inside, Max's room is dim and smells like sweat and industrial cleaner. I peek around and read the whiteboard on the wall with a nurse's name and some cryptic code I can't decipher. The blinds are drawn so only slivers of the evening light filter in, striping the floor with shadows. We left first thing Sunday morning, cutting short our weekend with Charlie, so I could see Max.

I step closer to the bed, rest my hand on the side rail, consider reaching out and touching Max's face, but I'm standing on his left where the cuts and bruises are the worst. Victor said Max was lucky—said they had to cut him out of the truck. Looking at him, so still in this bed, I know I should feel lucky, too.

He's alive. He'll be okay. He's alive.

But, instead, I feel a clawing inside of me, talons of fear scraping along my throat.

I close my eyes, feeling the tears burn.

I've been here before—maybe not this room, but one that looked like it, one full with machines and gray light and the stench of tears and bleach. I've looked over a bed rail at my best friend, held her hand, wanting to stay with her forever, while she told me to leave.

"Please," she'd begged. "Go. Take your brother and get out of here."

"But—"

"I don't want you here." Her voice was like a dull razor being dragged across my wrists. I tried to hide the tears that slipped down my cheeks. "Not like this, Becca. You can't see me like this. I don't want you to remember this."

But I do. I remember. I'll never forget. Just like I'll never forget the way Max looks now.

Irresistible force. The phrase just keeps playing on repeat in my brain. I can hear Max so clearly, from that day in the barn. "He wanted to see what would happen when an irresistible force met with an immovable object." Life is an irresistible force, and we're stuck in its path. Anything can happen at any time. There is no future. It's all an illusion.

I lean over the railing, pressing a kiss on Max's

forehead. His skin is warm on my lips and, under the assaulting smells of antiseptic and plaster, I can barely make out the smell of his soap, honey and cedarwood.

"I'm sorry." My voice is sandpaper.

If I leave, he won't be alone. He'll still be surrounded by loved ones. But I can't stay. I must resist the irresistible force that is trying to take my heart again.

Scene Ten

[The theater]

I avoid everyone at school the next day. I skip lunch and hide in the library. I even dare Mrs. Jonah to say one word to me about reading in her stupid literature class. I read two hundred forty-two pages. I hide in the back row of the theater waiting for Owens to call me to the stage, fully expecting Victor and the gang to pelt me with rotten vegetables when I do. I deserve it.

But without Max, everything is running slowly. Owens is even more erratic and high-strung than normal. I swear he thinks Max got in a car accident just to screw with his play schedule. He's been muttering to himself in the dark since the first missed sound cue.

Darby finds me and flops down in the seat beside me. My muscles instinctively tense. "I'm sorry to hear about Max. He okay?"

I grab a lock of hair and twist. "I don't know."

Darby blinks. "Why don't you know?"

"I couldn't stay at the hospital. I—" I break off and gnaw on the inside of my cheek.

"You left him?"

"He wasn't alone." My voice is too high, frantic. "Victor and everyone, they were there. Ask them. But I couldn't be there. He seemed—" I've been searching for the word since I left the hospital. Beautiful, brilliant Max, so full of life and warmth, with the smile like springtime, looked—and suddenly it's there. The word I've been searching for. "Fragile."

I'd come to think of Max as a rock, but even rocks can be worn away, or toppled in an earthquake. Nothing lasts.

Darby swears under her breath. "So you bailed?"

I nod. "But he wasn't alone. It won't matter if I'm not around."

"Wow," she says, sitting back in her seat. "I knew you were damaged, but this"—she waves a hand in my direction—"this is more like destroyed. Open your eyes, woman. You're not some invisible nonentity. You've jumped with both feet into the middle of a pond, and you're making lots of ripples. You've got to get your shit together."

"That's what I'm doing."

"By hiding? By reading?" Darby picks up my book and shakes the pages in my face. "What happens when the book ends?"

I snatch my novel back from her. "I get another one." Each of my words is enunciated with crystalline clearness.

"And that's how you want to live?"

If every move I make creates ripples and those ripples affect other people's lives, and then their lives send ripples out toward me like tidal waves, then yes, being very, very still is definitely the way to be. "That's how I intend to survive."

Darby nods. "Yeah. Okay. I see the difference." She

stands, and her seat cushion bobs up. "But that friend of yours, Charlotte, she would be pissed if she knew what you were doing to your life."

I jump up, too, shouting, "Don't you talk about Charlotte."

"See," Darby says, stepping toward me, her face six inches from mine. "That's just it. I get to do whatever the hell I want. I'm living my own life. Can you say that?"

Without waiting for me to respond, she whirls on her heels and stomps down the aisle. Her groupies are all giggling and whispering behind their hands. I want to slap them all. I want to rip out their hair and toss it in the air like confetti. I want someone else to hurt like I'm hurting. I want to scream in Charlotte's face. How dare she let me love her! How dare she die on me! How dare she ruin me!

Owens calls me to the stage, but I won't be going up there. Not today. I slam open the doors, letting the sunlight from the hallway flood the dark theater. When they close behind me, the sound reverberates in the soles of my feet.

Scene Eleven

[Darby's car]

The next morning as I'm getting my stuff together to wait for the bus, there's a sudden braying noise from the driveway. My traitorous heart skips a beat—Max!—before my mind catches up and reminds my heart to shut up. *Max is in the hospital*, my brain says, very rationally. *Right where you left him*, my heart hisses.

I run to the porch and find Darby, laying on her horn like she's trying to raise the dead.

"What are you doing?" I ask. Darby motions for me to get in. I walk slowly toward the passenger side door, like I'm walking through a land mine.

Darby pulls out of the driveway without a word. She fiddles with the radio instead.

"Am I being abducted?"

Darby rolls her eyes and turns out of the neighborhood. We drive in silence until she pulls into the drive-thru at the Dunkin' Donuts where she orders a coffee, black, and then motions for my order.

I wonder, briefly, if I should tell the barista about my

abduction. "French Vanilla with cream and sugar, please."

Darby pays at the window and hands over my drink. She inhales a large sip, grimacing as it must have burned the inside of her mouth a little, then turns to me with a bleary-eyed grin. "I'm rescuing you."

"From what?"

"At the moment, from the bus. We'll see what else needs work as we go along."

"What if I don't want your help?"

Darby slams on the brakes right as she's pulling into the street. A car veers, blaring its horn at us, and my coffee spills out the edge of my cup. The hot liquid singes, but my jeans soak up most of the pain.

"Christ," I swear at her. "How is *that* helpful?" I rub at the spot on my thigh.

"Becca, I don't give a shit if you want my help. It's not all about you. *I* want to help you. Therefore, that's what *I'm* going to do. You do whatever the hell you want."

"But why?"

"Because it's your life."

I furrow my brow, trying to piece together what she means.

She rolls her eyes. "Do what you want because it's your life. And don't ask why. Sometimes things just are what they are. Why did Charlotte like you?"

An invisible hand clenches my throat. "I have no idea."

"And in the end, did it matter why?"

I shake my head.

"Why does Max like you?"

"He shouldn't," I say. "He shouldn't like me. I'm damaged. Seriously."

"Oh, I know," Darby says, pointing at herself. "That's what I've been saying all year. But it's not like any of this is permanent, Becca. It's not like any of this is forever."

That I know.

"So enjoy it while you can." She takes another gulp of her steaming hot coffee and grimaces as it burns its way down her throat.

She sets her hands at nine and three o'clock on the steering wheel, just like we're taught in driver's ed—except she's got a cup of coffee balancing on the wheel in her hand at nine. "Now *I'm* going to go to school. Would *you* like a ride?"

"Yes." I take a sip of coffee.

Apparently I've moved out of the way of one irresistible force and directly into the path of another.

"Have you talked to Max yet?" She asks as we're pulling into school. The question freezes me, and it takes a moment to remember how lungs work. She nods, watching me. "That's what I thought. His leg wasn't as bad as they initially thought, just bruises and cuts. His arm is healing in a cast. I heard he'll be getting out of the hospital Sunday."

"You heard?"

"I asked Victor."

"You talked to Victor?"

Darby rolls her eyes. "Yes."

"Thanks."

She shrugs. "I was curious. That's all."

I nod, but I know she's trying to help me.

"It's my birthday," I say, fiddling with the strap of my bag. Darby's face pinches like she's sucking on a lemon. "Sunday," I explain. "It's my birthday."

"Well, what a lovely birthday present for you, then."

I run a finger around the rim of my coffee lid. Darby groans beside me. "You know," she says, like the words are painful, "I may have heard one more thing."

I look at her fearfully.

"He looks for you. Every time he wakes up."

My heart, already beaten, stops.

Scene Twelve

[On a road trip]

Charlie got home Saturday evening. I'd told him he didn't have to come home for my birthday. We'd just seen him at MIT, and I know his classes are crazy, and he can't afford to take a day off, and yet, bright and early Sunday morning, he barges into my room and sings a horribly out of tune version of the birthday song. It reminds me of baby rhinos jumping on pianos. When he finishes, he takes a low bow before sitting on the end of my bed. "Do you want to take a road trip?"

"Are you going to sing again?"

"Maybe."

"Then no. Definitely no." I pull my pillow over my face.

He smacks me with a pillow, the very pillow I'd been hiding under. "I said"—he emphasizes his words with more flurries of the pillow on my face—"Do you (pillow thump) want to take (pillow thump) a road trip (pillow thump, thump, thump)?"

I try to deflect the pillow with a blanket force field. "No."

Charlie studies me for a beat, hugging the pillow to his

chest, before asking, "You sure?"

I know exactly where he wants to go. I want to go with him. I do, but then again—"No."

He picks at a loose thread in the pillowcase. He looks lost. He looks like he did when he figured out the scientific improbabilities of Santa Claus actually living at the North Pole.

"Okay," I say, relenting, feeling myself stacking up the bricks in a heavy wall to protect myself from today.

"Good," Charlie says. His voice is soft like dandelion fluff. "Charlotte wouldn't want to miss your birthday."

I haven't been to visit my best friend since the day they buried her in the ground in a faraway cemetery in a picture-perfect mountain town. I mean it's far, but not that far. Charlie went back when he left for college. He said it was on his route up to Cambridge anyway, but I've studied the maps. I know.

We don't talk much on the drive up. We talk about Thanksgiving and whether Dad will make that god-awful gluten-free stuffing he made last year. We talk about Charlie's work with Dr. Bell at MIT. He tells me funny stories about Greta and James in California. He misses them. But they'll be home at Christmas. He'll see his friends at Christmas.

"How's Max?"

All of my insides feel like they are bolting for the exits, shoving and pushing at one another to abandon ship. "I, uh…"

"Mom said you haven't been back to the hospital all week."

"She noticed that, huh?"

Charlie gives me a sidelong look. "You know intelligence is partly genetic, right?"

I try to roll my eyes at him, but my heart's not in it (probably because it's too busy fighting my spleen to be the first to get out).

"Do you want to talk about it?"

I clamp my jaw shut and shake my head. Charlie looks both disappointed and relieved all at once.

Charlie puts an audio book on to fill the silence between us. I watch the trees as we pass them, and eventually I fall asleep.

When I wake, Charlie is standing outside his door, stretching his long arms up toward a clear sky that's the color of Charlotte's eyes. There's a rush of panic that starts clamoring up my spine, until I notice we aren't at the cemetery, but are parked along a main street with boutiques and beautiful pots of autumnal-colored mums.

"Where are we?"

"I need to pick something up. Plus, you're boring when you're drooling, so we need to get you some coffee." He waves an arm toward a very pink door on the street.

Inside the pink door, the world smells like vanilla and sugar. It smells like Charlotte. There's a dark-haired woman behind the counter with a wide white smile and lips as pink as the door.

Charlie steps right up to her, and I wouldn't have thought it possible if I hadn't seen it myself, but her smile gets wider. "Mornin', Miss Rose," he says, the southern drawl that he usually works to keep hidden, spreading out between them like butter on toast.

Miss Rose's pink lips twitch, and she tilts her head, birdlike. "Back again?" she asks, but like she already knows what he's going to say next, like Charlie and this baker woman are in some play together, reciting lines.

"I have it on good authority these are the best doughnuts in all of ever," Charlie says.

Miss Rose's eyes get glassy. "And who might that be?"

"Charlotte Finch," Charlie says. Charlotte's name goes through me like a bolt of lightning.

I must gasp or flinch or something because the next thing I know, Miss Rose is coming around the counter and gathering Charlie and me up in her ample arms and squeezing us so hard I can't breathe. Or maybe I just can't breathe because Charlie and Miss Rose have a whole play together and it centers around Charlotte and I've got nothing. Nothing.

"It's nice to meet you, Becca," Miss Rose says as she lets us go.

"I, uh—"

"Charlotte spoke of you when she visited."

I'm shocked she would remember something like that. Who is this woman?

Reading the question in my expression, Miss Rose smiles in her open way. "It's my business to know the Finch girls' business. Their momma was my best friend."

"Oh," I say, and I think I say it out loud, but I can't be sure because there is so much going on in my head, it's like a building being evacuated in a fire, a big, blazing, alarms-are-blaring kind of fire.

"Y'all need coffee," Miss Rose says, her hand still lingering on my shoulder.

"And I've got that special order to pick up," Charlie says.

Miss Rose winks at him, squeezes my shoulder, and then bustles behind the counter and into a back room.

"What's going on, Charlie?" And with that, I've successfully evacuated all the air from my burning lungs. There're black splotches blooming in my vision and my eyes are tearing up—probably from the smoke.

Charlie leads me to a small table by the window. "It's okay," he says, holding my hand. "You'll be okay."

But I don't believe him. I'm alone and adrift, and God this sucks so hard that I want to tear open my own damn flesh. Because how? How do we go on when we've lost so much? Charlotte was not just any friend but *my person*, the person I was put on this earth to befriend and, without her, what am I? Nothing. Nothing. It's just one more reason why I had to leave Max. I've got nothing to offer him.

"Becca?"

I force myself to look at Charlie. His ears are bright red, so red I imagine they'd be hot to the touch. And his mouth is a straight gash of a line across his face. And his eyes are so loud. Screaming eyes. Shouting with pain and worry and loss and hope.

Hope.

Charlie is looking at me with the barest shred of hope he can stand to hold on to.

And so I hold on to it, too.

"We're going to be okay," he says, leaning his forehead against mine, whispering the words for only us to hear. "We're going to be okay. Please, Becca. Can't we be okay?"

I nod and, with our foreheads pushed together, the motion makes him nod, too.

"Okay," I say. "Okay."

Scene Thirteen

[A cemetery]

When Miss Rose comes out from the back, she's got a large brown bag with twine handles, which she hands to Charlie. She bustles over to the coffee and pours out two large to-go cups. Charlie sets the bag down and takes the coffee over to the counter with the cream and sugar. I watch him tear the tops off three packets of sugar, splitting the contents between our two cups. He's got a funny little smile tugging at the corner of his mouth.

Miss Rose chuckles from behind the counter and, once again, I know they know something I don't know. It's theirs and not mine. I take a shaky breath, though, because I promised Charlie I'd try to be okay. And I can do that. At least for today.

Becca Hanson makes a stunning reprise of her role *Girl Being Okay* for one show only.

Charlie has topped off the coffees with thick cream and pressed the lids on them. He hands me mine and says good-bye to his strange friend in this strange town, while I linger by the door.

We drive in silence toward the cemetery with the windows cracked open so that the hissing wind is the only sound between us. The warmth of the coffee cup against my hands helps chase away the chill in the mountain air. I look out at the small town, which quickly thins to wider green pastures with houses leaning on the backs of mountains, and I wonder about Charlotte's life here. She didn't talk about it much. It was in the past. Charlotte lived in the present.

"How do you know Miss Rose?"

Charlie's lips curl into a smile. "Met her when I brought Charlotte here to see her dad."

"Just the once?"

"Well," he says, sipping his coffee, "I stopped in for coffee and doughnuts this summer, on my way up to MIT."

I nod.

I take a long sip of my coffee to wash down the jealousy that is sitting like bile at the back of my throat.

Charlie turns onto the cemetery drive. There's a tall brick archway with wrought iron gates swung wide open. As we drive through it, all my senses spark like fireflies at dusk.

Once the car is parked, Charlie reaches into the back to retrieve the bag Miss Rose gave him. He carries it and his coffee around to my door, opening it for me. "When you're ready," he says, nodding off in the direction in which I know Charlotte is buried.

I watch him through the open door as he heads for the path that will wind around the old gravestones, bleached white like bones themselves, toward a small pink dot near the back corner.

I can choose to stay here. I can just sit here in this car,

drinking my coffee, and being miserable, or I can get out, walk down that path, and what? Sit and be miserable by a pile of dirt and a broken-down angel wearing a coat of ugly pink paint?

I close my eyes against the bright sun and remember Charlie carrying that broken statue toward Charlotte's grave on the day of her funeral. He didn't want Charlotte to be alone. And I'd carried the paint and brush for him. And her wing. I'd carried the angel's wing.

I'd felt so calm then. I didn't feel good, but I didn't feel this constant panic inside—this need to peel away my skin so I can escape from the chaos inside myself.

I'd tied the angel's wing back on and kissed my brother's cheek and said good-bye to Charlotte. Then walked to the car without another look back, straight into Charlie's best friend Greta's arms. She'd held me and rocked me and shushed me, even though I wasn't crying anymore. And Charlie had sat by that grave and talked with his girlfriend and painted the angel that hideous shade of pink. What did he call it? Flamingo-ass pink.

When I open my eyes again, I find Charlie, a lone living figure amongst the dead. He's so tall, dwarfing the stones around him, like they are children frozen in a game of tag. I have the urge to run around tagging them all, shouting, "Unfreeze," with every touch.

Charlie suddenly doubles over, no longer taller than the stones around him. He's squatting next to the pink angel by Charlotte's grave. I'm struck with a realization like lightning to my system. He needs me. My big brother needs me. I launch myself through the graveyard. I can't get to him fast enough. He needs me.

When I reach him, he's got his hands wrapped around the back of his head, his elbows pinned around his ears, crouched down, rocking himself. And sobbing.

My brother is crying, loud bursts of pain like the sudden cawing of crows as they startle from a field.

Beside him is a headstone.

And Charlotte's name is on it.

This wasn't here last time. It'd been too soon. There were rolls of sod pressed with gaping seams over the fresh dirt. There were flowers, so many flowers. But there was no stone with her name. No stone summing her life up in the short line of *Daughter, sister, and friend*.

I want to scream. I want to kick at the stone, shove it, topple it. And I must make some sort of strangled sound, because Charlie looks up from his well of sorrow. Seeing me, he reaches out one of his long arms, catching my hand in his, and pulling me down with him, like we'll be safer down here—safer together.

He cries, and I silently scream until there is nothing but nothing inside of us.

We sit with our backs to the stone. It's a rosy color, the only one of its kind in the cemetery, and the pink I'd mistakenly thought was the angel. She's still here, but after so much time, her pink paint is chipping and faded. It wasn't meant for stone angels.

Her broken wing is missing, too—no longer tied on with a handkerchief. It must have fallen off and been thrown away by a caretaker.

Charlie's low chuckling breaks the silence between us. "*Now* we're going to try to be okay. Okay?"

I snort. It's like playing the quiet game on car trips

when we were little. One of us would say, "Okay, no noises starting NOW," and we'd both giggle and snort and make plenty of noise between us.

Charlie pulls a pink box tied with string from the brown bag Miss Rose gave him.

"Best doughnuts in all of ever?"

Charlie's smile flickers. He opens the box and pushes it toward me. Inside is a small cake, decorated with orange roses and a little brown rabbit with faded white spots. "Happy Birthday, Very Real Becca," is written in orange frosting.

Charlie's hand finds mine in the long grass. He squeezes my fingers before letting go. "Do you want me to sing?"

"God, no," I say, a trickle of hysterical laughter threatening to multiply into a deluge in my throat.

"Come on," Charlie whines. "You know I've got mad singing skills." He sings an even more horrible rendition of this morning's song. I wouldn't have thought it humanly possible to sing so terribly if I hadn't heard it myself.

But his appalling, earnest singing does the trick; it batters down the dam in my throat holding in all the laughter and the sadness and the anger, all the emotions that mean I'm still here. I'm still real. I'm still alive. And this is no act. All this stuff inside me is the real deal.

I join him in the last refrain, delighting in the sound of our voices echoing between the mountains—like we're multiplied and vast—an unstoppable army of two. *Does this count as yodeling? This terrible singing? I think so, Charlotte.* I pat the headstone beside me. That's one more from *The List* I can check off.

Charlie cuts the cake into three large pieces—one for me, one for him, one for Charlotte. Miss Rose has tucked three plates and three forks into the brown bag. I kind of love Miss Rose right now. And it's not only because she makes the best birthday cake in all of ever.

We spend the rest of the day with Charlotte. We stretch out in the grass on either side of her just like we always did, Charlie and I making a buffer around Charlotte, trying to protect her from nothing any of us can be protected from.

I tell Charlotte all about the play and Max and even Darby. I guess Charlie is listening, too, because he interrupts.

"You haven't even texted him?" He props himself up on his elbow to look at me.

"I'm afraid," I say, sitting up. I face Charlie across the grave. I finger the lines on the headstone of Charlotte's name. "Remember that dog that lived next door to Gran?"

He nods.

"Remember how they'd tie it up every morning to that stake in the backyard and it'd just walk circles around it all day, wearing a path in the dirt? And that one day, you just couldn't take it anymore, and you snuck over and set that dog free."

Charlie's smile is fragile. "But it refused to leave," he says. "I set it free, but it just kept circling and circling. Even when we called for it to follow us."

"I'm that dog, Charlie. My life is just circling and circling, tethered to the time when Charlotte was in it. I've tried this year to take new paths, make new friends, have new experiences, go new places, but I keep circling back to this." I lean against Charlotte's headstone. "I'm afraid I'll never get away. I'll never get over missing her. And I don't know if I even want to."

Charlie sits up. "Maybe," Charlie begins, clearing heaviness from his throat. "Maybe we don't ever get away from the grief. Maybe we aren't supposed to. Maybe we're supposed to carry it with us—always."

I study the short line on the headstone between Charlotte's life and death, the dash that sums up her eighteen years here so poorly. It is too small. I want a sharp object so I can etch the line farther, make it bigger, bolder, last longer.

I can't figure out how to keep going alone, not when every step I take away from Charlotte pulls me right back. Not when what I really want, in the deepest part of my heart, is to never have to walk away from her, to always be walking toward her.

"I can't lose anyone else."

Charlie nods. "Yeah, but that's not how it works, right? People—" He stops short, catching himself.

My fingertips buzz with adrenaline. "They die. They die, Charlie. People die. One day they're here, and then they're not. Could be cancer. Could be a careless accident. Could be getting flattened by a truck." The cake in my stomach is poisoning my insides, making them burn. "We don't know. All we know is that they die and they leave us and it hurts."

"Because we loved them." Charlie catches my eye before continuing. "It hurts because we love the ones we lose, and they love us."

"Are you trying to say it's worth it?" I grasp at my chest like I can hold the torn edges of myself together. "*This* is worth it?"

"I don't know, Bec," Charlie says, pulling at a clump of grass. "But I do know I wouldn't trade a moment I had with Charlotte. Not a second. I won't give an ounce of this pain back, because it's mine, and it means she was here and she was real and she loved me."

Charlie stands, brushing the grass off his pants. "But

I do know this," he says, looking down at me where I sit. "Choosing to be alone because Charlotte died isn't grieving for her. That's just plain old fear, and everyone suffers that, even the brave."

He stands above me, his fists clenched at his sides, the setting sun turning his yellow hair orange, like a flame.

"How do you know all this, Charlie?"

"Well, I am a genius." His body relaxes a bit. I reach up and take one of his hands.

I think about Romeo and Juliet, about how they were each too afraid to live without the other. I've always hated the end of the play, because if they're both dead, then what does it matter? Perhaps what matters is that they loved. The point isn't the end. It's the story that matters.

I need to write my own story. I need to make it matter.

I touch the rough top of the headstone. Is that okay, Charlotte? Can I keep writing even if you're not in the story any longer?

When we get back to the car, Charlie stops me before I slide into the passenger seat. He reaches into the glove compartment, giving it an extra hard slam to be sure it closes properly after pulling out a small box.

"What's this?"

"Birthday present."

There's a piece of paper taped to the box with a quote, written in my brother's cramped scrawl, from my favorite book.

> *You become. It takes a long time. That's why it doesn't happen often to people who break easily, or have sharp edges, or who have to be carefully kept. ~ Margery Williams, The Velveteen Rabbit*

"Charlie—" I begin, but my voice is broken. He's already given me so much.

"No, no, no," Charlie says, holding out his hands like he alone can hold back the tide of tears that are threatening to crush us both. "Cry later. Open now." He nudges the box in my hands.

I open the box to find a keychain inside with a single key. "What's it for?"

Charlie opens his arms like a maestro as he draws my attention to his beat-up blue car.

"Your car? Why are you giving me a key to your car, which will be with you in Massachusetts?"

"It's not my car."

"There are two pieces of shit like that in the universe? Seems impossible. And cruel."

Charlie's ears go red, but he chuckles. "It's the same piece of shit, but now it's your piece of shit."

"What?"

"The real Becca doesn't need to mooch rides anymore. The real Becca can go anywhere she wants, anytime she wants, provided her piece-of-shit car is running that day."

"Charlie—"

He holds up his hands. "Just take it. I don't need it. It sits in a garage, an expensive garage, for weeks on end. There's a train from home to Cambridge, and I can even do schoolwork while I'm on the train."

"But—"

"You're welcome," he says, shutting me up by enveloping me in a lung-crushing hug.

I whisper my thanks into the hair at the nape of his neck. "I don't deserve you."

Charlie holds me at arm's length, a fierce look in his eye. "You deserve to live your life outside the pages of a book, Bec. It's what Charlotte wanted. Take her with you. Keep her with you."

I'm smiling and crying at the same time and am acutely aware of the snot threatening to gush out of my nose. I give Charlie my most determined nod possible.

He smiles and tucks a hair behind my ear. "But could you drop me off at home before you go to Max's?"

"How'd you—?"

He points at his head. "Genius. Remember?"

I laugh, wiping my nose with the back of my hand. "How could I ever forget?" And while I never thought I'd have a birthday better than the one I had with Charlotte, this one is pretty damn okay.

Scene Fourteen

[Max's bedroom]

It starts drizzling as I turn onto the long gravel drive threading through the pines to Max's house. The rain does little to dampen the smell of dust and evergreens as I park by the barn. I run my fingers along the smooth, worn wood as I walk around it toward the kitchen door. I imagine I can feel every drop of rain as it falls on my face, each one a reminder that I'm still here.

I knock on the kitchen door before peeking my head in. This is protocol for the Herrera household. Once they've invited you into their life, you don't need to wait out in the cold, but let yourself in. Dezi explained it to me what feels like ages ago. It was really just months ago, though.

Inside, Javi and Victor are sitting at the kitchen table. They both look up at me as I enter. Javi gives me a big smile. Victor looks wary, like a predator has just cornered him.

"You're here," Javi says, pushing away from the table to grab my hand. "Victor made me hot chocolate. Want some?"

I glance at Victor and decide, no, I do not want

anything he might hand me. It'd probably be poisonous. "Where is everyone?" I ask instead.

Javi tells me how the house has been so full lately, aunts and uncles, cousins, friends all coming and going. "Mom said she needed some peace, so Dad took her somewhere, even though there's no one here but us." Javi points to himself and Victor.

I clear my throat. "I see. And where's—"

"Sleeping." Victor's reply is a barricade.

"Right," I whisper.

Javi chuckles. "He won't wake up. His medicine makes him funny. Then he sleeps and sleeps. Want to see him?"

I don't look at Victor, but nod at Javi. He drags me down the hall to Max's room. Victor follows like a shadow. Once we're inside, Victor tells Javi to go find the marshmallows for the hot chocolate. When we're alone, he crosses his arms and looks me in the eye.

"I should have been here sooner."

He nods.

"I shouldn't have run."

He nods again.

"I won't run again."

Victor sighs. "He may not want you here. You should have seen his face, Becca, every time he woke and you weren't here."

I swallow. "I'm here now. I'll be here."

Javi's victorious cry snakes its way down the hallway toward us. Marshmallows have been found. Victor glances at Max once before he brushes past me.

The rain continues to fall outside, tapping on the window with feather-soft fingers. The lamp on his desk is on, but otherwise the room is dark. I glance around, studying the drawings on his walls. They are sets, beautiful, modern sets for *Romeo and Juliet*. He's been working on them even though Owens would never look at them. I touch the firm ink lines, so solid and sure, and ache to touch Max.

His breathing is slow and rhythmic. His left arm is in a cast from just above the elbow down to his hand. The bandages on his head have been removed, and his sharp cheekbones seem even more pronounced in the semidarkness of his room. His hair is shaggier, too, with a long black lock that has fallen across his eyes. I push it back, savoring the warmth of his skin.

Watching him sleep with the rain beating a steady rhythm outside, I'm suddenly exhausted. Slowly, careful not to disturb him, I crawl into the space next to Max on the bed. I curl into his right side, the side not covered with bruises, and breathe in the sweet smell of him. The storm of fears that has been swirling around me since Victor called to tell me there'd been an accident suddenly stills. Actually, I've been lost in this storm longer than this one week. It feels like I've been fighting it my whole life. I think of Romeo's line, just before he drinks his poison.

Then, I defy the stars.

I can't change my past. I know that now. I wouldn't want to. But I'll be damned if I'm going to let something as fickle as fate decide my future.

I rest my head on the pillow, in the crook of Max's neck. I'll be here, unmovable, I think, just before I fall asleep.

I wake to the feeling of fingers playing in my hair. The rain is falling harder outside, and the desk lamp has been turned off, so the only light from the room filters in from a distant source down the hallway. I pick up my head and am inches from Max's face. His fingers freeze, and he eyes me warily.

"Are you really here?" His voice is a rasp.

"Yes."

"Are you going to leave again?"

"Not if I have any choice in the matter."

He smiles and closes his eyes. His fingers run gently through my hair again. I press myself forward, pressing my lips to his. His good arm tightens around me, and I think to myself, *I will not lose another chance to kiss this boy. I will not lose another smile from his lips*. Not because of fear.

This is my birthday present to me.

Scene Fifteen

[The theater]

I pull into Darby's drive Monday morning, blocking her car just as she's about to pull out. She doesn't recognize the car, so of course she hops out in full drama queen mode.

"Some of us have places to go, asshole."

I roll down my window and stick out my head, enjoying the moment Darby realizes it's me. "Stop your whining and get in, then."

Darby's smile is annoyance, humor, and admiration all at once. She reaches into her car for her bag and takes her sweet time strolling around to the passenger side of my car. Once she's in, she examines everything, from the clock on the dash missing most of the bits from each digital number, to the crack in the dashboard that makes the glove box door misalign. She settles back into her seat with a satisfied smile, propping her feet on the dash.

"Well, it's a piece of shit, but I do like having a chauffeur for once."

There's a smug grin on my face. "This car goes where I

want to go and nowhere else." It feels good to be in control.

"Is that right?" Darby laughs. "So how was your birthday?"

I know what she's hinting at. "I got everything I wanted." I catch a glimpse of a smile on her face.

"What finally made you go?"

"Charlie." I pull into the drive-thru line at Dunkin' Donuts. "And Charlotte."

Darby and I ask to go to the library in Mrs. Jonah's class. She doesn't even question us, just writes a pass. We head straight for the tech booth.

I sit in Max's chair, and I think I can smell his soap. He should be back next week. I can't wait to pick him up for school in my new piece-of-shit car.

Darby reads quietly beside me—Henrik Ibsen's *A Doll's House*. I smile inwardly, knowing she's going to have a lot to say about the play when she's finished reading it.

"Hey," I ask, breaking the comfortable silence. "What ever happened with that essay?"

Darby smiles. "I rewrote it."

I bite the inside of my cheek to keep from grinning. "Oh, well, I'm sure that was a good idea."

She chuckles. "We'll see. Of course, impressing that scout will go a long way, too."

"There's no way she won't be impressed by you, Darby."

She looks me in the eye. "Thanks."

My face feels like I'm sitting too close to a campfire, and I'm relieved (and amazed) when I realize Darby's blushing, too.

I make a big fuss pulling out my English notes, unable to say anything else. Darby retreats into *A Doll's House*. I consider reviewing for tomorrow's test. Instead, I turn to a clean page and pull out a pencil.

Without thinking about it, I start to write, just nonsense at first, but then it takes shape, turns into a dialogue, something I've never read before, but feel certain Romeo and Juliet might say to each other in a quiet moment alone. Not that they got too many of those. No, that's not true. The only thing they ever had was moments. What happens when the conversation goes on for more than three minutes? What do they say then?

Wryly, I know they'd probably just stop talking and start making out, but I force my hand back down to the page and try to imagine them in a more realistic setting.

I see them sitting opposite each other in a cafeteria, surrounded by their peers. Before I know it, the words are flowing onto the page. I'm lost in their conversation, until Darby scoots closer, leaning over my shoulder.

"What're you working on so diligently over here?" Darby asks, pulling the notebook from my grip.

I swipe it back and hug it to my chest. "Nothing."

She gives me one of her devilish grins. "Looks like something." She opens and closes her hands, making *gimme, gimme* motions. "Come on. Let me read your dirty fan fiction."

"It's not dirty," I scoff.

"But it's fan fiction? Lemme see. I'll be your best friend."

I snort. Darby takes the notebook and quickly reads what I've written as I try to make myself be still despite the nervous energy zinging through my limbs.

When she's done reading, she sets my notebook on her

lap and runs her fingers around the edges. "This is really good."

"But."

She smiles. "But nothing. It's just really good." She hands me my notebook.

Below, in the theater, we hear a door open. Owens appears in the booth window as he walks to his makeshift desk on the fourth row and shuffles through papers there. He gathers a few sheets and then proceeds to the stage, sitting himself in one of the banquet chairs. That's when we notice he's on his phone. Darby flips a switch and we can hear him over the hanging mics.

"No, no," he's saying, glancing down at the paper in his hand. "That shouldn't be a problem. I can start anytime, anytime at all. I thought you understood that when we spoke last week." He nods into the phone, listening. Darby and I exchange a look, careful to keep our heads barely visible in the window of the booth. "The school will be fine. This play has been plagued since the beginning. They'll understand why I'm leaving."

"Leaving?" Darby mouths.

"Plagued?" I ask.

"Wonderful," Owens says, throwing his arm out like he's accepting some silent applause. "I'll be in to sign the contract today."

Darby's fist tightens. "That bastard is leaving?"

"But we're in the middle of the play. And there's a scout coming."

"Ass," Darby hisses. She stands, and I try to pull her back down, but there's no stopping her. She slams the button to turn on the spotlight, blinding Owens. "You conniving sneak," she shouts, but not until she's flipped the public address system on so that her voice thunders through the theater like an angry god.

Owens clutches his phone to his chest while using the papers in his hands to shield his eyes from the spotlight. "What's going on? Who's up there?"

"Were you even going to tell us? Or were you just going to disappear?"

You can see the moment Owens figures out who is speaking. A ripple of fear washes over his face.

Darby doesn't wait for an answer. "You know what? Fine. Good riddance. I hope you're happy making other actors miserable, because I'm done with you." With that she flicks off the spot. The little emergency lamps along the aisles are the only pinpricks of light in a black galaxy.

Darby deflates in the darkness beside me. It's like watching her shed a costume. "What are we going to do?" One of her soft dreads has broken away from the band at the nape of her neck, and it falls across her cheek as her head slumps forward. "The school will cancel the play. Without the play, I'm stuck."

I look down at the notebook in my lap, fingering the edges of the pages. Something inside me breaks open, and not in a sad, terrible kind of way. This feels new. Like a rift opening, toppling the old and allowing possibility to take root and grow. I toss my stuff in my bag.

We don't need Owens to make this play a success. If anything, his leaving is a blessing. He'll take his ego and melodrama with him, and we'll be left with a theater full of talented actors and techies with nothing to lose.

"Let's go," I say, grabbing her bag, too. It's time to defy fate. Time to make our own reality. "I've got a plan."

"You do?" She asks as we breach the doors of the theater into the gray corridor.

I pull her along behind me, heading back to Mrs. Jonah's room. "Well, an idea. You'll help with the plan part, right?"

"Right," she says, sounding a bit like a cheerleader. "So we're going to come up with a plan."

"Together. But we'll need Max, too."

She rolls her eyes, but her smile takes up most of her face. "Of course."

Act Fourth
Scene One

[Max's room]

Practice is cancelled after school today (shocking, right?), so Darby and I head straight to Max's. He's been getting steadily better each day. I mean, he's not about to win an arm wrestling contest any time soon, but he can stay awake now for hours at a time.

I've been here every day since I showed up Sunday night. Max has forgiven me. Victor can almost look at me. Everyone else is somewhere in between. It's those ripples again. By hurting Max, I hurt them, too.

When Darby and I arrive, Dezi is bustling about making the strong black coffee he drinks. I introduce them and leave Darby in the kitchen while I check on Max. When I peek in Max's room, he's awake. He's got a pad propped up on his cast and is sketching with his good hand. I'm suddenly overcome with gratitude that it wasn't his right arm that was broken.

"Whatcha working on?" I ask as I steal across the room

and crawl up beside him. His face opens with a wide smile as he wraps an arm around me.

"I missed you," he says, nodding at the sketch in front of him.

I reach out to trace the lines of my own face mirrored back at me. He's drawn me with my mouth open, laughing. I look happy. He's made me happy. I tilt my head and pepper his jaw with kisses. He turns and catches my lips with his, and his kiss is so sweet it makes my heart feel like it's swelling, too big for my ribcage.

"This is adorable, but do you think you could wrap it up?"

I pull away from Max too quickly, rattling the bed and disturbing his bruised leg. He winces, gritting his teeth. "We cannot get a break, can we?" He kisses my nose before greeting Darby. "What are *you* doing here?"

"Oh, um," I begin, and when he looks at me incredulously, I bite my lip to keep from laughing.

"You're kidding me," he says, studying my face. "You guys are friends now? How long was I asleep?"

"Well, not friends, but—" I peek at Darby. Her arms are crossed over her chest, and she's got one purple booted foot jutted out, but suddenly she's not so scary anymore. "Allies?"

"I wouldn't put up with your whiny shit if we weren't friends, Becca." She steps into Max's room, pulls out his desk chair, and sits, getting down to business. "Now about this plan."

"What plan?" Max asks.

I explain about Darby and I overhearing Owens and the idea we had about revamping the play.

"We're thinking Mrs. Jonah would step in as our faculty advisor. Owens never saw any merit in modernizing the play, but with him gone, we can do whatever we want. We don't need to change the language, that speaks for itself, but let's change the tone."

"If we bomb, at least it'll be because of us, not anything Owens did," Darby finishes.

"So what do you need from me?" Max asks. I notice his eyes cut to his bandaged side.

I point to the sketches over his desk. "I want to build them."

"You?"

"Well, me and the gang." I take Max's right hand in mine. "I know I can do it. Most of the hard work is done, really. We've already built the most important piece together." I point a finger out his window at the barn, where the catwalk we made has been waiting for its destiny to arrive. "I'll only need to repaint flats and make a few adjustments."

Darby stands to look over the set sketches. "You're going to be a little busy, Becca. If we're changing the play, you'll need to relearn the blocking as Juliet. The tempo is going to change, the mood, everything. That's going to take some work. I don't see how you'll have time to do the tech work and the acting work."

"You're right," I say, standing and meeting her. "I wouldn't have time. But since I signed up to be a techie"—I point at the sketches—"that's what I'm going to do. You'll be Juliet."

"What?" Both Darby and Max ask.

I lay a hand on her shoulder. "That scout is going to be in the audience, which means you need to be onstage."

"But I will be onstage. There are no small parts, only small actors, Becca. If I can make an impression on that scout as Tybalt, that'll be a real testament to my skill."

My hands fist on my hips. I know what I want. I want to work backstage. I want Darby to play Juliet. And for once—I peek at Max—okay twice—I will get what I want. "Yes, that's all very noble, but I'm not playing Juliet. The show must go on. What are you going to do about it?"

Darby studies me. My confidence wanes under her acute glare. My hands fall from my hips, and I push my hair behind my shoulders, giving one lock a quick twirl. I try not to look away, but my eyes keep slipping like hers are made of ice. Finally, her wicked grin flickers into place.

"I'm going to make Owens beg to take us back. And then I'm going to laugh in his face."

Victor and the rest of the gang show up at Max's. We explain the situation, Darby and I. With a nod from Max, everyone jumps into action. Kelli pulls out her costume sketches, and with Victor and Darby helping, she sketches the period costumes to look more modern. Miles, Greg, and I help Max. We sketch out plans for reworking the sets he's built, adding new modern pieces to the old ones. What we'll end up with is an almost steampunk Romeo and Juliet, a blending of old and new, then and now. Everything about it feels perfect.

When Max's eyes start to drift and close, I shoo everyone out of his room. I can hear them in the kitchen where Dezi has made what smells like the most delicious pot of stew ever. But I don't want to leave Max yet. I only have a few quiet moments with him before he'll drift off to sleep.

"I still owe you a date," he says, his voice thick with exhaustion. I finish putting the new set plans in my bag before turning to him. He pats the bed next to him, and I nestle into my place there. "We were supposed to go out, just the two of us. I haven't forgotten." His eyes close, and the half smile drifts away from his face.

I push his hair back from his face, tracing the lines of his cheekbone and jaw. "I'm looking forward to it. I seem to remember a promise of ice cream?"

He nods, and I think he's fallen asleep, but then he asks, "Why did you come back?"

I frown, thinking of how stupid I was to have thought I could walk away from him. "There are many choices I need to make about my life, Max. But you aren't one of them."

"I'm not a choice?"

"This feeling, the one I get when I'm with you, it isn't a choice. It just is. It's part of me, and I can't walk away from it any more than I can try to escape from myself." He tries to open his eyes, but I press small kisses to them. "And I don't want to. Not anymore."

"Becca?" Max says, his breathing slow and steady beside me.

"Hmm?"

"Tell me a story about Charlotte."

I cradle his head on my shoulder and run my fingers through his shaggy black hair, settling in next to him to tell my story. "Charlotte taught me to drive. I mean, I took driver's ed and all, but I never did the practice hours."

Keeping his eyes closed, Max turns his face, snuggling into the crook of my neck. I kiss his temple before continuing. "Charlotte thought it was nuts that I didn't care about getting my license. She just couldn't understand why I'd forfeit such a freedom. Freedom meant a lot more to her than to me."

It is the best gift he could ever give me—the willingness to share my memories. It makes me feel less lost. It makes Charlotte feel more real. It makes her a part of my present—a piece of my old life that will always be part of my new one, too.

Scene Two

[The theater]

I climb the stairs to the stage, my whole body threatening to mutiny, stomach feeling weak, and legs like overcooked noodles. The stage is dimly lit, Max's beautiful traditional sets pushed to the sides. The house lights are also dim, so that when I stand at the edge of the stage and look out, I'm not blinded by the event horizon, but by faces. Mrs. Jonah sits grading essays in the back of the theater. Everyone else is in the front, center section, but there is an unspoken boundary between the techies and the drammies. Max is in the booth. Esperanza brought him just for this announcement.

Mr. Owens was wrong about one thing. The school administration most certainly did care that he was leaving. Especially since they found out about it from us. Darby and I met before school and marched into Mrs. Jonah's room to propose our plan. None of us thought Owens wouldn't have already resigned. Actually, maybe Darby did.

Mrs. Jonah went to the administration to confirm everything, and that's when the clichéd shit hit the fan. Once it was all cleaned and disinfected, we had a new advisor, an extra two weeks until production, and permission to create the performance our way.

Now we just have to get everyone else to join us.

"The stage is yours, Bec," Max says, his voice like a warm river flowing through my earpiece, smoothing all the jagged edges of my thoughts that are threatening to tear me apart.

I let go of the lock of hair I've wound up to my third knuckle and clasp my hands behind my back until my fingertips tingle. I glance to my right and left; I'm flanked by Darby and Victor, but they both nod at me to start things off.

"Right," I say before I exhale what feels like hurricane-force winds. "We're going to do the play without Owens, and it's going to be brilliant, but only if we work together." In a rush, hoping to get all the words out before they start throwing rotten tomatoes or stones or calculus books, I outline the plan, telling them about the new vision for the play. Everything will be set in a theater. Romeo and Juliet are from warring acting troupes.

Thomas stands, and I stutter in my explanation. Suddenly the only word in my vocabulary is "uh." Those sitting close to Thomas volley between watching him and turning their attentions back to me. I stop talking altogether, trying not to gnaw off the inside of my lip in a flurry of nerves.

"What if this plan of yours doesn't work?" There are murmurs all around the theater. "You've never done this before, Becca. Why should we listen to you?"

"Because I'm the only one with a foot in both camps." I take a step closer to the edge of the stage. "And it's going to take all of you, techies and drammies, to make this play happen. Owens played you against one another, encouraged the tension. But this way you'll get your chance to prove how amazing you are to that School of the Arts scout—together."

There's silence in the theater. The only sound on the stage is that of my own excited breathing.

Darby steps forward to stand beside me again. Victor joins us. "Sounds good to me," she says.

The queen has spoken.

"Max," Darby shouts, turning to face the booth. "Get your ass down here and tell us what to do."

Max's chuckle over the speakers sounds like the distant rolling of thunder, the kind that lingers as a storm moves farther away. "Yes, Your Majesty."

"Screw that," Darby says. She pantomimes taking an invisible crown from her head and tossing it up toward the booth. "This thing always gave me a headache."

I catch Max's shocked expression as he leans close to the window in the booth, and it makes me smile. But it's a short-lived smile that slips away when I notice Thomas. He's standing with his shoulders set crookedly, like half of him is ready to join and the other half is holding him back. When everyone else moves to meet Max at the back of the theater, I jog down the stairs from the stage and grab Thomas by the elbow.

"What're you thinking?"

"Does it matter?" he asks, his voice as flat as the polished floors of the stage. "I'm just a pawn, remember?"

"You matter, Thomas." My fingers are still perched at his elbow. His blue eyes gaze down at them, and I itch to remove them, but I don't. "Owens is an idiot, but he was smart to cast you as Romeo. Don't walk out on us now. The play needs you."

"What about you?"

"I can't do this without you."

Thomas puts his hand over my fingers, his callused fingertips tapping a rhythm I can't understand. "Yes, you can."

I sigh. "You're right. I can"—I grin up at him—"but I don't want to. And that's not all you're right about. I *don't* know what I'm doing."

He chuckles and rolls his eyes (almost as impressively as Darby herself). "Don't worry, Becca. I'm not going anywhere. I need this play. I need this chance. At least I still get to make out with you onstage."

I smack him in the chest with my free hand, and he squeezes my fingers at his elbow before we take a step apart.

"Actually, about that." I glance at Darby.

He raises an amber brow. "She took your role?"

I shake my head. "It was never really mine. I was just playing a part. In the end, I think I look better in black."

"You were good out there."

I wrinkle my nose. "Maybe, but I'll be happier back there." I point up at the booth.

Scene Three

[The J & R Salvage Yard]

The gravel crunches under the wheels of my car as I pull slowly down the winding drive that cuts through the salvage yard where Max's truck was towed after the accident. The hollow, crumpled bodies of vehicles and machines surround us as we make our way to the office where the owner's son, Reid, has agreed to meet Max.

We've got one week left before we open the play. Things have been progressing—maybe not smoothly, but in a generally forward-ish manner. It's like Dr. Wallace said, sometimes we take a step forward only to stumble back a few. This, I've learned, is true both of grieving and living.

As we get closer to the small office building, the smell of rust and rubber tickles my nose. The beat-up cars and junk are packed tighter together the closer we get, like a maze of ruins. The overwhelming volume of wreckage is making me feel like all the goodness in my life is leaching away. The terrifying realization of what might have been threatens to spill from the safe place I'd locked it away and flood my car, washing Max and me out the doors, setting us adrift in different directions.

I park outside the shabby office. Max leans closer, kissing my shoulder. "Breathe, Bec," he whispers. When I look at him, he smiles and it chases the Dementors away. "I'm right here. I'm okay."

I nod and touch the bruises on his face. "You're the boy who lived." It's cheesy. I know it. Instantly, I'm blushing. I toss him a smile so he knows I know I'm nuts.

Max's laughter, not my fear, is what floods my car, and it's beautiful.

Inside the office, Reid, tall and skinny, just like his name suggests, shakes Max's hand and nods at me as I linger by the door pretending to read the J & R Salvage Yard policies hanging crookedly on the back wall.

"I emptied out the glove box for ya," Reid says, holding out a rumpled plastic Walmart bag. "The dashboard figurine you wanted was busted, but I put all the pieces I could find in here. You oughtta be able to glue her back together. You'd be surprised by what superglue can fix."

Max opens the bag, and I inch closer to peek over his shoulder. Mary's broken at the waist. One of her outstretched hands is gone. And it looks like there's a chunk of her mantle missing, too. But she's still smiling.

She reminds me of the one-winged angel sitting by Charlotte's side.

Max thanks Reid, closing the bag, and we're about to go when—"Wait."

"You okay?" Max asks. He takes my hand and squeezes.

"I want to see the truck."

"That's not a great idea, Bec. I don't remember much, but it can't be a pretty sight."

But I look at Reid. "May I see the truck?"

Reid looks between us a few times before shrugging. "Sure, but he's right. It ain't pretty. Think you can handle it?"

Something's missing, and seeing the truck may be the last piece I need to finish the puzzle. I can't quit now. "I need to see the truck."

"She's not far." Reid ducks his head as he goes through the door. Max and I follow. I have to take two steps for each of Reid's long strides, and Max is still slower than normal, so we fall behind quickly.

The sun is setting behind the tall pines that border the salvage yard, turning the sky into a watercolor palette of pinks, reds, and oranges. I zip up my hoodie to keep out the slight chill that is creeping in with the shadows.

"Why are we doing this?" Max asks.

It's a fair question. I don't have an answer, though. Not one that I can put into words. Instead I lace my fingers with his and pull myself closer so that our elbows and shoulders bump each other as we walk.

We catch up to Reid, who's standing in a posture similar to one seen at art museums, but instead of studying the *Mona Lisa*, he's looking at the half-mangled hunk of metal that was once Max's truck. The darkening shadows of the early evening drip from the twisted frame like blood pooling under a corpse.

"You were in there?"

Max nods. His face is suddenly ashen, like he's back inside that wreck. His shoulder is now firmly pressing against mine. He's leaning on me like his bad leg is about to give out.

"And you survived." I squeeze his hand.

He survived. He really shouldn't have. The driver's side is completely concave. It looks a little like a giant hauled off and punched the side of his car. Where the emergency officers used the Jaws of Life to pry him out, the metal is torn and twisted, the door hanging off at a crazy angle.

I look at Max, and I just know my face looks ridiculous—my eyes are bugging out and my lips are pursed like a duck's bill—but I can't contain the tidal wave of amazement that is knocking me on my ass. "Whoa."

One of Max's dark brows rises, along with a corner of his mouth. "Whoa?" He straightens up, his legs regaining their strength. He presses his lips together, trying not to laugh at me.

"You survived. In that. And that's... I mean, I don't know, but that's a miracle or something. Right?" Max keeps grinning. I look to Reid for confirmation. "I mean, right?"

Reid opens his arms and turns this way and that, taking in all the wreckage around us. "Miracles as far as the eye can see."

My knees feel like they're made of rubber bands. "Whoa," I whisper, and plunk myself down on the gravel.

Reid shoves his hands in the back pockets of his faded jeans and starts down the path back to the office. "I'll just give y'all a minute."

Max thanks Reid as he slowly lowers himself down next to me. "I didn't think I wanted to see the truck again. I'm glad we did, though."

I rest my head on his shoulder. "Me, too."

We watch the shadows slide along the truck's bruised side, creeping toward us as the sun continues to set. I reach into the bag at Max's feet and pull out broken Mary's torso. "I have a confession."

"Oh, yeah?"

"I was angry at her." I squeeze the little figurine and feel the broken edge dig into my palm. "I had all these crazy emotions, and it was simpler to just be mad, except I didn't know who to necessarily be pissed with, and she was an easy target, you know? I mean she had one job. Protect you. And she pretty much sucked at it."

I scoot so I'm facing Max. "But I was looking at it all wrong. Wasn't I?"

"How's that?"

"She did protect you."

"Well, she did have a few tons of steel helping her."

I roll my eyes like the drammie I am. Max's mouth twitches into a giant smile. "But you're here. With me."

His fingers push a tangle of hair behind my ear and then trace the line of my cheek down to my chin. "I'm here. With you."

"Then I'd say she did her job." I open my hand and hold out the Mary figurine. "Will you fix her?"

Max studies her in my hand for a while before he answers. "No." He takes her from me and runs a thumb over her face. "I think it's time to let her go."

Maybe Dr. Wallace would say that's progress for Max. He doesn't have to hold on to a physical representation of Beni any longer, because he's realized Beni will always be a part of him. Like every time he looks in the mirror and sees the scar along his left cheekbone, he'll remember how he survived the irresistible forces at work against us, even if Beni succumbed.

And that's all well and good, but I've only just made my peace with this Mary here, and I'd like to see her stick around a little longer. "Have I ever told you about the time I fixed an angel's wing?"

Max blinks, his smile widening. "Excuse me?"

"Yep." I laugh. "My brother ran her over."

"He ran over an angel?"

"Oh, yeah." I stand and hold out a hand to help Max up, too. "Tore her wing clean off."

"So what you're saying is that you have experience with celestial healing."

"I'm a real miracle worker." I lean into him and touch his scarred cheek with my fingertips.

Max opens my hand and places a kiss and then the Mary figurine in my waiting palm. "Save us, Becca Hanson."

I tilt my face up and rock onto the balls of my feet to press my lips to his. His arms encircle my waist, and I'm enveloped by his woodsy scent, the warm softness of his flannel shirt, and the sound of his steady heartbeat. And all I can think is *whoa.*

Scene Four

[The theater]

Marcus Zimmerman and I are probably the only people in this theater right now who are not hoping to pursue a career in the arts. Well that's not entirely true, because what is bird calling if not an art, and Marcus Zimmerman wants to be a professional bird caller. I don't even know if that's a thing, but it's what he's just confessed to me as we wait backstage for Max and Victor to fix yet another missed light cue in the sequence.

"The toughest for me is the nightingale," Marcus says, cupping his hands around his mouth and making a screeching sound that is more of a cross between a train squealing to a stop and a microwave timer going crazy. It sounds like nothing that could ever exist in the natural world. Ever. He's convinced it's his ticket to the big show, though.

"Wow," I say, shielding my eyes and looking up at the catwalk, where Miles and Kelli are repositioning a light. Nothing has gone right this entire dress rehearsal. Darby actually tripped and impaled herself on Romeo's weapon at their first meeting. From then, it's all gone downhill, like a snowball set loose on the top of Everest.

"Okay," Max says in my earpiece. "Tell them to try from the top of the scene."

Beside me, Marcus is bobbing his head and making cooing sounds. "Dove?" I ask.

"Yesss," he hisses, extending a hand for a high five.

My head is throbbing, and I want to smack Marcus between his eyes rather than on his well-padded palm. "Max says you guys should try again."

Marcus looks confused for a beat and then recovers. He takes his place next to Darby onstage. By the time Thomas enters as Romeo, they've messed up every third line.

When we reach the end of act four, I'm beyond the end of my rope. I crumple in a seat in the audience next to Darby. "Why is this sucking so hard?"

"Theater tradition."

I glare at her. If I could stab her with my corneas, I'd do it right now. Why is she so calm?

"The more disastrous the dress rehearsal, the better the opening night."

"Really?"

She nods, but the muscles of her neck are so tight, they look like thick cords just under her skin.

"Besides that, we've only had four weeks to pull this together."

"We need more duct tape."

It's true that we've redone all the set pieces, reconstructed costumes, and refurbished props, but it felt like a whirlwind. Everyone has been working together, and no one has killed anyone else, so that's a plus. Still, it feels like something is missing. Like we're all playacting at being a team.

I wish I could just wave a magic wand and make it

all work out. I hate being a Muggle. What we need is something that will truly pull us together.

Help me, Charlotte. What can I do?

Thomas flops down in the seat behind us. "We're going to be here all night, aren't we?" It isn't a question, though. He rests his head in his hands.

It's true. We need to trudge through this disaster at least one more time. We need to prove we can do one freaking scene without messing up. Yet when I look around at everyone with exhausted, mannequin expressions, I can tell we need a big break.

You need a distraction, Charlotte answers.

She always claimed that distractions were a good thing. I don't know that you can categorize them as good or bad, but sometimes they are necessary.

"Think Owens is all moved in and comfy in his cushy new office?"

Darby thunks her head back on her chair, puffing out her cheeks and then letting the air leak from her pursed lips like a punctured balloon. "Who gives a shit? Not me." Her voice is thick bitterness, with a side of rage.

"You said your dad is busy with a bathroom remodel, right?"

She opens one eye and looks at me like I'm Hamlet's Ophelia.

"What'd he do with the old toilet?"

"Ew, why?"

"Because I think we should help Mr. Owens decorate his fancy office at his fancy job over at The Actors' Studio." I make sure to infuse my voice with the appropriate amount of snootiness as I say the community theater's name.

Thomas looks up from his hands and leans forward,

gripping the back of my seat. "What do you have in mind?"

"Well, it seems like such a king of a man deserves a real throne of his own."

Darby laughs, an explosive sound that ends in a snort. The snorting sound makes her laugh even more. We're all just a hair shy of delirious.

"Yes," she says, jumping to her feet and punching a fist in the air. She jogs to the stage, grabbing a broadsword from the prop table and pointing it out at all of us. "We've got a mission. A mission so important the entire success of the play may just lie in its completion."

Thomas and I chuckle from our seats. He puts a hand on my shoulder. With a gentle squeeze, he whispers, "Thanks."

Scene Five

[A dumpster]

Max, Victor, Darby, and I head to the jobsite where her dad's been working. My piece-of-shit car may not be much of a looker, but it's got a giant trunk. I pull up to the curb and cut the lights as Darby instructed. Outside the beautiful old home, its porch decorated with twinkling lights that look like icicles, there sits an ugly brown dumpster.

"It'll be in there," Darby says, leaning up into the front seats to point at it as we pull up. "The Jamisons are staying in the house during the reno. We've got to keep it down."

"Who's gonna care if we take an old toilet off their hands?" Victor asks.

"It's called trespassing," Darby says, looking over her shoulder at him.

We sit in silence, making sure we haven't been spotted. All the houses on the quiet street are dark, except for the house with a million Christmas lights still blazing three doors down. We've got the windows cracked open so that I can hear the night sounds of a distant neighbor's dog barking out a staccato rhythm. The winter air is finally getting the barest tinge of chill in it, and a finger stroke of that coolness works its way into the car, brushing along my cheeks. It makes me shiver.

Max glances my way, drawn by my sudden movement. His dark eyes pick up the soft reflection of the yellow streetlight. My mind reels with what I'd like to do with him in a dark car, that is, until Darby thumps the headrest of my seat.

"Let's go," she says. "This place is a graveyard."

Since Max's still got the cast on his arm, he'll wait by the car as lookout. He opens the trunk, and the old metal squeals in protest. We all freeze. My skin is electric as I wait, expecting Mr. Jamison to come out shooting. Not that someone in a neighborhood like this would come out with a shotgun acting like the dude from *The Beverly Hillbillies*, but still, when breaking laws, my mind tends to run to the extreme. Not that I break a lot of them, but if I did, my imagination would get in the way.

No one moves for a minute, which is an awfully long time to have your system overflowing with adrenaline. By the time Darby gives the all clear, my hands are shaking and my legs feel like they are on fire.

We pick our way over to the dumpster.

"How're we supposed to get in there?" I ask.

Darby puts her hands together to boost me over. "Ladies first."

"What?"

"This was your idea. Let's go," she says, a ghost of her evil grin flitting across her face. I wonder for a second if she's setting me up. Maybe I'm wrong about us. Maybe she still hates me. Maybe she's going to toss me in the trash can and the three of them are going to pull away laughing their asses off. Maybe my face has gone completely pale because Victor steps up beside me, thumping me on the shoulder, before he jumps and catches hold of the top of the dumpster. He pulls himself up.

"Come on, Becky dearest," he says before dropping down on the other side. "I'll catch you."

When I look back at Darby, she chuckles. "Trust me?"

"No," I laugh, but I put my foot in her hands and reach for the rim of the bin. It's not graceful, but I manage to wriggle my way up and over the top. I wave Victor off, determined to stick the landing on my own. Darby drops down next to us.

"Over here," Darby calls in a whisper. "Help me move these boards."

Victor high-steps his way through the rubbish to help her shift some boards that were tossed on top of the toilet we need. Together they heft the two pieces, the bowl and the water tank, over toward the edge, and I wonder for a moment, *what the hell am I doing in this trash if they don't even need my help?*

"Uh, guys?" Max calls.

Victor pulls himself up to peek over the rim. "What?"

"Late-night dog walker."

He must point because Victor turns his head to the left and sucks in a curse. I scrabble up some debris so I can glimpse the dog and walker. They are far enough away that they appear only as moving shadows.

"Who walks their dog in the middle of the night?" Victor asks, his voice hitching up a few octaves.

But I knew a certain girl who loved to take late-night walks with her dog and my brother. Loved them because she couldn't sleep and walking was doing something, whereas lying in her bed waiting for the end wasn't doing enough. I'm mesmerized watching the shadows, wishing without real hope that when the walker approaches I'll see those short black curls. And then I realize I don't have time for some existential dilemma right now because—"They're coming this way."

"What do we do?" Victor asks.

"We move our asses," Darby says.

Victor heaves himself over the side, and Darby stands on the toilet bowl to boost herself up to straddle the rim of the dumpster. For a second I think, *I knew it! They're leaving me here.* But Darby looks back at me and leans down with her arms outstretched. "Hand me the bowl."

I was already reaching up for her to pull me out, so I freeze with my arms in the air like I'm surrendering. "What?"

"The toilet," she says, pointing. "Can you lift it?"

I can. Darby grabs it from me and heaves it over the top, lowering it to Victor on the other side. I grab the water tank and pass that up as well.

"Go," I say, eyeing the debris all around me. "I can push this over and get out. Get it all loaded."

"You sure?"

I try to mimic one of Darby's don't-question-the-queen looks. She chuckles and disappears on the other side. I quickly move a few boards, stacking things near the edge so I can climb up. I move a piece of plywood and think I hear a funny hiss somewhere close by. What the hell is that?

Darby's voice, a shade below panic, calls out. "Move it, Becca. He's almost here."

I ignore the sound and reach for another board, but just as I'm moving it, there's another hiss, followed by an insane yowl. I yelp and pull my hands away just as a huge mass of fur comes barreling out from under the wood I've moved, claws gleaming, aiming all its fury right at my face.

I scream and turn my back on the attacking beast, scrabbling up the wobbly boards I've stacked so far, clawing and leaping for the top of the dumpster. My fingers connect with the rim and I hold on as the beast digs its claws into my sweatshirt and spits fury in my ear.

I can hear Max calling my name, and just as I pull myself up to the top of the dumpster, his face appears there. For a second we're inches apart. His eyes are huge, his mouth open even wider. "Holy shit," he swears, grabbing my shoulder and hauling me over the edge. Unfortunately, the monster on my back comes over with us.

"Hey," shouts a man's voice, and it's accompanied by the low howl of a dog. "What's going on over there?"

Max and I lie in a tangled pile on the ground by the dumpster. My hood has fallen up over my head, which is probably good, or the crazy animal would have its paws all tangled in my hair. "What is it, Max? Is it rabid?"

"Cat," he says, ducking his head away as a white-footed paw strikes out at his face from over my shoulder. "Very pissed cat."

"Get it off," I scream.

The dog howls again, deep and raspy, and I can hear the chain of his leash clinking as he pulls to get away from his master.

"Heel, Harry," the man calls, but he is no match for the huge dog, and it pulls away. The cat must see the dog coming, because it screams in my ear before using my head as a springboard and dashing away. As soon as it flees, I roll off Max, pulling him up with me, and we light out for the car. Darby's already in the driver's seat, and the engine roars to life as Max and I dive into the backseat together.

She pulls away from the curb like an Indy driver on the final turn.

"Did he see the car? Did he get the license?" Max asks, holding me close to his chest with his good arm.

"Naw," says Victor. "Too busy chasing his dog."

"Are you okay?" I ask, hoping our fall didn't damage any of Max's healing bruises.

"Fine," he says and then swears under his breath. He loosens his grip on me so I can slide off his lap and into the middle space between Victor and him. The car is filled for a moment with four sets of lungs trying to remember how to breathe properly as the shock wears off.

"Crazy cat," I huff.

A snicker whistles out of Darby's nose.

I glare at her.

She glares back, hers a mockery of my own expression.

I giggle. "I was attacked by a cat."

She giggles. "Yes. You were wearing an angry cat hat."

My whole car is filled to overflowing with laughter. Perhaps Charlotte was right. Distraction feels good.

Scene Six

[The Actors' Studio]

Kelli and Thomas are leading everyone else to The Actors' Studio once they've gathered the rest of our supplies from the workshop at school. Miles and Greg were already here when we arrived. They said Kelli had sent them early to scout the place which, for the gregarious Greg, meant walking straight in and making friends with all the people staying late to finish painting sets. When we showed up, Miles directed us to a back door and knocked five times quickly.

"Finally," Greg says, pushing open the door. "I thought you guys'd never sh—" He pauses and looks me over. "Becca, dear, what the hell is wrong with your hair?"

Darby starts giggling beside me, and I glare at her. "It's a long story, how 'bout I tell you when we're all done?"

Greg raises a brow at me, but helps me prop the door open anyway. The rest of the cast and crew arrives, and we all carry in armfuls of materials. Miles leads us to a door with a brass nameplate that reads:

Anthony W. Owens
Director

I open Owens's office door and the techies and drammies flow into the office around me like floodwater from a damaged levy. There's no other way to describe the focused frenzy with which they all work except as organized chaos.

Within minutes, Greg, Kelli, and three of Darby's minions move Owens's desk, chair, and the two wingback chairs out of the office, depositing them down the hall in a storage closet. Next, Marcus Zimmerman and a few techies bring in a four by six foot platform they'd hastily built back at the shop at school. Behind the installed stage, more people drape the walls of Owens's office with yards of musty red velvet. A few of the curtains in the wings had recently been replaced, but the fabric had been saved for making sets and costumes. I help Darby hang a large canvas banner that reads, ALL HAIL THE KING. BOWEL BEFORE HIM. It's lit with a string of round lights like a marquee. The paint is still damp.

Finally, Victor and Thomas bring in the discarded toilet, setting it up on the platform. We plug in the lights and stand back to admire our handiwork—snapping off a few pictures for posterity, taking turns sitting on the throne and wearing a paper crown someone made back at school.

When Miles gives a warning whistle, we all take off running for the back door, scrambling into cars.

"I'd give anything to see Owens's face tomorrow morning." Darby yawns. She leans her head against the window in the back of my car and looks up at the stars flying by as we make our way back to school.

"Bet it'll look like this," Victor says, pulling his face into a wide-eyed gape.

Max chuckles. "My guess is more like this." He presses his lips together, puffing out his cheeks, and draws his brow down in a scowl. "I swear he'll have steam coming out of his ears."

We all laugh, and then the car gets quiet, each of us imagining our own victory over Mr. Owens.

It's late when we get back to school, and everyone is tired, but they are also content. More importantly, techies and drammies are no longer tripping over one another backstage, dropping cues, and snapping at each other like turtles in a fishbowl. We pull off the rest of our dress rehearsal with few problems, which may fly in the face of theater traditions, but that seems to be what we're all about. We're making our own history now.

Scene Seven

[The theater]

The theater is packed for opening night. Kelli prances backstage, her glossy curls whipping from side to side. "Guys, guys, guys," she's saying, her voice leaping in time with her feet. "I saw her. I saw the scout."

Thomas grabs her elbow, steadying her beside him. "She came?"

"Miles seated her. Recognized her from that staff photo you guys showed us."

It looks to me like Thomas is attempting to swallow an entire school bus. All around me, the words "she's here" spread like a disease through the crowd backstage. Smiles evaporate into grimaces. Already filled with fidgety nerves, the wings shiver like a fever patient with chills.

"This is good news, right?" I ask.

Thomas finally swallows the last wheel on his bus and croaks a "yes," but I can tell things are coming unglued, and we don't have time to find all the pieces and put them back together before the curtain rises. I don't care what Reid says about superglue. Sometimes it's best to hold things together rather than let them fall apart.

"Max," I hiss into my headset. "They're losing it back here."

"Owens normally gives a speech right about now that bores everyone enough to calm them."

"So you want me to do some extemporaneous speaking? Have you met me?"

Max is silent.

"I'm getting Darby."

Darby is sitting alone with earbuds in, listening to music. She's leaning against the wall, hidden between a set piece and a bucket of swords. Her eyes are closed, her head lolling a bit to one side. She looks peaceful. Too bad.

I nudge her shoe with my foot. "Help."

Her eyes open slowly, her head straightening. "What?"

"Everyone's freaking out because the scout is here and Owens isn't here to do the boring speech thing."

A soft smile curls Darby's lips. "She came."

I nod and hold out a hand to help pull Darby off the floor. She reaches up, and I yank her to her feet. She threads her arm through mine, but I stop her before we join the others. "Hey, Darby?"

"Yes."

"I just wanted to say thanks—for everything."

"Don't thank me yet." There's a saccharine-sweet glimmer in her eye that makes my insides bunch up with a cramp of worry. We reach the milling group of energy, and Darby pushes us through to the center, calling out, "People, please, calm down."

Around us everyone quiets and struggles to keep their nervous tics in check. Darby waits until she has everyone's attention. She squeezes my arm, and I squeeze back.

"I just want to say," Darby says, stalling to be sure everyone is listening. "Becca has something to say."

At the sound of my name, my whole body goes rigid. All eyes swivel to me, including Darby's traitorous ones. In my headset, I can even hear Max chuckling. He's been listening in.

"Uh." I dig my fingernails into the crook of Darby's arm where my fingers are resting. She pats my hand before disentangling herself and stepping away into the ring of people around me. I'm suddenly center stage in their attentions. I have no idea what they want to hear. No idea what they need to hear.

"Well, I guess, I want to say…" I hate you, Darby Jones. Yes. That's what I want to say.

But it wouldn't be the truth because when I look at her, she's watching me, not in the way she used to, like a predator waiting for me to screw up so she can pounce. She's watching me, waiting to see if I'm up to the challenge. Waiting to see me.

"What I want to say is thank you. You're all talented and tenacious and are seriously going to kick ass out there."

I blink to clear my vision and catch sight of their faces—smiling, nodding, hopeful faces.

"The School of the Arts would be lucky to have any of you. So, as a friend of mine once said to me," I pause and find Victor at the fringe of the crowd. "Let's go break all the legs that ever were."

There's applause and laughter and suddenly hands and arms and faces crushing me from all sides in a beastly group hug.

Goodness, these theater folks sure are emotional.

Act Fifth
Scene One

[The theater]

We've made it to act five of opening night. Romeo and Paris are dead and all that's left is for Juliet to kill herself. Then all the living characters will feel like crap and forgive one another, and those new relationships will help them carry the weight of all that shared grief.

Because that's how it works for those of us left behind. We have to feel like shit for a long while, and then we have to move forward. And that doesn't mean that we ever get over the loss. No, because Charlie is right. We don't set down our grief and walk away from it. We carry it always, and thank goodness for that, because I'd hate to lose my Charlotte again.

From the stage, I hear Darby as Juliet. "I'll be brief." There are tears on my face as Darby jabs the prop dagger under her breastbone, saying, "O happy dagger! This is your home."

I peek at the scout, sitting in the audience, and my heart feels like a balloon about to burst as she wipes her eyes with a wilted tissue. Darby's done it. That scout is going to snatch her up as the brightest jewel in The School of the Arts crown. I just know it.

Seems like fate is trying to take away yet another friend, but this time at least I can visit, as long as my piece-of-shit car will make the hour-long drive to The School of the Arts.

Max's hand, warm and steady, reaches out to cover mine in the darkness.

Poor Juliet. Tybalt was dead. Paris was dead. Romeo was dead. She was alone. But alone isn't a permanent condition.

Alone doesn't have to be forever.

Yes, Juliet. You should have stayed longer. Who knows what else you could have done and seen.

The lights on the stage go down as the curtain closes. When it opens for the curtain call, the house lights come up. They remain dim, but there's enough light that I can make out faces in the crowd.

Everyone is here tonight. Charlie and his friends Greta and James are home for winter break and sitting together in the row behind Mom and Dad there in the center section. Mrs. Jonah is in the front row. Dr. Wallace is near the back. Even Darby's three wriggling little siblings are sitting sandwiched between her mom and dad and big brother. They take up almost an entire row on the right side of the theater.

And everyone is clapping. The whole place is applauding, the sound like distant rolling thunder.

"We did it," I whisper, standing to take in the whole view—the audience, the actors onstage, the techies coming out to take bows with them.

Max stands beside me. "Yes, we did."

He's looking at me. I can feel the weight and balance of his eyes on me. I feel like a boat finding its center after a storm. I step into his arms, my insides tingling when his eyes drop to my lips. I cup his face in my hand, running my thumb across the pink scars from his accident. His arms envelop me, the scent of cedar making me dizzy. And those lips, those beautiful lips—those are mine. All mine.

He lowers his head, our lips are inches, now centimeters, now only a whisper away from meeting, and then there's nothing separating us.

I know this kiss will end. But that's okay. Because if it never ended, I'd never have the pleasure of waiting for the next one. And the next one. And the next.

We're pulled apart by catcalling and loud whistles.

Max's eyes widen, holding mine in his gaze, before he turns us both to face the booth window. Everyone onstage and in the audience is clapping for us.

"Take a bow," Max says, grinning in the wide way that shows off that beloved crooked canine.

Onstage, Darby has her fingers in her mouth, whistling loudly. Kelli, Greg, and Miles are off to the side, holding hands and laughing. I spot Charlie, clapping and shaking his head with a silly smile. I give him a quick wave before I bow.

"'Scuse me," Victor says, barging into the booth and pushing us to the side. He flicks a lever up, and we can all suddenly hear Darby.

"Ladies and gentlemen," she says. She meets Kelli, who is holding a large bouquet of roses, at center stage. "We'd like to take a moment to thank a new friend to the drama club this year. Without her, this production of *Romeo and Juliet* wouldn't have been nearly as special."

Darby shields her eyes as she looks up at me. "Will the real Juliet please join me onstage?"

I shake my head. Nope. Not going to happen.

But Victor and Max are pushing me out of the booth. Just before he shuts the door in my face, Max gives me a quick kiss on the lips and a devilish grin.

I take a few deep breaths at the top of the steps, listening to the applause from the crowd. Slowly, careful not to trip and fall in front of everyone, I make my way down the aisle and up to the stage.

Kelli meets me at the edge and drags me the rest of the way to the center. Darby gives me the bouquet of flowers, the scent immediately intoxicating me, and whispers in my ear, "Would you like to say a few words?"

Would I? I'm suddenly transported back to the church with the too-still body of my best friend. I look out into the audience and immediately spot my brother, sitting too tall in his seat, waiting to finally hear what I have to say.

I do have something to say. Something important. I touch the petals of the roses in my arms, taking a deep breath.

I will say the things.

I am brave.

I am.

"Thank you, Charlotte."

Acknowledgments

This is it! This is my curtain call for *Life after Juliet*! It's my chance to applaud all the beautiful people that helped bring this story to the stage.

Thank you, reader. Thank you for your time and for giving yourself up to possibility and story. I've loved hearing from readers and meeting you at bookish events over the past year. There have been many moments in the writing of this story, that a kind note or hug from a reader was exactly what I needed to keep going. Becca and the gang thank you for helping me bring their story to light.

Thank you, Heather Howland, for planting the seed of this story in my heart. I hadn't considered giving Charlie's little sister a chance to grow until you asked, "What happens to Becca?" Knowing you, Heather, has changed my life.

Thanks to everyone at Entangled Publishing. You all deserve a standing ovation for helping to put this book together. Jenn Mishler, you have been a wonder to work with. Thank you for always making time for me, for your enthusiasm, and your earnest guidance through the revising process. Thank you Nancy Cantor for your keen eye. Liz Pelletier and Stacy Cantor Abrams, thanks for giving Becca a chance to share her story. Big hugs to the entire Entangled publicity team. You are all so talented, creative, and driven, and we authors are blessed to have you on our team.

To Jessica Sinsheimer, my lovely agent, thank you for all your tireless backstage work. It is incredibly empowering to know I have someone as smart, kind, and talented as you walking beside me on this writing journey. Continued thanks to everyone at Sarah Jane Freymann Literary Agency for your support.

Cheers to the YA Cannibals, my beloved writing group, who has been there for me during every stage of the writing process. You are more than a critique group. You are family.

For my friends, Charlie's Angels, hugs, kisses, and coffee for all!

When it comes to thanking my family, I feel a bit like Becca. I've read hundreds of thousands of words in my lifetime, but I still can't find the right ones to tell you all how much I love you. Thank you for always supporting me. Thank you for the pep talks and candy. Thanks for believing in me, even when I can't find the will to believe in myself. You are the best family in all of ever.

I'd love to have my own high school drama family join me onstage for one last bow. Janice Schreiber, my drama mama, you taught us with heart, passion, and professionalism. You made the stage feel like home. Thank you.

Before the last curtain falls on this story, I have one thing more to say. Thank you, Em.

Check out

Love and Other Unknown Variables!

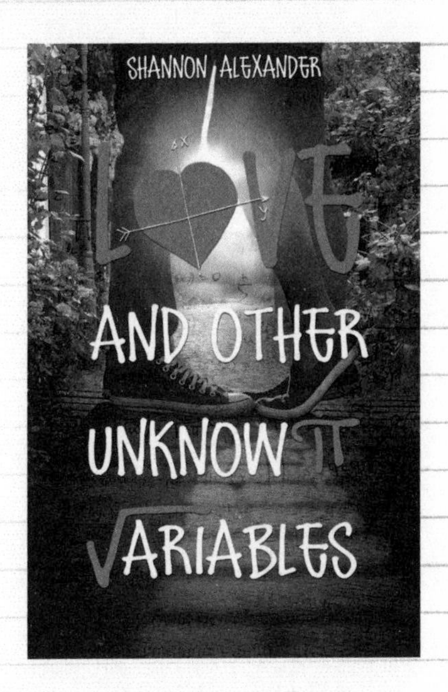

Charlie Hanson has a clear vision of his future. A senior at Brighton School of Mathematics and Science, he knows he'll graduate, go to MIT, and inevitably discover solutions to the universe's greatest unanswered questions. He's that smart. But Charlie's future blurs the moment he reaches out to touch the tattoo on a beautiful girl's neck.

The future has never seemed very kind to Charlotte Finch, so she's counting on the present. She's not impressed by the strange boy at the donut shop—until she learns he's a student at Brighton where her sister has just taken a job as the English teacher. With her encouragement, Charlie orchestrates the most effective prank campaign in Brighton history. But, in doing so, he puts his own future in jeopardy.

By the time he learns she's ill—and that the pranks were a way to distract Ms. Finch from Charlotte's illness—Charlotte's gravitational pull is too great to overcome. Soon he must choose between the familiar formulas he's always relied on or the girl he's falling for (at far more than 32 feet per second squared).

Grab the Entangled Teen releases readers are talking about!

The Sound of Us
by Julie Hammerle

When Kiki gets into a prestigious boot camp for aspiring opera students, she's determined to leave behind her nerdy, social-media-and-TV-obsessed persona. Except camp has rigid conduct rules—which means her surprising jam session with a super-cute and equally geeky drummer can't happen again, even though he thinks her nerd side is awesome. If Kiki wants to win a coveted scholarship to study music in college, she can't focus on friends or being cool, and she *definitely* can't fall in love.

The Society
by Jodie Andrefski

Not everyone has what it takes to be part of The Society, Trinity Academy's secret, gold-plated clique. Once upon a time, Sam Evans would have been one of them. Now her dad's in prison and her former ex-bestie Jessica is queen of the school. And after years of Jessica treating her like a second-class citizen, Sam's out for blood. But vengeance never turns out the way it's supposed to...and when her scheming blows up all around her, Sam has to decide if revenge is worth it, no matter what the cost.

Love Me Never
by Sara Wolf

Seventeen-year-old Isis Blake has just moved to the glamorous town of Buttcrack-of-Nowhere, Ohio. And she's hoping like hell that no one learns that a) she used to be fat; and b) she used to have a heart. Naturally, she opts for social suicide instead...by punching the cold and untouchably handsome " Ice Prince"—a.k.a. Jack Hunter—right in the face. Now the school hallways are an epic a battleground as Isis and the Ice Prince engage in a vicious game of social warfare. But sometimes to know your enemy is to love him...

Thief of Lies
by Brenda Drake

Gia Kearns would rather fight with boys than kiss them. That is, until Arik, a leather clad hottie in the Boston Athenaeum, suddenly disappears. When Gia unwittingly speaks the key that sucks her and her friends into a photograph and transports them into a Paris library, Gia must choose between her heart and her head, between Arik's world and her own, before both are destroyed.